PRAISE FOR

You Must Not Miss

★ "Leno (*Summer of Salt*, 2018, etc.), channeling early
Stephen King at his best, offers no neat conclusions, and
her frank examination of depression, grief, alcoholism, and
the ruinous aftermath of sexual assault is grim yet effective.
Readers will ponder this exceedingly creepy gut punch of a
tale long after turning the last page."
—*Kirkus Reviews* (starred review)

★ "Compelling and harrowing....Leno doesn't shy away
from challenging themes...and she brings lyrically haunting
language to a story filled with inherent darkness."
—*Publishers Weekly* (starred review)

★ "Leno...takes a concept...and executes it with beautiful,
brutal precision. Between the lines of spare and dreamlike
prose lurks a girl who, though quiet at first, demands to
be seen, and readers will not soon forget her."
—*Booklist* (starred review)

"This unusual blend of realistic fiction, fantasy, and mayhem
begs debate wherever it is read!"
—*VOYA* magazine

You Must Not Miss

KATRINA LENO

LITTLE, BROWN AND COMPANY
New York Boston

Copyright © 2019 by Katrina Leno
Cover art © 2020 by Tran Nguyen. Cover design by Karina Granda.
Cover copyright © 2020 by Hachette Book Group, Inc.

Little, Brown and Company
Hachette Book Group
1290 Avenue of the Americas, New York, NY 10104
Visit us at LBYR.com

Originally published in hardcover and ebook by Little, Brown and Company in April 2019
First Trade Paperback Edition: August 2020

Little, Brown and Company is a division of Hachette Book Group, Inc. The Little, Brown name and logo are trademarks of Hachette Book Group, Inc.

The publisher is not responsible for websites (or their content) that are not owned by the publisher.

The Library of Congress has cataloged the hardcover edition as follows:
Names: Leno, Katrina, author
Title: You must not miss / Katrina Leno.
Description: First edition. | New York ; Boston : Little, Brown and
    Company, 2019. | Summary: "When seventeen-year-old Magpie Lewis
    discovers a magical world in her backyard, she uses it and its powers to enact
    her revenge on all those who have wronged her"—Provided by the publisher.
Identifiers: LCCN 2018023693| ISBN 9780316449779 (hardcover) |
    ISBN 9780316449793 (pbk.) | ISBN 9780316449809 (ebk.) |
    ISBN 9780316449786 (library edition ebook)
Subjects: | CYAC: High schools—Fiction. | Schools—Fiction. | Family
    problems—Fiction. | Revenge—Fiction. | Magic—Fiction.
Classification: LCC PZ7.L5399 Len 2019 | DDC [FIC]—dc23
LC record available at http://lccn.loc.gov/2018023693

ISBNs: 978-0-316-44979-3 (pbk.), 978-0-316-44980-9 (ebook)

Printed in the United States of America

LSC-C

10 9 8 7 6 5 4 3 2 1

To Wendy Schmalz:
grateful to call you my agent,
even more grateful to call you my friend.

ONE FOR SORROW,

TWO FOR JOY,

THREE FOR A GIRL,

FOUR FOR A BOY,

FIVE FOR SILVER,

SIX FOR GOLD,

SEVEN FOR A SECRET,

NEVER TO BE TOLD.

EIGHT FOR A WISH,

NINE FOR A KISS,

TEN FOR A BIRD,

YOU MUST NOT MISS.

— A variation of "One for Sorrow," a nursery
rhyme concerning magpies, birds that have
often been considered ill omens (and perhaps
for good reason)

ONE FOR SORROW

The smell of chlorine had always reminded Magpie Lewis of summer, and summer in turn reminded her of a much happier time, a time before her life had gone so completely wrong. Last summer her sister had been home, her father had been discreet, her mother had been sober, and Magpie had spent three untouchable months on a pizza pool float in their small aboveground pool while her former best friend, Allison, had floated alongside her on a white swan. The swan was full of razor-blade slashes now, and the pizza was deflated. When Magpie put her mouth on the pizza float's nozzle and blew, she tasted chemicals, sunscreen, sweat, regret. She pulled back and tried to spit away the taste.

Magpie's skin tingled where she'd spilled some of the powdered chlorine on the back of her hand. She'd searched the internet on her phone. (*will powdered chlorine on skin fucking kill me hopefully*; the answer, regretfully: no.) She had run her hand under the garden hose for a few minutes. The water was freezing, so now her hand was numb instead of tingling, which she considered a slight improvement.

She found an old tire pump in the garage and took it to the backyard, where she sat cross-legged on the grass. The pizza float was faded from three months of sitting out every day last summer. She thought she could almost see a Magpie-shaped pattern of more vibrant color where her body had blocked the sun. She'd worn 50 SPF sunblock and hadn't tanned at all.

You were not supposed to get into a pool immediately after adding chlorine, but this was May 1, and it was unseasonably hot in New England, practically July-warm, and besides, Magpie would hardly touch the water at all from her perch on top of the float. If she were honest with herself, she would admit she was hoping very much that the pool or the float or some combination of the two would act as a time machine and shoot her backward to a day when her heart did not constantly feel so wilted and sick.

Magpie hoisted the inflated pizza float over the side of the pool, then she climbed up the ladder to the small, raised pool platform and lowered herself gingerly onto the float. She removed her straw hat from her head and placed it over her face and breathed in deeply, the smell of chlorine, the sharp knife of it, the hot burn. She'd put too much in, but the pool hadn't been taken care of in the past year and it was slightly green with who knew what—moss or fungus or whatever.

"Algae," she remembered suddenly, and spoke the word aloud, her voice so soft that it got trapped inside the sun hat and reverberated there for a moment. Through the cracks in the woven hat, Magpie could see sun, blue skies, trees. There was one month left of her sophomore year of high school, and she had decided, after a mountain of evidence to support it, that the entire world was a joke.

But the sun felt good and the pizza float drifted lazily and knocked gently into the sides of the pool and there was a warm breeze and Magpie felt, momentarily, a cautious sort of peace.

She let her hand dip over the side of the pool float and linger, wrist-deep, in the cool water; then she remembered the fresh chlorine and took it out again.

Inside, the house phone rang. Only a handful of people knew and used that number, and most of them were telemarketers. She knew her mother, Ann Marie, was inside, drunk early and watching TV, but the phone rang a dozen or so times, then went silent, unanswered. Ann Marie had disabled the voice mail months ago, but Magpie's father still called every day at six o'clock, waiting for someone to pick up. Magpie liked to imagine what he might say if he could leave a message. It would be in a low, pleading voice. It would drift out of the house and slink over the grass and crawl up the side of the pool and swim across the water right into Magpie's ear.

He would say something simple, something like:

Ann Marie, please call me back. Please talk to me. Please give me a chance to explain.

What this translated to, roughly, was:

Ann Marie, I am sorry that our daughter caught me having sex with your sister in our bedroom six months ago while you were out of town visiting friends and Magpie was supposed to be at school but instead was skipping third period to root around in your bedside table for our little bit of weed so she and Allison could get stoned and eat four bags of BBQ potato chips. I am sorry for how naked I was, and for how naked your sister was, and for how long we stood looking at our daughter/niece not knowing what to say, not knowing even how to hide ourselves. It was as if time hiccupped and got stuck, and the three of us could not figure out how to undo it, how to get it moving again. Ann Marie, I am sorry for the image of my naked, semierect dick that will forever be emblazoned on the insides of the eyelids of our youngest daughter. Ann Marie, please call me back. Please talk to me. Please give me a chance to explain.

A crash from inside broke Magpie's daydream; this was Ann Marie throwing the phone against the wall. But it was the oldest and sturdiest phone known to man, and it would inevitably survive this minor inconvenience, and Magpie would pick it up later and piece it back together, and the whole charade would repeat tomorrow, and the day after tomorrow, and on and on into infinity.

Magpie spent enough time on the pool float for the sun to go down and her mother to pass out on the couch with the TV on too loud, then she toweled off on the swim platform and went inside.

The house she shared with her mother on Pine Street was dark, blinds pulled tightly closed, heavy blackout curtains hung at almost every window. Air-conditioning units blew stale, chilly air that raised goose bumps on her skin every time she got too close.

She had been making herself dinner for six months with little variation, because food did not interest her much; she ate it so she did not lose too much weight and raise the suspicions of the school guidance counselor, whose own daughter's kidneys failed after a slow burn with anorexia. The school guidance counselor was now very obsessed with the weights of the students who went to Farther High School, and she regularly roamed the hallways, peering at bodies, looking for too-prominent bone structures: clavicles and elbows that pulled at skin until it turned three shades lighter than it ought to have been.

Magpie set a pot to boil on the stove and got a box of macaroni and cheese out of the cabinet. They were out of milk and butter so it would be dry and the powdered cheese would clump together in little tumors.

She went and muted the TV. Ann Marie slept noisily

on the couch: big, raking breaths that shook the pictures on the living-room walls. Sweating on the coffee table within arm's reach of her, there was a large tumbler of vodka and ice because it looked like water and they could both pretend, if they wanted to, that it *was* water. Magpie rarely got close enough to the glass to smell it, but she could smell her mother, who hadn't showered that morning and bled pure ethanol from every pore. It made Magpie's nose burn, even worse than the chlorine.

When her dinner was ready, she ate it standing up in the kitchen, straight from the pot, with the only clean utensil in the house: the wooden spoon she'd used to stir everything together. The macaroni tasted like cardboard dusted with dry sawdust, but somehow that was comforting to her, a familiar taste, something very small that she could rely on.

For lunch every day Magpie bought a greasy grilled cheese sandwich and a small container of apple juice, and for breakfast there was sometimes a spoonful or two of cottage cheese if she remembered to eat it, if it hadn't gone green with mold.

She hadn't had vegetables in a while.

Magpie opened the fridge and found broccoli so covered in a sickly white film that she almost couldn't identify what it was—just a tiny spot of green remained. It did not occur to her to throw it out.

"There aren't any vegetables," she whispered into the fridge. Then she shut the door and trapped her voice inside to cool.

Magpie always arrived at school early. This was for two reasons: She wanted to be out of the house before her mother got up, and she wanted to get to her locker before Allison, whose own locker was next to Magpie's.

She removed every single book that she would need throughout the day so she wouldn't have to return to her locker until thirty minutes after the last bell rang, which allowed her to give Allison a wide berth, ensuring Magpie wouldn't see her after school. Her backpack groaned audibly with the weight. Her back groaned audibly with the weight.

She went to her first class, English, and found it predictably empty. Magpie liked predictability; she liked that Mr. James arrived only five minutes before class every day and that she would have the darkened classroom to herself for forty blissful, quiet minutes. She sat near a window in the back and pulled out the homework she was supposed to have done over the weekend, staring blurrily at the syllabus as she struggled to bring it into focus.

Read the short story "Where Are You Going, Where Have You Been?" by Joyce Carol Oates. Answer the following study questions:

Why does Connie leave with Arnold Friend?
What is the significance of the name Arnold Friend?
What is the significance of Connie's obsessive hair brushing?
What is the meaning of literally anything?

Magpie squinted and read question four again. It dissolved and reformed in front of her eyes into something that made more sense.

Magpie hadn't read the story. She removed her English textbook from her backpack and opened to it.

Her eyes refused to work properly.

She couldn't manage even a single sentence.

So Magpie pulled a spiral-ring notebook from her backpack, a cheery yellow notebook that stood in stark contrast to the dark cloud that hung permanently around her. In ink, on the top right corner of the cover, she had written one word. *Near.*

The notebook was well-worn and used; the yellow had faded and peeled around the edges, revealing the cardboard underneath. Magpie had been writing in it for months—six months, actually. She'd picked it up the morning after she'd walked in on her father and her aunt. She'd written the word—*Near*—on the cover, then she had turned to the first page and scrawled: *I wish I lived somewhere else. A tiny perfect place. A town called Near with no people, no traffic, no noise. Just a green sweeping hill and grass so bright that it's almost lime.*

She opened now to an empty page somewhere in the middle, the first one not completely filled with mostly neat tiny handwriting, and she wrote: *In Near it is always warm enough to go swimming.*

In Near I always feel like I am floating.

In Near the water is as warm as a bath.

And then she heard someone set their bag down on the front desk. It was five minutes till class and Mr. James was right on time.

"Good morning, Margaret," he said. She closed the yellow notebook and slid it into her backpack. Mr. James walked over to her desk and tapped the English book. "Ah, refreshing your memory? What did you think about that one? Dark, I know."

Magpie didn't know what she thought about it because she hadn't read it, so instead of answering, she tried not to make eye contact.

Mr. James tilted his head, looked at her with what could only be described as careful optimism. "Margaret?"

"I'm sorry," Magpie said. She struggled halfheartedly to come up with some sort of excuse, but her mind was blank, a large white expanse of nothingness.

"Margaret, did you not do the assigned reading? You really can't afford to miss another homework credit."

"I can do it tonight," she said.

"I don't allow late assignments, Margaret. We've been over this."

"I can do it in study hall."

"But you had the entire weekend—what excuse can you possibly have for not reading one short story?"

What excuse could she have?

But even if she had been able to think of one, she didn't get a chance to use it—the warning bell had sounded and her classmates were filing diligently into the room, filling up the space, taking all the air. Magpie lowered her head and tried very hard to get enough to breathe.

———————

Lunch. A grilled cheese sandwich that dripped grease onto her lunch tray.

She always used to sit with Allison. Back then, she never knew who else she would find at the table. The occupants constantly changed as people fell in and out of Allison's favor.

A quick glance at the table now showed people Magpie once considered friends—Elisabeth, Nicole, Brittany—eating and laughing together.

Six months ago she had chosen a new table. One that was across the cafeteria from Allison's. She'd seen the empty chair and asked if she could sit there.

Brianna had said, "It's a free country, girl."

Luke had said, "You're Mags, right?"

Clare had said, "Welcome to the Goonies; are you cool with blood sacrifices?"

And Ben had said nothing but shifted his chair to the side a little to indicate that she could sit next to him.

They had accepted her, she knew, because they each had a past.

Brianna had gotten her period in class one day as a

freshman and bled through her jean shorts and was theretofore banned from all civilized conversations because everyone knew periods must be kept quiet and denied at all costs.

Luke had been dating the blondest cheerleader on the squad until he'd come out as bisexual and started dating a quarterback on one of Farther's rival football teams.

Clare's father had killed himself when they were all in middle school and thus became something to avoid, as if grief were perhaps contagious.

Ben had transitioned to male sometime last year, to the acceptance of few outside of that small group.

And Magpie.

Whose transgressions against Farther High School were too egregious to list.

Or at least that's what Allison had said.

And people listened to Allison.

Her version of events was so convincing that it sometimes confused even Magpie, who'd been there.

Magpie had sat between Ben and Brianna ever since because she did not believe, like the rest of the school, that there was very much to worry about regarding transgender people and people with periods.

She ripped her grilled cheese into two pieces, then four, then eight.

"Do you want this?" Ben asked, handing her some sort of yogurt in a tube. "I've told my mom these are disgusting, but she keeps buying them."

Magpie took the yogurt tube and turned it over slowly. The flavor was bodacious blueberry.

"You think it's disgusting, but you want me to have it?" Magpie asked. She'd been trying to make something of a joke, but it ended up just sounding a little rude.

"I'll take it," Brianna said, and plucked it out of Magpie's fingers.

"What about that short story for Mr. James? Fucking *dark*, huh?" Clare said.

"I would read whatever Mr. James wanted me to read," Luke said. "I would read his grocery list."

"Gross, you can have him," Brianna said, rolling her eyes. "I don't see what the fuss is about."

"You can't deny the smolderiness of those eyes," Clare said, sighing into her container of applesauce.

Magpie didn't contribute; she didn't really have much of an opinion about Mr. James's looks. He was just another teacher who assigned homework she didn't do.

"You should eat something," Ben whispered to Magpie, leaning closely. "Mrs. Henderson is on the prowl."

Magpie looked around the cafeteria; sure enough, the school guidance counselor was walking from table to table examining lunch choices.

Magpie took an exaggerated bite of her sandwich.

"Thanks," she mumbled to Ben.

"You're welcome. How's your day so far?"

Magpie looked at him. Ben had one of those open, honest faces. Everything was laid out on the table with him. Magpie liked that.

"I'm tired," she responded. She hadn't slept much the night before. She had lain in bed for hours and stared at the ceiling and felt the weight of the night as if it were something you could put on a scale and measure.

"You *look* tired," Ben said. "Here." He handed her the rest of his coffee. Magpie hadn't really drunk coffee before meeting Ben, but now he often shared his with her. She had a sip and felt the warmth flow almost dramatically down her chest into her stomach.

She had sat at this table and known these people for only six months, but in that time, she had become comfortable with them. They were acutely aware of the unfairness of the world, of Farther High, of their own unique circumstances. They didn't know Magpie's full story, but they had all heard the whispers that followed her down every hallway: *slut*.

"Thanks," Magpie said again, about the coffee. Ben knocked his shoulder into hers.

"You're welcome, Mags," he said.

Different names for different people.

To teachers: Margaret.

To this table: Mags.

To herself, her mom, ~~her dad, her sister, Allison~~:

Magpie.

Ben and Magpie both had history after lunch, so they walked together, taking a very roundabout way that Ben never questioned (to avoid Allison's locker). Magpie hadn't known Ben well before she'd switched lunch tables, but now she might call them friends—even though they generally saw each other only in the cafeteria and the hallways that connected the cafeteria to history class.

They walked in silence for a minute until they reached a water fountain where Ben paused to have a sip.

When he straightened up, he said, "Have you thought about Ms. Peel's assignment?"

Magpie hadn't paid attention in history for six months; she couldn't confidently say whether they were in World War I or World War II or the Cold War or maybe no war at all, maybe just the California Gold Rush or something.

"Assignment?" she repeated.

"The final project," Ben said. He waited a moment, but Magpie's eyes showed no recognition. "She's been talking about this since January, you really don't...?"

"Oh, yeah, of course," Magpie said. It was the safest answer. Ben looked relieved.

"Well, I was wondering if you wanted to be my partner?" he asked.

"Sure."

"Did you have an idea for the topic?"

"I dunno. Maybe you should choose."

"How about…Amelia Earhart? It fits the criteria, you know, women who've positively impacted history."

"That sounds great."

"Cool," he said. And then—quietly enough so she almost didn't hear him—he added, "Hey…is something going on?"

"What do you mean?"

"You're usually quiet. And that's fine! It's just today you seem a little quieter than usual."

He stepped to the side as a senior boy Magpie didn't know paused to use the water fountain. He took a sip, pulled away, looked from Magpie to Ben, then said, "I wouldn't drink after her if I were you."

Magpie felt her cheeks grow hot as the boy melted away into the crowded hallway. Ben looked as if he wanted to say something else but didn't know quite where to start.

Finally, he cleared his throat, and said, "That was…I'm sorry."

"Oh, it's fine. It's totally fine. That was tame."

"Really? People are still…saying stuff?"

Magpie laughed quietly, a laugh that was more like a scoff. "I know you hear them," she said after a second.

"I don't listen," he said earnestly. "I learned a long time ago not to listen."

"But you still *hear*."

He smirked a little at that. "Fair enough," he said. "I still hear. But I don't listen."

"You might as well," she said with a shrug. "Everything they say about me is true."

Ben tilted his head. As if he was looking at her from another angle. Then he frowned slightly, and said, "Well. I don't believe that for a second."

———————

When the last bell rang, Magpie waited thirty full minutes in her algebra classroom, then went to her locker. As usual, she left all her books at school. Her backpack was mostly empty; it contained only her house key, the yellow notebook, and her cell phone, a pay-per-use thing she hadn't used in weeks.

She walked to the grocery store.

There were two grocery stores in town, Baker Farms and Kent's.

Allison worked at Baker Farms.

Magpie went to Kent's.

She had her mother's credit card in her back pocket. She knew exactly how much was on the card because she opened the bright-red bills that came in the mail every month. She paid the minimum with money stolen from her mother's wallet, just enough so they wouldn't turn off the card. There were many little obstacles to figure out now that Ann Marie had given up all her responsibilities, but Magpie was navigating them deftly.

Her sister, Eryn—

Magpie didn't like to think about her sister.

But Eryn hadn't been interested in navigating those obstacles anymore. Eryn had told Magpie once, a year or so ago, how bad it used to be. Eryn was six years older than Magpie, and Magpie had been too young to remember the last time her mother had been drinking.

Eryn had said that if their mother ever started drinking again, she would leave.

Eryn, true to her word, had left.

She wasn't physically that far away—she was a senior at Fairview College, barely thirty miles from Farther—but it felt as if she were in another country, on another planet. It felt as if Eryn had died and nobody had thought to tell Magpie when the funeral was.

She didn't know what was worse.

Her father calling every night at six o'clock to remind her of his naked pink body standing up with everything hanging everywhere, how he had tried to hug her after he'd finally put his clothes back on, his shirt clinging to his damp skin, his hair falling limply around his face, tears pouring down his cheeks and apologies pouring from his mouth.

Or her sister, who never called.

Or her sister, who changed her phone number.

Or her sister, whose last words to Magpie were: "I'm sorry, okay? But I cannot sacrifice my mental health just because you're not old enough to leave yet. Call me when you're eighteen."

Magpie consulted the mental list of groceries that she kept folded up in some easily accessible part of her brain. A dozen or so boxes of macaroni and cheese, milk, butter. Dish soap.

But how was Magpie supposed to call Eryn when she was eighteen if Magpie didn't know Eryn's number? Would Eryn come back for her?

She remembered the wilted, smelly broccoli in the otherwise bare refrigerator. She couldn't remember how long it had been since she'd eaten something green. She vaguely heard some employee ask her if she needed help finding anything, but she ignored him until he shrugged and walked away.

She gathered up the few things she needed, already forgetting the broccoli, then grabbed a tiny orange to eat on the way home, so she wouldn't get scurvy.

Scurvy? she thought. *All the shit you're swimming in and you're worried about* scurvy?

It was not warm enough that evening to go in the pool, but Magpie went to the backyard anyway and tended to it, skimming drowned and bloated bugs off the surface and sprinkling more chemicals in to shock all the winter germs away. She dumped the contents of the filter into the grass and dragged the dead swan to the trash cans around the side of the house.

She gave the garden shed a wide berth. It was filled with things that belonged to her father, the things he hadn't had time to pack: lawn mower and camping equipment and ski poles, all linked together by an elaborate network of spiderwebs.

She did the dishes while her macaroni cooked. Her mother was semilucid and had even gone to work. She kissed Magpie vaguely on the cheek and asked her about school.

"School is great," Magpie said.

"How is Allison?"

"Allison is great."

"She hasn't been around in a while."

"She was here the other day; you were out."

The delicate ecosystem of the house was maintained only if Magpie carefully avoided certain truths: She had not spoken to Allison for six months; her mother was an alcoholic; her father had slept with her aunt.

This was easy to manage because her mother generally lost interest in talking to Magpie after a few minutes.

"I think I'll order pizza," Ann Marie said. "Would you eat some pizza pie, little Magpie?"

"Yeah, Mom, that sounds great," Magpie said, knowing that her mom would not order the pizza, knowing that her mom would pass out soon, knowing that if she actually did want pizza she would have to order it herself.

Magpie tended to her macaroni and cheese; it was marginally better this evening because of the milk and butter. She ate standing over the sink, looking out the little window at the backyard, the pool, the pizza float she'd pulled onto the pool's platform so it wouldn't get too soaked in chemicals, the little shed just beyond the pool that contained all her father's things.

Maybe one of these days she would burn it down.

On Tuesday morning Mr. James arrived fifteen minutes before class instead of his usual five, and he sat down at the desk next to Magpie's and asked her if she'd read the story yet.

"I'm sorry," she said.

"Forget *I'm sorry*," he said. "I need a little more than that from you, Margaret. Do you realize you're looking at repeating sophomore year? I'm trying to help you out here, but I'm getting the distinct impression you don't want to be helped."

Magpie was very practiced at giving the bare minimum of information to satisfy the questions of a nosy entity. "I'm sorry. I mean—my father left a few months ago. It hasn't been easy on my mother and me. I'm trying my best. I really am trying my best."

Mr. James let out an enormous sigh; maybe he was

thankful she'd given him something to work with. "All you have to do is ask for help; I guarantee you there are plenty of people willing to give it to you. Let's see…Why don't you go home tonight and do the reading? The Joyce Carol Oates story. Read it, and then tomorrow I'll get here a little early and we'll talk about it. Sound good?"

"Thank you," Magpie said.

Mr. James nodded.

Then he saw the yellow notebook that she had hurriedly closed when he had walked into the classroom. He touched its cover and Magpie felt the touch on the inside of her body. That notebook was as much a part of her as her blood, her soft tissue, her large intestines. It was as if he'd run his fingernails across her heart. It wasn't a nice feeling.

"I always see you writing in this," he said.

"It's nothing," she replied quickly.

"Are you a writer, Margaret?"

Was she a writer? Only if you could count writing about make-believe worlds.

Well—*one* make-believe world.

A place she knew as intimately as the real town she lived in.

A place she returned to again and again and again.

The only place she knew she belonged.

"Not really," she replied.

"It's none of my business," he said. "But if you ever want to share anything, I'd be honored to read it."

Before he had gotten to class, Magpie had written one new line in the yellow notebook.

In Near I will be able to protect myself from the people who have hurt me.

"I'll think about it," she said.

But what she meant was something closer to:

In a thousand million years, no.

———

At lunch everybody was talking about the end-of-the-year party that Brandon Phipp was throwing at his parents' house.

Magpie's stomach gave an uncomfortable lurch when his name trickled through the cafeteria and reached even their table, the lowest of the lows. Only Ben noticed her pushing her tray toward Brianna, suddenly unhungry. He offered her a small Tupperware of baby carrots. Ben's mother still packed him lunch every day; she sometimes even wrote him little notes that made him smile and made Magpie's heart break into forty-seven million pieces inside her chest. She took a carrot and smiled weakly at him. He pushed the rest of his coffee toward her.

Everything they say about me is true.

Why had she said that?

Why hadn't he believed her?

Because he's a nice guy, she realized.

"I think it's pathetic that everyone is so excited about a party," Brianna was saying.

"I think you think it's pathetic just because you won't be invited," Clare said, laughing. Brianna threw a potato chip at her.

"I'm definitely going," Luke announced. "It will be fun."

"Brandon Phipp once bought me a powdered donut. The kind with jelly inside," Brianna said.

"See, that's nice!" Clare said.

"With a note that said, *Next time you bleed through your pad, you can blame it on this*," Brianna finished.

"That doesn't even make sense," Ben chimed in.

"I mean, the jelly wasn't even red. It was purple," Brianna added. Then she shrugged. "I still ate it."

"So Brianna's a *no*." Luke laughed. "Clare's a yes. I'm a yes. What about you, Mags?"

Magpie looked up from her coffee. She stole a quick glance across the cafeteria.

And there they were, sitting together as usual: Allison and Brandon. In the split second she allowed herself to look at them, Brandon was drinking from a can of soda. Allison was inspecting a fingernail.

Magpie turned back around, and she made herself smile.

It was a trick she had learned from Allison, actually.

How to act like you didn't care about anything in the world.

You smiled but not *too* wide. More like a smirk. And you

tilted your head a little, as if you found something vaguely entertaining.

And you took an idle sip of coffee, and said, "I'm probably a no."

And you tried to ignore the memories of that night. Of the last party you had been to at Brandon Phipp's house. When you were so drunk you could barely see straight. When you were so drunk you had to rely on other people's version of events. When you weren't sure you trusted your own memory enough to contradict them.

Luke shrugged. "Suit yourself. I think it'll be fun, though. Ben, what about you?"

"Oh, I don't know," Ben said. "I mean, Brandon's house is enormous; I heard he has an indoor swimming pool and everything. It would be sort of cool to see it. But on the other hand..."

"On the other hand, it's Brandon Phipp," Brianna interjected. "And let's not forget that donuts aren't the *only* things he gives girls."

Nobody had to ask what Brianna meant; everyone had heard the rumors about Brandon slipping things into girls' drinks.

The rumors about how, between Brandon and his college-age brother, a girl couldn't set her cup down at a Phipp party.

"So we watch our drinks," Clare said a little impatiently. "And we go and have a fun time. It doesn't have to be more complicated than that."

But Magpie knew—sometimes it *was* more complicated than that. Even if you didn't want it to be.

———

Magpie went to sleep late that night and woke up hours later to an enormous crash. She lay motionless in bed listening to someone attempt to pick up what they had knocked over and then to another crash as they dropped it again and then to a sort of stumbling, shuffling sound as whoever it was knocked up against various furniture.

Ann Marie, home and drunk.

Magpie crept quietly out of her bedroom and down the short hallway that led to the living room. Her mother had turned on a lamp, but it lay overturned on the floor, along with the phone, a stack of dirty dishes, and the end table that had held it all.

Her mother sat on the floor now, cradling the phone. The dial tone was muffled against Ann Marie's shirt. Magpie took it from her mother's hands. Ann Marie looked up and blinked.

"I fell," she said.

"You're bleeding," Magpie replied.

Ann Marie had a thin cut that ran the length of her forehead, as if someone had gently pressed the tip of a knife into her skin and dragged it a few inches. She raised her fingers to the cut now, pressing gingerly, her face revealing no pain.

"I don't remember," she said.

"Just go to bed, all right? I'll take care of all this."

"The mother is the one who's supposed to take care of the kid."

"I think that ship has sailed," Magpie said.

"Have you talked to Eryn lately?" Ann Marie's voice was surprisingly steady for someone so clearly inebriated. She hardly slurred at all. But Magpie could tell that she *was* drunk, very drunk, not only because she had fallen and cut herself but also because of her bloodshot eyes, her dry lips, the smell that pulsed off her and permeated the room, the thick, choking, lingering smell of alcohol.

"Eryn changed her phone number," Magpie replied. She righted the end table and carefully set the lamp back on it.

"I tried to call her, but nobody answered," Ann Marie said. "I've tried to call her so many times."

"That's because she changed her number."

"But is she all right? How are we supposed to know if she's all right?"

"She's fine, Mom. She's probably a lot better off than either of us."

"I don't think she even said good-bye. I can't remember...."

Magpie could remember. And she knew why Ann Marie couldn't: because she had been so drunk that she had fallen asleep on the bathroom floor in a small pile of vomit. Eryn had opened the door and found her there and cleaned her up and put her into bed and then left. Magpie had watched her go as she stood on the front steps with the door open behind her and a growing hole opening wider and wider in her stomach, an open wound that ached and throbbed more and more as Eryn backed her car out of the driveway and drove away down the street.

Magpie had stayed outside for a long time, ignoring the incessant ringing of the house phone (her father) and the incessant chirping of her cell phone (Allison).

When she'd finally checked her text messages, there were eleven from her soon-to-be-former best friend, who was tipsy and insisting that Magpie meet her at a party in the rich part of town. A party at her boyfriend, Brandon Phipp's, house.

Magpie went back inside.

Ann Marie had left a half-empty bottle of vodka on the kitchen counter.

Magpie had never tried it before, never even had a sip, but she poured herself a glass of orange juice and added a heavy splash of vodka. She drank the glass quickly, liking the burn of it, pouring herself another and another, each with less orange juice and more vodka, until she had finished the bottle and felt warm and numb from the inside out.

She got dressed and went to the party and if she could have changed anything about her life, she would have chosen to just get in bed instead. She would have faced Allison's inevitable wrath the next day; she would have been able to apologize for not being in the mood to leave her house. She would have turned off her phone and gotten into pajamas and locked herself in her room and cried herself to sleep and woken up the next day having done nothing to cause her best friend to hate her so violently and completely that any hopes of rekindling their friendship were dashed as soon as they entered her mind.

But she'd gone to the party because she was the stupidest person in the world, because her heart had been broken twenty times already that night, because she wasn't capable of making the right decisions, because her mother was passed out, and because she didn't want to be in the house with her for one second longer than she had to be. Because Eryn had left and Magpie's father had left and Magpie's entire family—extended aunts and uncles and grandparents and cousins—would all soon take Magpie's aunt's side. Because she would get to them first, and it is so very hard to believe anything except the first side of the story that you hear. Magpie knew this; it did not make it easier when she and her mother were not invited to Christmas dinner.

"You need to get some sleep," Magpie told her mother now. "You need to drink some water."

"Please tell Eryn to come home," Ann Marie said, but she allowed Magpie to help her to her feet, and she followed her obediently into the master bedroom. "Please tell her it's okay to come home now."

"I'll tell her," Magpie said, pulling off her mother's alcohol-stained shoes and pushing her back on the bed.

"I have to get changed," Ann Marie said.

"It doesn't matter," Magpie replied. "Nothing matters."

"These aren't my pajamas."

Magpie pulled the covers up to her mother's chin and tucked them in too hard. She had a wild idea that just a few more inches of blanket would cover her mother's mouth and nose, blocking her airways, suffocating her. Magpie could sit on her mother's hands and Ann Marie wouldn't be able to move and she wouldn't be able to breathe and then she would die and everybody would think it was the alcohol that had done it. Magpie would be removed to—

Where?

To her father?

No, she would simply not tell anyone her mother had died.

She could live that way until she turned eighteen. She would buy the first ticket out of Dodge. When they finally found Ann Marie's body, it would be only a skeleton, and Magpie would be only a memory: a whisper of a real girl. Gone, gone, gone.

She held the blanket over Ann Marie's face for just a moment.

Her mother whined softly through the cotton.

Magpie tucked the blankets underneath her mother's chin.

———

Magpie read "Where Are You Going, Where Have You Been?" the next morning before school, and when Mr. James arrived twenty minutes before the bell rang, she was just finishing the last paragraph.

It wasn't a very nice story at all. It was about a girl, Connie, who is home alone when a man named Arnold Friend shows up at her house. They talk a lot—weird, rambling conversation about how Arnold Friend knows Connie is going to leave with him. And at the end she *does* leave with him for no reason Magpie could figure out. It's pretty clear things won't end well for Connie. It's pretty clear Arnold Friend doesn't have anything good planned for her. But he just talks to her, and she leaves. It didn't make any sense at all.

Mr. James sat at the desk next to Magpie. She had her textbook open; her yellow notebook was safely inside her backpack. She didn't want Mr. James to touch it again. He tapped the English book instead.

"What did you think of it?" he asked.

"I didn't like it."

"Okay! Tell me why." Mr. James settled back in the chair.

"She just let him take her. She just *went* with him. And he's clearly going to kill her. It doesn't make any sense."

"It's an interesting bit of psychology, isn't it?"

"But why would she go with him?"

Mr. James was very quiet. He had an expression on his face, a very hard-to-read expression, but one that made Magpie enormously self-conscious. She thought he must know, that the gossip of the student body had inevitably reached the teachers, that everywhere she went in this school everyone must see her for what she really was.

But then Mr. James shook his head a little, and the expression was gone.

"I think you've got a really unique perspective on this story, Margaret. I'd love to hear more of your thoughts. How about you write me up a little essay—nothing huge, just a few paragraphs—expanding on your ideas. Get it to me next week. No page requirements, no word count, just your opinions down on paper. Does that sound good?"

"I can do that," Magpie said, and in that moment she felt like it was the truth.

The hallways were mostly deserted as Magpie headed to her locker thirty minutes after the last bell. She felt still buoyant after her talk with Mr. James, but that buoyancy popped the moment she turned the last corner to her locker.

She froze in her tracks.

The back of Allison was at her locker, putting away her things.

The back of Allison was only ten feet away.

The back of Allison had heard footsteps approaching in the otherwise abandoned corridor and was turning slowly—

Magpie darted back around the corner and ducked into

the first door she saw: a restroom. She had never before felt so thankful for a restroom's impeccable placement. She went into a stall and shut the door, and she counted to five hundred before she let herself come out again.

The back of Allison was gone.

Magpie put her books into her locker, and she left the school as quickly as she could.

━━━━━━━━━━

Ann Marie had not gone to work.

The kitchen looked like a small explosion had gone off, but Magpie figured out that her mother must have tried to make pancakes, the only thing to eat in the house besides her stockpile of macaroni and cheese. Ann Marie, asleep on the couch, was covered in powdered mix and sticky with syrup and smelled strongly of the cheap vodka she drank. Magpie covered her mother with an afghan—not out of any affection, but so she wouldn't have to look at her.

Then she took out her yellow notebook and scribbled something in the margins of a free page.

And I can get there whenever I want. And I will know it when I see it.

Then she went into the kitchen and began to pile dirty bowls and frying pans and measuring cups onto the counter, and that is when she saw it through the window over the sink...

In the backyard, in her father's shed...

The light was on.

Magpie froze, a perfect imitation of a statue, a glass batter bowl in her left hand, her right hand outstretched to turn on the sink faucet.

Nobody had been in her father's shed for six months. Magpie knew that for a fact. The key hung on a hook next to the back door, and it had a dusting of filth on it from six months of no one vacuuming or dusting or bothering to take her shoes off when she walked into the house.

The door of the shed was still shut, which meant the padlock was still on it because the door would swing open if the padlock wasn't there. And that meant no one could possibly be inside because you couldn't lock the door while you were inside. So the door's being shut meant the door was locked meant nobody was inside...So how was the light on?

Magpie placed the glass bowl on the counter and leaned forward, looking through the window up at the evening sky. Had it been raining? A bad thunderstorm had once tripped their house alarm; maybe something like that had happened? But the sky was clear and blue, and the backyard was empty, and her mother was snoring, and the garden shed's light was on, and her hands were shaking, she realized suddenly. Her hands had started shaking.

She walked to the front of the house.

The simplest explanation was, more often than not, the correct one, and Magpie would find her father's truck parked in the driveway, and he would have come for his things and brought someone to help him load the heavier machinery into his truck, and he would have done it at night because, Magpie hoped, he was too ashamed to show his face in the daylight. That is how she wanted to picture her father: too ashamed to exist before the sun went down.

But his truck was not in the driveway, and Magpie went outside and stood in her front lawn with bare feet, and his truck wasn't parked anywhere on the street that she could see.

She turned back to the house.

Everything looked normal.

Her neighborhood was filled with the normal sounds of a neighborhood: someone's radio on too loud, crickets, a whir of a car's engine as it raced down the street parallel to hers.

Magpie decided she was overreacting.

She walked around the side of the house.

The light in the shed was still on, and she could see nothing moving inside; everything was still through the two windows that sat high on either side of the door.

She glanced at the pool to her left, glistening and serene in the low light of dusk. The pizza float was resting on the small platform.

She turned back to the shed.

And nothing had changed. Not a thing out of place; not a thing touched or disturbed.

Except the light.

The light was off.

TWO FOR JOY

At lunch the next day Ben greeted Magpie with a few books on Amelia Earhart and asked if she wanted to get together that weekend to work on the project, either at the library or at one of their houses, and Magpie said sure, that sounded fine, but really what she meant was *I think there's something wrong with my eyes.*

Because the shed's light had gone on and off, on and off, on and off three more times the night before, and each time Magpie had stepped outside to check on it, it was as dark as the night sky above her.

That afternoon after school, in the safety of the bright, bright sun, she would open the door and go inside and unscrew the single light bulb that hung on a chain from the ceiling and was turned on with a string.

Obviously, there was a faulty wire. Obviously, Magpie's eyes were fine.

"Do you have a preference?" Ben asked, and Magpie looked at him for so long that finally he added, "I mean, do you want to go to one of our houses or the library?"

"I like the library," Magpie said.

This was true, she *did* like the library, because she liked quiet places where you were explicitly not allowed to be louder than a whisper. But there were other reasons for her choice: She did not like her house; she did not like other people's houses. She liked neutral ground, neutral territory, a fair and fighting chance for everyone.

She tried her best not to close her eyes and see a single light bulb lit up when it should have been dark.

"That works for me. Saturday around one?" Ben asked.

"One is perfect. I'll look over the books before then," she said.

As if to prove this—to herself or to Ben or to the universe—Magpie took a daily planner from her backpack. It had not been opened in a while; the last six months were white and pristine. She found May 7 and wrote neatly: *Read Amelia Earhart books.*

"Okay, I better get going," Ben said. "Got a meeting with the guidance counselor."

"Are you going to eat that?" Brianna asked, leaning over Magpie to point at the remains of Ben's sandwich.

"All yours," he replied. He handed her the sandwich, then pushed his almost-full coffee cup and a small Ziploc baggie of apple slices toward Magpie. "See you in history, Mags."

The lunch table without Ben felt suddenly off-kilter, tipped on edge. Magpie ate a slice of apple and washed it down with coffee.

Magpie concentrated on the coffee so intently (a trick she had learned: look intimately interested in whatever you had in front of you and people tended to leave you alone) that she almost didn't notice something brush against her left arm. A small clearing of a throat. The coffee cup lifted up, stolen. Magpie looked to where Ben had been sitting.

Clare, smiling, pretended to take a sip of the coffee but then set it back down in front of Magpie.

"Earth to Mags," she said lightly, tucking her short blond hair behind her ears.

Up close, Clare was thinner and paler than Magpie had noticed before. Her eyes had deep circles underneath them; the mascara had rubbed off in a dark smudge. Sensing Magpie's scrutiny, maybe, Clare wiped a finger underneath her bottom lashes and let out what Magpie thought was a rather affected laugh.

"Sorry," Magpie said. "Zoned out."

"Totally different view over here," Clare said, indicating the table. Then she leaned back, grinned, and added in a whisper, "So, you and Ben, huh?"

"What do you mean?" Magpie asked, feeling the back of her neck go hot.

"Don't worry—our little secret. Ben and I are friends. I know he likes you."

The dynamics of the lunch table were still being revealed to Magpie. She'd previously thought the inhabitants of the table sat together out of necessity rather than any sort of kinship, but every now and then, little alliances presented themselves to her. Clare and Ben, for example, and before that, she'd learned that Brianna and Luke often got high and went shopping together. She filed away this new information and forced herself to smile.

"He told you that?"

"Yeah. He thinks you're—wait, how did he put it?—a real sweet piece of ass."

The heat on Magpie's neck cooled instantly, leaving her cold and uncomfortable.

"I'm totally kidding," Clare said quickly. "He just said he thinks you're really sweet and smart."

"Oh," Magpie replied. "That's nice."

"I shouldn't have said that," Clare added. "The sweet piece of ass thing. Sorry."

"It's totally fine. It just caught me a little off guard."

"He would also literally murder me if he knew I was talking to you about this. But I just had to ask...Do you like him?"

"I'm not sure," Magpie said honestly. "I *do* like him, of course. As a friend. I just never thought about...I just have..."

"Baggage, sure," Clare finished. "Why else would you be sitting at this table? Why else would you be talking to me, Clare 'McBaggage' Brown?"

But she was smiling. It occurred to Magpie that this was

the most she had spoken to Clare in her entire life. Had Magpie, like so many of her classmates, ostracized and avoided Clare when her father had killed himself? They'd been eleven or twelve; the news had spread through the school like a brushfire; Clare had been absent for a full month and returned an untouchable stranger. Whispers had followed her in the hallways. Students had turned their eyes downward to avoid her. Teachers did not call on her.

"Baggage," Magpie repeated, but what she really wanted to say was more along the lines of *I am so sorry if I let them erase you.*

"Honesty is the best policy," Clare said, shrugging, a little apropos of nothing. "I just mean, it's okay if you don't know what you want yet. Just be honest with him and yourself, and shit will all work out. Not like you asked for my advice, of course. But I know Ben's put up with a lot in his life. A lot of people saying one thing, doing the other, that type of thing. People supporting him initially, then flaking. Wait—do I sound like his protective older sister right now?"

"Sort of, yeah," Magpie said, but she was still smiling. She liked Clare. She liked Ben. Everything was normal. Everything was okay. She had made it up, the light bulb in the shed. Her eyes were playing tricks on her. She needed to eat more vegetables.

"Gosh, I don't mean to. I'll stop now," Clare said. "Hey— do you want to do something after school? My mom works late; we could watch a movie at my place or something."

Magpie considered—a week ago, maybe a few days ago, maybe even five minutes ago, she would have said no, the word would have been out of her mouth before Clare had even finished speaking. But today, now, she thought about it. And instead of no, she said: "I don't think I can."

Clare rolled her eyes an impressive distance back in her head. "Look, if this is about your baggage or whatever, lemme just say that I think Allison Lefferts is a huge shithead, not to mention a liar. I wouldn't believe a word that came out of her mouth even if she was pointing at the sky and telling me it was blue, okay? For what it's worth."

Magpie felt something very much like a swell of happiness in the pit of her stomach. And even though she knew the truth (or at least she thought she did sometimes), she said, "Sure, I'll come over."

"Great. My locker's 309. Meet me after last period."

Clare's locker was nowhere near Magpie's, which meant it was nowhere near Allison's, and in the interest of not being too late, Magpie arrived with her backpack full of books.

"Geez, that thing's loaded. Do you want to put some stuff in here?" Clare offered. She moved aside, and Magpie began scooping books into Clare's locker. Clare regarded her with confusion, then something clicked. "Ah...Lewis, Lefferts. Your lockers are right next to each other, aren't they?"

Magpie froze a little, brought a book to her chest, and squeezed. "I just…"

"It's fine. I wouldn't want to run into that dickhole in the hallways, either," Clare said.

Magpie relaxed a little. She put another book into Clare's locker. Then her fingers found the yellow notebook, and she squeezed it so tightly that she knew, when she let it go, she'd have spiral-ring imprints on her palm.

When Magpie finally finished putting her stuff away and turned around, Clare was smiling, but it was a sad smile.

"You know—somebody once told me that my dad probably killed himself because I wasn't good enough." She laughed softly. "Good enough? What does that even mean, right? Like how do you be a *good enough* daughter?" She took a deep breath. "Anyway, my therapist and I have talked a lot about how to let those things just roll off your back. Because those things…they say way more about the person who said them than they say about *you*. I mean, of course they do. Who says something like that. And who *still* calls Brianna *bloody girl* in the hallways. And Luke the *f*-word. That doesn't say anything about *them*, you know?"

Clare fidgeted for a second, put on her backpack, and coughed. "I just thought I should say something. I mean—I understand. Because Allison's the one who said that. That my dad killed himself because I wasn't good enough. So I can only imagine what she's said to you."

Clare didn't linger long enough to see Magpie's reaction.

She turned and started down the hall, and Magpie struggled to catch up to her, suddenly embarrassed, as if she were somehow accountable for Allison's actions.

That's not me, she reminded herself. *I didn't do that.*

And from another part of her brain, a different voice answered.

Ah, but you didn't stop it, either.

It never made sense: Allison and Magpie. Allison was never not popular, never not beautiful; there was not even a ten-minute period in her life where she underwent the so-called awkward phase. Her school photos would stand the test of time as the perfect example of the right clothes, the right hairstyle, the right shade of baby-pink lip gloss.

"Guys like when you wear lip gloss, Magpie," Allison had said once. Fourteen. Heart-shaped sunglasses. Yellow-and-white bikini. "They like it *especially* when you suck their—"

"Ew, Allison," Magpie had replied, stuffing her fingers into her ears.

Allison hadn't always been like that—so vulgar, so gross. They'd met when they were five years old in swim class at the local YMCA, and back then Allison had been a quiet, gentle girl who had won Magpie's favor by always breaking her string cheese in half and sharing it with her. But something had happened to Allison around eleven or twelve.

She'd started to become obsessed with her own self-worth, which she based entirely on how she looked and how many people wanted to be her friend. She became a true crafts-man of her own image; her aesthetic was carefully cut out of magazines and pasted into a binder kept hidden away in the deepest depths of her soul. And while she still clung to Magpie fiercely, she also began to make and set up little fac-tions of other friends. Magpie noticed this but did not say anything. When she questioned Allison, all hell broke loose. Allison had once gone so far as to throw a dinner plate into the wall above Magpie's head, exactly like they had seen in countless movies.

What had caused it? Magpie had suggested they go ask Allison's father for money so they could walk to the gas sta-tion on the corner and buy candy. It was something they always did, something they'd done a thousand times, but Allison had said no. And when Magpie had pressed her, she'd thrown the plate, still dirty with leftover lasagna, bits of cheese and vegetables flying in every single direction.

Afterward, Allison had sunk to her knees (also exactly like in movies, the well-established stance of extreme emo-tion, be it anger, happiness, or embarrassment) and cried, her hands covering her face and her shoulders heaving.

"I'm so sorry," she sobbed.

Were they fourteen? Thirteen?

The years blurred together.

Magpie picked up the pieces of the dinner plate and held

them in her cupped bare hands, careful not to cut herself. She used her foot to open the lid of the Leffertses' trash can and dumped them inside.

They waited a moment, the two of them, but only Mr. Lefferts had been home, and he was holed up in his study on the other side of the house. After a few breaths, it became obvious he hadn't heard it.

And if nobody had heard it, it could be just as if it hadn't even happened.

Magpie stood over Allison, and for just a moment, a brief moment that lit up the kitchen in blinding yellow light, she saw that something inside her friend, something very important and fragile and tender, had snapped in half. She saw into Allison's body as if her friend's skin were transparent. She saw that Allison's heart was cracked open, and what was spilling out of it was something very unpleasant. She felt bad for her despite Allison's almost breaking open her skull with a plate a few minutes ago. She bent down and put her hands on Allison's knees.

"I'm so sorry," Allison repeated.

"What's going on with you?"

What Magpie *should* have asked, what she would have asked if she could do it all over again, was so much more complicated.

Why would you rather throw a dinner plate at my head than ask your father for ten or twenty dollars?

"I'm *sorry*," Allison repeated, still crying. "Please don't tell my dad, okay?"

"I won't tell," Magpie said. She wrapped her arms around Allison and squeezed her tightly. "I promise."

Why hadn't it upset her more, that Allison had thrown a plate at her head? If it had hit her, it could have broken her nose, or sliced open her forehead, or blacked an eye.

Maybe it was because, when she looked at Allison, she still saw the only kid in swim class who hadn't laughed when Magpie had jumped out of the pool too late to make it to the bathroom, a stream of urine running down the insides of her legs as she'd stood frozen at the edge of the water.

Maybe it was the way Allison had introduced herself that very same day during snack break when all the other five-year-olds had found other little groups to sit with. The way she had pulled the string cheese out of her bright-blue lunch box and broken it in half without saying a word, handing it to Magpie with a smile. The way she had leaned in to whisper, "It happens to me sometimes, too. It's okay."

Maybe it was because Allison was like that—when you were on her good side, she defended you fiercely. An unwavering protector.

Until you gave her a reason not to be.

And Magpie *had* been upset, of course, when Allison had thrown the plate at her head, but underneath that anger there had been Allison, at five, hair wet from the pool, a fierce expression on her face as she pushed a snotty little boy into the deep end because he had laughed at Magpie for her accident.

Allison, at seven, poking holes into the tires of a bike that belonged to a boy who'd stolen colored pencils out of Magpie's backpack.

Allison, at ten, sticking gum into a girl's long curly hair after that girl had called Magpie ugly.

So maybe she had been upset for just a moment, but she could never stay mad at Allison for long.

"I don't know what's happening," Allison said. "It's like I'm not even me anymore."

Magpie could not argue with that.

Clare's house was small and homey. Her little brother, Ringo ("His real name's Teddy, and I have no idea who introduced him to the Beatles, but it wasn't me."), greeted them at the door, fully launching himself into Clare's arms before she'd even stepped into the hall.

Magpie knew his story. Clare's mom had been nine months pregnant with Teddy—Ringo—when her husband had shot himself in the family car after pulling into the garage after work. They had a different car now. They had a different house, a different garage. The boy was four.

Magpie tried to make herself as small as possible in the foyer. The walls were lined with school photos of Clare and one from Ringo's nursery class. There was one photo of the family before Mr. Brown had killed himself; Mrs. Brown's belly was full and Clare was laughing, laughing. Clare caught Magpie looking at it.

"We go back and forth," Clare said quietly. "You know. About how much to tell him. That photo is a compromise."

Ringo had darted back down the hall; Clare watched him go.

"I'm so sorry," Magpie said.

"It sort of gets easier," Clare said. "It sort of doesn't."

She led Magpie down the short hallway into a small kitchen. An older woman was stirring something in an enormous pot.

"Hi, Linda," Clare said. She dumped her backpack on a kitchen chair, and so Magpie did the same. "This is Mags."

"It's nice to meet you, Mags," Linda said. She peered into the pot, saw something she didn't like, made a face, and then threw a bunch of dried herbs into it. "You're okay with Teddy, Clare? I can't stick around today."

"Ringo!" the boy said, shooting in and out of the kitchen so quickly that he was more blur than boy.

"Ringo," Linda said, rolling her eyes. "I'd prefer it if he wanted to be called George, but what do I know?" She crossed the kitchen and gave Clare the wooden spoon and a kiss on the cheek. "Simmer until you girls get hungry, okay? Tell your mom I'll come a little early tomorrow so she can make her meeting. She worries too much, you know?"

"I know," Clare said. She took her place behind the stove as Linda left. "Ringo!"

47

"Yeah?"

"Do you want to watch a movie?"

"Yeah!"

"Go pick one out, okay?"

"Okay!"

"Sorry," Clare said to Magpie. "I forgot Linda had to leave early today. She usually stays until my mom gets home. I didn't know we'd have to babysit."

"I don't mind," Magpie said.

And she didn't—it was nice, sitting in the Browns' kitchen watching Clare adjust the dial on the stove and stir whatever was cooking in the pot. Clare looked far more at ease than she ever did at school. She leaned over the pot and breathed deeply, smelling. "Are you hungry? I'm starving."

"Yeah, actually," Magpie replied.

"ROBIN HOOD," Ringo shrieked, running into the kitchen, somehow without the shirt he'd just been wearing.

"Sure, Ringo. Stop stripping and go turn the movie on, okay?"

"ROBIN HOOD," Ringo repeated, running back into what Magpie assumed was the living room.

Clare opened a cabinet and took two bowls from it.

"Isn't Robin Hood a little violent?" Magpie asked.

"Oh, not the bloody one. The one with the talking animals."

Magpie watched Clare ladle two heaping portions of soup into bowls, and her stomach growled audibly, suddenly aching for something other than macaroni and cheese.

"Linda makes stew in the summer and salads in the winter. It makes no sense," Clare said. She dropped a spoon in the first bowl and nudged it toward Magpie. "Come on, you can eat it while we watch the movie."

Magpie took the warm bowl in her hands and followed Clare into the living room. The opening credits of the movie were already playing, but Ringo was stretched out on his stomach on the carpet, snoring loudly.

"Did he just—"

"Fall asleep in .2 seconds?" Clare said, laughing. "Yup. He goes from ten to zero and back again. Which is lucky for us, because we don't have to watch *Robin Hood* anymore." She found the remote and turned off the movie, flipping through a few channels before she landed on a rerun of some crime show. She kept the TV on but turned down the volume so they could barely hear it. She blew into her soup and took a bite. Magpie did the same. It was filled with vegetables and beans and little macaroni elbows. Her stomach was so unused to anything that didn't taste like artificial cheese, she was worried she wouldn't be able to keep it down.

"Good, right?" Clare asked.

"So good."

"She's a good cook. My mom is hopeless. Without Linda and Ben, I'd never eat a decent meal."

"Ben cooks?"

"He's the *best*, seriously. He makes this veggie lasagna, oh my God."

"Have you been friends for long?"

Clare smiled a little sadly. "Since my dad died, yeah. We'd been friends before, kind of, but after that, he was really there for me. A lot of people just disappeared, but not Ben."

"He's always been nice to me, too," Magpie said.

"He's the best. I don't know what I would do without him."

That choice of wording: *I don't know what I would do without him.*

At one point Magpie didn't know what she would have done without Allison. Without her sister. Without her father. If she had learned anything in life, it was that you could always do without people. You could always find a way to do without them.

"Mags?"

"Hmm?"

"I just wanted to say, about the party... It's totally okay if you don't want to go. I know Allison is going to be there. But I meant what I said before. I think Allison is a liar. And even if she *isn't* lying? It's not like you killed anyone. We all make mistakes."

We all make mistakes. Wasn't that the truth?

The thing was—there were some mistakes you couldn't come back from.

Magpie arrived home to a dark house. She'd had two enormous helpings of Linda's stew, and her mind and her heart and her body felt full, and she turned on the light in the living room and was silently overjoyed that her mother wasn't lying passed out on the couch. It was eight o'clock; Magpie and Clare had done a little homework together after watching TV, and it had felt like the most normal night she'd had in a while.

She dropped her backpack on the couch and walked down the hall to her bedroom. She could do this. She could have friends again; she could graduate high school; she could go on dates and forget about her father and forget about Eryn and forget about Allison. She could do all of these things and—

But no.

She could not.

Because as much as she tried to convince herself that the sour, acidy smell that drifted into her bedroom and brought tears to her eyes was not vomit, the rational part of her brain understood that she must get up, must go check on her mother, must get the bleach out of the bathroom cupboard, and must do what she had to do to scrub that smell out of the carpet.

She walked to her mother's bedroom.

The smell grew greater, more urgent.

Something buzzed in Magpie's skull, a tiny warning alarm that sounded only in the most desperate of emergencies.

Something was not right.

Her mother's door was slightly ajar; she pushed and it

swung open, revealing a dark cave stuffed full of the sharp fumes of vodka and the thick, heavy scent of vomit.

"Mom?" Magpie whispered into the darkness. Her hand fumbled along the wall for the light switch, and the room was thrust into an immediate wash of color.

Her mother was lying on the carpet next to the bed, half-naked, her shirt around her neck and one breast hanging loose from her bra.

It was the breast Magpie concentrated on, the breast that confused her, because her mother's skin around the nipple and out across the mountain of her boob was all blue. A pale, tender blue.

Vomit was arranged in a perfect halo around Ann Marie's head. Magpie took two noiseless steps closer to her and noted the empty bottle of vodka just out of reach. The blueness turned her mother's entire body into something foreign, something Magpie did not recognize. She thought wildly of Smurfs, of those cat creatures from that James Cameron movie, of the bottle of Dawn dish soap at their sink.

She knelt at her mother's feet and laid one hand on her shin, then pulled it back, recoiling. She had never felt a body so cold, and for one minute she thought—

But no.

Ann Marie's chest rose and fell slowly, slowly, slowly.

Up and down.

Slowly.

Up...

Down...

Magpie stood up and ran back down the hall and tripped and fell and pulled herself up and dove across the living room to reach the phone, and she dialed 911 even as some tiny voice in the back of her head thought—*Wait.*

What if you don't?

What if you let her die?

Would that be so bad?

But then Clare's words echoed through her brain: *It's not like you killed anyone.*

So Magpie ignored the other voice.

She did the right thing.

She cried her address into the phone and waited for the ambulance on the front steps like on the night she had watched Eryn drive away.

She heard the sirens and hoped they would find her.

Then hoped they would not find her.

Then she just waited, without much hope at all.

***

Magpie settled into the sick glow of the waiting room at night, a particular kind of light that is not found anywhere else on the entire planet.

She had ridden in the back of the ambulance with her mother. The paramedics worked very quickly, sticking things into Ann Marie's skin and cutting away the remainder of her clothes with big sharp scissors. Magpie pressed herself against the back doors and made herself as small as she could, and Ann Marie sometimes breathed and sometimes did not, but she didn't die.

Now, in the waiting room, Magpie took a seat in the corner again, always in the back corner, always as far from the front as she could manage. She shivered against the metal of the chair. She had brought her backpack with her, and she removed the yellow notebook now and wrote in its pages.

I am always warm.

Then she put it away again.

The doctors hadn't told her much—nobody had told her much—but it didn't take a genius to figure out that Ann Marie had finally done it. She'd finally drunk enough to land herself in the hospital. Magpie imagined a long, strong clear tube inserted in her mother's mouth, the slop of all that poison in her stomach suctioned out by a great machine, a pumping sound like a new mother filling a bottle with milk. Magpie's eyes had tears in them, but she didn't think she was crying. It was only that the pale blue of her mother's exposed breast was a little too much for her mind to wrap itself around.

She'd hung up on the 911 operator even after she had asked Magpie to stay on the phone. But the 911 operator had sounded so calm, so peaceful, so serene, and that was not what Magpie needed. Magpie needed someone to scream, someone to match the rising tumult in her brain with a sound loud enough to drown it out. The beat of her heart sounded to her like a steady drum of *fuck fuck fuck fuck*.

She wanted to call Allison. She wouldn't.

She wanted to call Eryn. She couldn't.

She wanted to call her father.

She let herself imagine, for one moment, her father walking into the hospital waiting room.

Magpie rises up to meet him. Her father, already crying, runs to embrace her. There are no more people; it is just the two of them. There are no chairs, no TVs, no beeps from hospital machinery. The walls melt away and Magpie and her father are standing on a cloud and it is suddenly six months ago and her father did not sleep with her aunt and Eryn did not leave and her mother did not start drinking again and Magpie did not do anything to upset Allison and the world is too small to contain all the happiness now bursting from the tips of Magpie's fingers, the heels of her feet.

She decided not to call her father.

She felt fatigue as if it were a cold, heavy hand on the back of her neck. She closed her eyes and leaned into it.

The doctor came out a little while later. The waiting room had thinned out. An elderly woman in a blue housecoat had left wailing. Magpie's eyes were like dinner plates, watching her, terrified. The distinct horror of being witness to another person's tragedy.

The doctor was a short woman with neat black hair. She introduced herself as Dr. Cho. Magpie stood up to meet her.

"Margaret," Magpie said.

"I wanted to tell you that your mother is stable," Dr. Cho said. "And to ask you a few questions, maybe, if you are up for it?"

"Sure."

"Do you know if your mother took any pills tonight? Anything other than alcohol? Any drugs? I'm sure the paramedics asked you; I just wanted to see if you had remembered anything between then and now."

"I don't think she took anything else, no. I only saw a bottle of vodka."

"I see," the doctor said. "Tell me, Margaret...Has anything like this ever happened before? Does your mother drink to excess often?"

Magpie was sixteen; if this doctor wanted to get Child Protective Services involved, they would force her to go live with her father. They wouldn't care about what he had done, because in the scale of evils, his was surely the lesser of *blackout drunk and almost dead.*

"Never," Magpie said. "Honestly, she rarely drinks. I think this must have been a terrible mistake. She would never have meant for something like this to happen."

"We rarely mean for things like this to happen," Dr. Cho said quietly. She looked around, maybe confirming that

Magpie was alone. "Do you have anyone you can call, Margaret? Your father, a family member...?"

"My father is on his way. He was out of town for a business meeting. He should be here any minute," Magpie assured her.

"Would you like to see your mother now?"

"I'll wait for him."

Dr. Cho nodded. She arranged her glasses on the bridge of her nose and took a seat in the closest chair. She gestured for Magpie to do the same. Magpie did.

"Margaret... Is there anything you'd like to tell me?" Dr. Cho asked.

"Like about..."

"About anything. Your mother's drinking, where your father is. Life at home. Anything."

"I told you, my father is on his way. He was out of town for a business meeting."

"What town?"

"I don't know; I don't memorize his schedule," Magpie snapped. Her eyes burned. She pressed her palms into them. "I'm sorry. I'm didn't mean to... I'm just worried about my mom. I would like to go see her, okay? I've changed my mind."

She did not actually want to see her mother; she only wanted Dr. Cho to go away as quickly as possible. Surely she must have other patients; surely she couldn't spend too much time prying into Magpie's personal life.

Magpie stood up again, concentrating only on smiling

and not running full speed out the front door of the hospital. She tried to look eighteen, to look legal, to look appropriately worried while also self-assured and honest. And when that didn't work, when Dr. Cho stood up and eyed her suspiciously before leading her to her mother's room, Magpie let her shoulders slump and resigned herself to appearing exactly as she was: a sixteen-year-old liar who didn't particularly care if her mother lived or died.

Dr. Cho led Magpie down a series of identical hallways, then stopped outside a door indistinguishable from the ones on either side of it.

"She'll be moved later tonight," Dr. Cho said. "Anyone at the front desk will be able to tell you where she is once they assign her a room." She dug around in her white coat pocket and pulled out a business card. "In case you need someone to talk to," she added, and handed the card to Magpie.

"Thanks. For all you did for my mom. I really appreciate it."

Dr. Cho nodded. Magpie watched her walk down the hallway and turn a corner, then Magpie hauled ass in the opposite direction, following the welcome glow of the bright red exit signs until she hit the warm night air.

———————

At home Magpie opened a fresh bottle of vodka and made herself a pitcher of lemonade.

She hadn't had anything to drink since the night of the party, six months ago, but something about seeing her own mother lying lifeless on the floor of her bedroom had stirred an itch in the pit of her belly. Maybe more than anything, she wanted to prove that it was possible to have a drink without having seven or eight immediately after it. Maybe more than anything, she just wanted to feel a little numb.

Magpie poured herself a tall glass of lemonade, added the vodka, then she sat down at the kitchen table with her yellow notebook and opened it up to the first blank page and wrote.

Only I will be able to get there. And anyone else I decide to let in.

And I will know the way like I have been waiting for it all of my life. Like it's been waiting for ME all of my life.

Because it has. And it wants me to come home now.

And before she really realized it, she had begun to cry.

She watched one fat, round tear splatter onto the page, blurring the word it landed on—*ME*—and she stood up angrily, wiping at her cheeks.

And then she stripped naked in the living room and pulled on her bathing suit and walked outside and dunked herself into the pool, which was blissfully chilly and made her break out in goose bumps.

"Are you having a crisis?" Magpie asked herself out loud, liking the way her voice lit up the quiet of the night. She was thinking about many things: about what a long day it had been, about Clare Brown wanting to be her friend, about Ben maybe liking her, about her mother almost killing herself, about Teddy Brown growing up without a father and wanting to be called Ringo. She thought about Linda's stew and how warm it had made her feel. She thought about Mr. Brown driving home and pulling his car into the family's garage and shutting the door behind him and shooting himself in the temple with a small handgun they kept locked in the tool cabinet. She thought about the car: Who had cleaned it? Who owned it now? Did they know what had happened in it? Was the used-car salesman required by law to disclose that information?

Magpie floated on her back and looked up at the perfect darkness of the sky, the mess of stars, a brighter dot she thought might be Mars or Venus, a very faint speck of light that moved impossibly slow: a satellite. She counted three planes. She counted twelve spots of blackness on the surface of her heart. She tried to name them all, but it was hard to tell, sometimes, where dark heart spots came from.

She righted herself in the pool and drank half the glass of vodka lemonade, then threw it violently across the yard. It came to rest on the grass halfway between the pool and the garden shed.

It did not shatter, only bounced once and was still. But stranger than that was...

The garden shed, with its light on and blazing.

The quick jolt of vodka had warmed Magpie's stomach, but now she felt a chill that had nothing to do with the night air or the cool water. She pulled herself out of the pool and wrapped herself in a threadbare beach towel embroidered in one corner with her sister's initials: *ERL*. She stood dripping on the pool platform.

The shed's light did not go out.

Magpie climbed carefully down to the lawn.

She took a step toward the shed, the light like a beacon, casting a circle of yellow on the grass around it.

Magpie felt her heart was like a fluttering thing, like a bird.

She was close enough now to touch the shed, and she did, letting her hand fall upon the padlock, which was locked one moment and lying open in her hand the next though she didn't have the key, though she hadn't even tried to open it.

She let the padlock fall to the ground.

She let the shed door open; she let the light pour over her.

The light was a tangible thing, a warm, soft blanket. She could wrap herself up in it; she could let it protect her.

She took a step into the shed, and it was as if the shed had split into two distinct places, one on top of the other. The lawn mower, the skis, the treadmill her father had bought and never used. All those things were here, and she could see them, and yet there was something else. There was another place, and it was all around her, opening up in front of her.

She looked out into it.

She was at the top of a green, green hill.

The grass spread out all around her, sloping downward

gently. There were dandelions growing here and there. Crisp white daisies with bright-yellow centers. Patches of buttercups.

In front of her, down the hill, was a little town. She could see the tops of the houses, the buildings. Cars parked in driveways. A white picket fence encircling everything.

She felt warm looking at it.

She felt safe.

She felt that fence around her heart, protecting it, keeping it away from anything that might want to get in and hurt her.

Oh, and it was beautiful.

It was like nothing in her life at all.

And she could step through; she could see that. It would be the easiest thing just to step through from one place to another.

So she did.

She stepped through.

And she let the towel slip away and fall to the grass.

And she was swallowed up into light.

And it was exactly like going home.

THREE FOR A GIRL

Here is what Magpie could remember when she woke up the next morning in her own bed, unsure of how she got there.

The light. Spreading through her entire body; seeping into her skin, her bones; moving through her veins, through her lungs, through her stomach.

A gentle feeling of peace.

A warm summer breeze.

A rolling expanse of green, perhaps a grassy knoll or hillside.

Grass so green it was almost lime.

She felt underneath her pillow for her yellow notebook and pulled it out, holding it to her chest the way a young child might clutch a teddy bear.

She let herself stay in bed for long minutes, let herself enjoy the feelings rolling through her: feelings of safety, of being full, of being light.

Her memories of last night were even now fading away.

Had she dreamed of something warm? Why did she feel so nice, so calm?

She could see the shed through her bedroom window, and it looked as ordinary as it ever had. It was just a standard, run-of-the-mill garden shed, sitting unused and neglected right at the back edge of their property.

But there was something there. A dream about the garden shed? The cut of sunshine through the darkness of a New England night?

The more she tried to remember, the more it slipped away. It *must* have been a dream. But a dream that had left her feeling so happy. So full.

But then she remembered her mother, and all the good feelings inside her were replaced by guilt. Her mother, alone in a hospital room. A cup of wiggling Jell-O.

"It's just ground-up cow bones, sugar, and a little bit of food coloring. That's all it is," Ann Marie had said of Jell-O once when Magpie was younger and wanted a little plastic cup of her own to unwrap in the school cafeteria.

She would have to go see her today before school. It would look suspicious if she didn't.

She took her time showering, getting dressed, her own small silent protest. It was not *her* fault that Ann Marie had drunk herself straight into an ambulance.

She rode her bike to the hospital.

She stood for a long time in front of the gift shop and wondered if she should use her mother's credit card to buy a small bouquet of flowers. And because her goal was to arouse as little suspicion as possible about her situation, she decided that she should.

She picked out the most inexpensive gathering of flowers, then she asked the man at the front desk what room Ann Marie Lewis was in.

Her mother was on the third floor. The walls were pale blue. The tile was white with flecks of dark gray. She found the right door and didn't let herself pause before she walked inside because she had enough foresight to understand that the pause would be eternal, a trap from which she would never be able to free herself.

Her mother was in a double room, but there was no one in the other bed.

Ann Marie was sleeping, mouth open, a thick line of drool running down the right side of her chin. There were tubes still plugged into her skin. She looked pale, no longer blue but a sickly grayish color. She looked exactly like you'd imagine someone who drank a bottle of vodka the night before might look.

Magpie gently set the flowers on Ann Marie's nightstand, not bothering to find a vase, not bothering to put them in water. Then she wrote her mother a note and left it on top of the flowers.

Hi, Mom. I stayed for a long time, but you didn't wake up. I hope you're feeling better. I'll come back later after school if I can. x, Magpie

She did not wait one single second more. She was in and out in less than a minute.

———

The lunch table had shifted to allow Clare to sit on one side of Magpie and Ben on the other.

"This is disorienting," Luke complained. "I don't know who's who anymore."

"Ditto," Brianna added. "I never bothered to remember your names, just where you sat."

"Clare's the cute one, I think," Luke replied. "Mags is the dark, mysterious one. Ben's the one who still won't let me dress him."

"No offense, but you're wearing a shirt with ice cream cones on it," Ben said.

Luke feigned indignation. Brianna, to his left now, pretended to lick the ice cream cones. Everyone settled into the idea of a new seating chart.

"Are you guys, like, best friends forever now?" Brianna asked Clare and Magpie. "Did you buy matching charm bracelets?"

"Yes," Clare said. "To both of those, yes."

"That's sweet," Brianna said. "Okay, Mags, I forgive you for not wanting to sit next to me anymore. If you still want to give me your leftovers, though, that would be totally cool with me."

"Of course," Magpie said. "Unless Clare wants them. That's part of the charm-bracelet pact we made."

Everybody laughed except Luke, who looked a little shocked. "I think…" he said, pausing for dramatic effect. "Mags, I think that might be the first time I've ever heard you make a joke."

Magpie smiled. "I've been practicing in the mirror."

The subject of Brandon Phipp's party was resurrected shortly after that, with a very clear line of who wanted to go and who didn't. On the didn't side: Brianna and Magpie. On the did side: Clare, Luke, and, surprisingly, Ben.

"I dunno. I like parties," Ben explained, opening his lunch to reveal celery sticks instead of carrots. He frowned at them momentarily before biting one in half. "Parties are fun."

"Excellent point," Brianna said. "I've changed my mind entirely. *Parties are fun.* Is someone writing this down?"

"It *will* be fun," Clare insisted. "We could take my mom's car; we'll all fit."

"Nobody has to go if they don't want to go," Ben added, looking quickly at Magpie.

"Oh, thank you, Ben, for excusing us," Brianna said, rolling her eyes.

Clare leaned over to Magpie as the rest of the table continued to debate the issue. "I'm not trying to pressure you," she whispered. "But I've been thinking about it, and I *do* think it would be good for you to come. Just to show Allison you don't give a shit what she says about you, you know? I mean—she *wants* you to sit at home being miserable. Which is exactly why you shouldn't."

"Sure, maybe," Magpie said. It was a good idea in theory, but she didn't really buy it. There was no winning. Whether Magpie showed up to the party or didn't—Allison had won six months ago.

Clare pulled away to continue arguing with Brianna, and Ben leaned in close. "Don't let Clare pressure you into anything," he said. "We could always do something else that night. If you wanted to."

"Like what?" Magpie asked.

"Like, we could go to . . . the movies."

Magpie tried to remember the last movie she had seen in the theaters, but she couldn't. When Eryn was sixteen and Magpie was ten, they used to go to the movies together. Magpie found out much later that Eryn had been paid for this; it was essentially a babysitting job. Her sister would sit next to her and text through whatever new animated movie they'd gone to see. Magpie had felt very grown-up riding in the car with Eryn and hadn't really minded her sister's refusal to hold her hand or buy her popcorn or pay attention to the movie. Sometimes Eryn left halfway through and came back during the credits smelling of cigarettes and something dark and bitter that Magpie would later understand had been her sister's boyfriend's cologne.

"What do you think?" Ben asked.

Magpie struggled to return to the present. All she could see was the glow of Eryn's cell phone in the darkened theater, the smell of boy and buttered popcorn, the dull pang of being short-term abandoned, a dozen movies Eryn had never actually been interested in seeing.

"That sounds nice," she managed finally, hoping her answer hadn't come too late to sound sincere. Because it *did* sound nice.

"All right, great!" Ben said. "We'll ditch the party for the movies."

"Ex-squeeze me, you'll do *what*?" Clare asked, leaning far over Magpie's right side to stare down Ben.

"We're just exploring different options," Ben said.

"You better explore the option of going to the party, or else you better explore the option of finding a new best friend," Clare retorted.

Magpie thought she was probably kidding, but she had never been good at reading people, and she didn't want to be the one to cause a fight between Ben and Clare. Before she could really give herself time to think about it, she said, "We can do both. Clare, we'll come to the party for a little bit, and then we'll go to the movies."

Clare narrowed her eyes. "I require at *least* an hour at the party."

"Deal," Magpie said.

Clare shifted her gaze to Ben.

"Deal," he said, smiling now.

"Fine," Clare said. "I hate you both, but fine."

———————

Magpie spent Saturday morning on the pizza pool float after finally scrubbing her mother's vomit off the carpet in the master bedroom and throwing her mother's sick-covered clothes into the washing machine with the last scrapes of detergent they had.

The hospital had called to say Ann Marie would be released on Monday.

Magpie avoided looking at the garden shed. The light remained off, but it still left her with a strange feeling in the pit of her stomach. As if there was something she couldn't remember.

She walked to the grocery store around eleven to put money on her phone and buy a box of cheap laundry detergent.

She wrote Ben a text message in the parking lot.

See you at one!

And he texted her back.

Sounds good!

When she got home, she put another load of clothes into the washing machine, and she took the Amelia Earhart books out to the backyard. She had a little more than an hour to look over them before she'd have to leave to meet Ben. She sat on the pool deck and let her legs dangle over the side into the water, which was no longer green but still smelled of chlorine, which made her feel calm and happy.

The pool was a normal pool. The backyard was a normal backyard. Everything was normal, even the garden shed, with its light off and its door shut and locked.

She was early to the library; she waited out front on a bench because it was a nice day and she didn't want to miss Ben—who arrived precisely at one o'clock, riding a pale-blue bicycle.

Magpie always thought it was jarring to see people out of their firmly established settings, and she had only ever seen Ben in school. Here, outside the library, atop his bicycle, Ben looked almost like a stranger. He wore a bicycle helmet, for one thing, and when he removed it, his hair was a little sweaty and matted to his head. He waved to her, and she got off her bench and walked over to him as he locked up the bike at the bike rack.

She wondered if she also looked a little bit like a stranger to him.

She was wearing a spaghetti-strap tank top, which she wasn't allowed to wear at school (shoulders were very slutty, apparently) and shorts, which she also wasn't allowed to wear at school (because, when she held her arms at her sides, the shorts were higher than the tips of her fingers).

At any rate, Ben had no trouble recognizing her, and he

even made a movement like he was thinking about giving her a hug, but Magpie was thankful he decided against it and chose instead to readjust the straps of his backpack.

"Hi," he said.

"Hi," she said.

"It's nice out, huh?"

"Really nice."

"What have you been doing today?"

"Not much. Some laundry. You?"

"Helping my parents with yard work," he said. "I think I got a little burned." He held up his arms, which had indeed turned a pale shade of pink.

"Aloe," Magpie said. And then she spent a few moments wondering if, instead of the Amelia Earhart books, she should have read a manual on how to be a better conversationalist, because certainly the offering of *aloe* was not doing her any favors.

"Well, should we go inside?" Ben asked.

They found an open cubicle in the back of the library; Magpie took the Amelia Earhart books out of her bag and set them on the desk.

"So where should we start?" Ben asked.

"I don't know." Magpie shrugged. "I think it's kind of interesting that they still don't know what happened to her. Even though they keep looking, you know? I mean, one week they think they've found her bones, the next week they think they've spotted her in an old photograph. But nobody *knows* yet."

"Isn't that the saddest part?"

"I don't think so. Because it means she could have survived. She could have orchestrated the whole thing in order to disappear. Start a new life somewhere."

"Forgetting for a moment that your scenario is *hugely* unlikely," Ben said, smiling, "*why* would she do that? She had a husband and everything."

"Everybody has a reason to want to change their lives," Magpie said quietly.

She hadn't meant it to be so honest, so prickling and sharp, but there it was.

Prickling and sharp and oh so honest.

Ben looked at her for a moment as if he wanted to ask her something. But then he shook his head—almost imperceptibly—and said, "I think this could be our entire project. I mean, you're right—lots of people have guesses about what happened to her, but nothing has been proved yet. We could research the major theories and maybe assign, like, a likelihood to each of them. A probability ratio or something."

"History is bad enough; now you want to bring math into it?" Magpie joked.

Ben laughed. "Probability is fascinating."

"Sure, sure."

They spent almost four hours at the library. Magpie

hadn't had lunch or breakfast, and her stomach turned pain-fully as she biked the two miles home. It was past five when she arrived, and she made herself dinner without turning on the kitchen overhead, enjoying the late light streaming in through the window from a sun almost ready to call it quits.

She looked out the window as the pasta water boiled.

Everything was still normal.

The world was quiet and ordinary.

After dinner, she would work on her essay for Mr. James. He wanted it next week, and she was determined to have it done early, to show him she was trying not to have to repeat sophomore year.

She poured herself a glass of lemonade from the pitcher she'd left in the fridge, then added a few splashes of vodka to it.

She made it weaker than she had the other night, just a hint of the burning vodka against the sweetness of the lemonade.

Magpie ate her macaroni and cheese in the kitchen stand-ing over the sink, her eyes darting every now and then to the backyard, just checking, just making sure.

Nothing out of the ordinary.

When she was done, she changed into her bathing suit and brought the drink outside to the pool.

She liked the quiet numbness that the first few sips of the drink provided, the spreading of calm she could feel in her chest that moved ever outward to her fingers and toes. It was especially pleasant while lying on the pizza float, enjoying the last few bits of sunlight that filtered in through the trees lining the backyard.

She took another long sip from her vodka lemonade, then rolled off the float and let herself be consumed by the water.

That was the word for it—*consumed*—the way the water slipped over her head and buttoned itself back up again. It felt like silk as she ran her hands through it. She felt it tugging at the edges of her eyes, her mouth, filling up her ears, trying to get inside her.

She surfaced after forty-eight beats measured by the thrum of her heart. She took a great gulp of the evening air and brushed her hands over her forehead, slicking back her wet hair.

When she opened her eyes, she thought she was imagining things; she blinked rapidly to get the water off her lashes, and every time she blinked, she expected him to be gone, but every time she blinked, he was still there, stubbornly standing in the backyard with his arms hanging limply by his sides and his expression so confused, so many things: hurt and lost and lonely and unsure of how he had come to be there.

"Dad?" she said, and the word bounced off the surface of the pool and was so much louder in the quiet than she had meant it to be.

Her father didn't respond right away. He just looked at her. Once, when Magpie was only a toddler, she'd opened the cabinet under the sink where her parents kept a plastic container of recycling. Her mother had forgotten to put the child lock back on the cabinet, and she'd gone into the other room for something, and Magpie had waddled immediately to the cabinet and pulled it open. She gazed at the tub of recycling as if it were a treasure chest filled with untouchable and priceless jewels. Laughing, she thrust her hands into the middle of it. Her laughter had turned into a squeal of betrayed pain as something sharp sliced into her finger. She pulled her hand out. Blood everywhere.

It was her father who had run into the room first. He gathered Magpie in his arms and set her on the kitchen counter and examined the wound, a worried but determined look on his face.

"You're all right," he murmured as Magpie wailed, throwing her head back and kicking her tiny feet against his stomach and chest. "You're going to be just fine."

The little cut had bled a lot but wasn't too deep. Her father cleaned it off with soap and water, and wrapped a bandage around her finger, and gave her ice pop.

For one full year afterward, she showed everyone the "boo-boo" on her finger even when it had healed completely and you couldn't see it anymore.

Magpie's heart twisted uncomfortably inside her. She remembered the sharp stab of pain on her finger as clearly as if it had happened a minute ago.

"Magpie," her father said.

Everything looked pale in the evening light. Her father, the pool water, the backyard. Magpie felt as pale as a shadow; she was surprised he could even see her.

"What are you doing here?" she whispered.

It seemed to her that she had split into two Magpies, that one Magpie was happy and swimming in her pool and drinking a vodka lemonade and making friends and the other Magpie was trapped in time, six months ago almost exactly, and when she looked at her father, all she could see was the dull pink of his naked body.

The two Magpies raged inside her: the first Magpie was overjoyed to see her father again, wanted nothing more than to pull herself out of the pool and run to him dripping wet; the second Magpie felt as if she would never get a full breath of air again as long as she lived.

"I've missed you so much," he said.

He took a step closer to the pool, and she moved farther away, keeping enough space between them, sending ripples of water spreading out around her. He looked a little wild, as if he hadn't slept.

"You've been gone for *six months*," she said.

"Your mother made it very clear that—"

"*Six months*. And then you just show up like a stalker and think that's going to make everything better?"

"I'm not...I wasn't...I've been calling."

"Right. For *her*. Did you forget I'm the one who actually walked in on you?"

He winced exactly as if she'd crossed the distance between them and slapped him across his face. It wasn't as if she hadn't considered it. She just wasn't ready to get that close.

"Magpie, I made a terrible, terrible mistake," he said.

"They won't even talk to us anymore. Did you know that? Nobody will talk to us anymore."

"Who…?"

"She got to them first. Everybody somehow thinks *we're* the bad guys. For Thanksgiving we watched TV and ate cranberry sauce out of the can. *Nobody wanted us.*"

"Magpie, I had no idea."

"Do you know Eryn left? Do you know Mom's in the hospital?"

"Slow down," he said, putting a hand over his eyes. "Slow down, Magpie."

Magpie climbed the ladder out of the pool. She looked around for her sister's beach towel, but it wasn't there. Where had she left it? She stood angry and dripping on the pool platform, looking down on him, feeling cold and vulnerable in only her swimsuit.

"Your mother called me from the hospital," he said. "She told me what happened. She doesn't want you to be alone."

Get him where it hurts, a tiny voice said in the back of Magpie's skull, a bright chirping voice that sounded almost like a bird's.

"I'm already alone," she said. "I've always been alone, and I will always be alone. Don't you see that?"

Her father looked as if he were on the edge of something, as if he might either cry or run or spit or scream.

"I'm so sorry," he said. "I did everything wrong. Please, Magpie, let me make it up to you. Please come home with me."

"Home? Where's *home* for you now, Dad? A motel? A one-bedroom apartment?"

"Please stop shouting," he said, and rubbed at the back of his neck. "I'm trying to help you. I'm trying to do the right thing. Come with me, Magpie."

"I'm not going anywhere with you."

"I'm not leaving you here alone," he said, and his voice was suddenly so stereotypically dadlike that Magpie half expected him to attach a *young lady* to the end of his sentence. "You are not staying in this house by yourself. You are underage and I am your father."

What could she do?

She couldn't go anywhere with him; she *refused*.

So what could she do?

What would *Allison* do?

Allison always knew the exact right thing to say, the exact right flick of hair or roll of eyes to inflict the most emotional harm on whoever her victim of the moment was. Magpie tried to conjure her now, to summon that sense of courage and fearlessness.

She laughed, and it was a strong laugh. A mean laugh. An Allison laugh.

Her father looked wounded, unsure. As if he did not recognize his own daughter.

"You're my father? That's a news flash. Since when, exactly?" she asked.

"You can't stay here by yourself," he said again, but his voice was quieter now, and his shoulders had sagged just a little.

Magpie could see the way in front of her clearly. The steps were easy and obvious.

"I won't be by myself," she said, relaxing, rolling her eyes in an easy, light way. "Don't be so dramatic. I have a friend coming over."

"Allison?" he asked.

But Magpie had been prepared for that; hearing Allison's name did not pierce into her heart like it could have. She smiled lightly.

"No. My friend Clare. You haven't met her. Her mom is out of town, and her dad isn't around anymore, so we're having a sleepover."

The carefully chosen word: *sleepover.* The carefully chosen vocal cadence: that of an innocent, tired daughter.

"Clare," her father repeated, as if he was thinking.

"Dad, I can't cancel on her now. We've already planned it. She has nowhere else to go."

The carefully chosen word—*Dad*—to evoke an emotional response from him.

It worked.

He softened.

He nodded.

"All right, I...I think that will be okay. As long as you're not here alone. But I want to meet this girl, Magpie. I'm going to wait until she gets here, okay?"

"Fine," Magpie said, shrugging, as if she couldn't care less. "But you can wait outside. You can't come in. This house doesn't belong to you anymore."

Magpie padded barefoot across the cooling grass and let herself in the back door. She could feel her father's eyes burning holes into the back of her swimsuit, but she wasn't worried about that anymore. Her feet left wet spots on the carpet. Her phone was on her bed. She picked it up and wrote a message to Clare.

Ugh, long story and I'll explain later but can you come over? And pretend like your mom is out of town and you're sleeping over? But you can leave as soon as my dad's gone.

Clare was a quick responder; she started typing right away, and Magpie held her phone in her hand, waiting for her response.

I'm bored out of my skull, sounds like a plan. What's your address?

Magpie gave it to her, and Clare responded that she would be over in fifteen minutes.

Magpie showered slowly, turning up the water as hot as she could stand it.

When she got out, her skin was pink. She got dressed and stepped out the front door onto the stoop.

Her father was sitting in his truck, waiting. He was both closer and farther away than he had been in six months, and Magpie so acutely felt that disparity that it took her breath away.

He got out of his truck.

He looked as if he wanted to say something to her, but a car pulled up next to the curb, interrupting the moment. Clare jumped out of the passenger's seat and waved her hand at her mom. Her mom waved back.

That simple exchange—that most normal of interactions— was enough to stab Magpie in the heart over and over again until she was sure she'd bleed to death before Clare reached the front door.

"So what's the story?" Clare whispered.

"Your mom is out of town. We planned this a few days ago. My mom's in the hospital."

"Wait—what? Is she okay?"

"Not now," Magpie said, because her father was walking toward them.

Clare smiled and turned around to greet him.

The smile was an expert smile, one pristinely crafted to fit a specific goal: fool a parent.

"Hi, Mr. Lewis," Clare said, and stuck out her hand. "I'm Clare Brown."

Magpie's father took it. He looked happy to have something to hold on to even for just a moment.

"It's a pleasure to meet you."

"Likewise. Hey, thanks for being okay with this. My mom is out of town and my aunt—that's who just dropped me off—well, she's got a newborn and twin toddlers, so it's basically, like, rock-concert levels of noise all night long, you know? So when Mags told me what happened to Mrs. Lewis, well, I'm just glad I can be here for her." She shifted her overnight bag from one arm to the other; Magpie thought this was a nice touch.

"Of course," Magpie's father said, and she watched him relax visibly into the intricate lie Clare had just told. "It's very nice to meet you."

"It's nice to meet you!" Clare said, and then she had the good sense to not add *Magpie's told me so much about you* because, of course, Magpie had not.

"Well—call me, all right? If you two need anything. Anything at all. Get spooked or want pizza or... Here, actually."

Magpie's father took two twenty-dollar bills out of his wallet and handed them to his daughter. Magpie closed her fist around them and tried not to let her skin touch her father's skin.

"Don't spend that on booze, okay?" he said, his voice shaky, his joke missing the mark by eighty-seven miles, approximately.

"Thanks, Mr. Lewis," Clare said.

"I'll be home. All right, Magpie? I'll be home if you need anything."

Magpie's father walked to his truck and got inside and drove away, and the two girls watched until it turned a corner, then Clare turned to Magpie, and said, *"Magpie?"*

"It's just an old nickname," Magpie said, forcing a smile. "Thank you so much for doing this, you can leave whenever. Here."

She tried to hand Clare one of the twenty-dollar bills, but Clare pushed it away. "What are you talking about? I'm staying over, and we're ordering pizza. Come on, *Magpie.*"

Magpie followed Clare into the house, her heart beating an uncomfortable, pounding beat against her ribs. The house was disgusting; nobody had dusted a shelf or mopped a floor in six months.

Clare paused just inside the living room, and Magpie knew she must have seen it, the wealth of filth that had collected on every surface, the neglect and misuse that had settled over the house like a film.

But far from making fun of it, far from calling attention to it, Clare turned around and looked Magpie dead in the eyes, and said, "What happened to your mom?"

"Oh," Magpie said, and although everything inside her was urging her to lie, to make something up, to run and hide, she made herself clear her throat and tell the truth. It was her truth to tell, and she would tell it when she wanted to. "She drank too much. Way too much. I think...I think she almost died."

"Jesus," Clare said, and she put her hand on Magpie's

arm, and Magpie learned that Clare's hands were warm and soft and surprisingly strong. "I am so sorry." She paused and nodded to the front of the house. "He doesn't live with you guys anymore? Your dad?"

"No," Magpie said. "But I'm sure you know why."

Clare looked confused. "No idea."

"You haven't heard anything about it?"

"Nope. But even if I had—I'm well aware that you can't believe everything you hear. I mean, people actually think my father shot himself. In our garage!" She rolled her eyes, and Magpie felt her face go hot. "It makes no sense to me, because anyone can just search his name and..." Clare mimicked fingers on a keyboard, then she caught sight of Magpie's face and stopped. "Oh, crap. That's what you thought, too."

"I'm so sorry," Magpie said. "I'm such a hypocrite, Clare, I—"

"It's fine, honestly," Clare insisted. She took a deep breath, looked around the living room, decided something. "He took pills," she continued in a small voice. "And not in our garage. He rented a hotel room. Told my mom he had a business trip, but he was really just a few miles away. I guess I'm glad he did it there instead of in our house. And no, we didn't move, either. That's our same house we've always lived in."

"I'm really sorry," Magpie said. "I had no idea."

Clare shrugged, and said, "It's all right. Should we order the pizza?"

Magpie got the phone number from a menu in the kitchen

and dialed as Clare put her overnight bag down on the couch and looked out the back door.

"You have a *pool*? I wish you told me; I would have brought my suit."

"You can borrow one of mine," Magpie said, holding her hand over the mouthpiece. "What do you like on your pizza?"

"Cheese, eggplant, mushrooms, olives, whatever," Clare said. "I'm starving. Where's the bathroom?"

Magpie pointed down the hall, and Clare went off in search of it.

She finished ordering the pizza and hung up the phone.

She should have gone to see her mother today, she shouldn't have been so foolish to think that nobody would come looking for her, a sixteen-year-old with terrible decision-making capabilities alone in a house without supervision.

But this was much better.

Clare, pizza...

This was infinitely preferable to hospital lighting, the harsh way it cut right into your skin, the smell of rubbing alcohol and blanched food sticking to your clothes like smoke.

And here was a weird thing: Even though she hadn't even been thinking about it, even though she had succeeded in pushing it to the farthest corner of her brain, even though she had written it off as a thing that had never happened, as a thing that was impossible and made up in her head, she somehow knew.

The shed light was on and she ought to show Clare.

She ought to bring Clare out to the backyard and show her all the beautiful things there were in the world if only you knew where to look for them.

Magpie heard a shuffle from behind her.

"Hey, what bathing suit can I borrow?" Clare asked.

With immense concentration, Magpie pulled herself away from the window. "I'll get one," she said. She went into her room and found one of her smaller suits, something she thought would fit Clare.

"When did they say the pizza will get here?" Clare asked from the doorway.

"Like, fifteen minutes." Magpie tossed the bathing suit to Clare. "I should put some chemicals in the pool. They're in the shed."

Her voice was not her voice. Her voice was that of a person who sounded almost exactly like her. Clare would never be able to tell.

"Oh, okay," Clare said, shrugging. "Want me to come with you?"

"Sure."

They went outside.

It had gotten dark.

The night was unnaturally quiet, pierced not even by the chirping of crickets, the buzzing of flies. The pool water was still and dark blue, reflecting the sky above it. Magpie dipped her hand into it as they passed. Not too hot. Not too cold.

Neither was Magpie too hot nor too cold; instead, she felt exactly right. Exactly the perfect temperature and exactly perfect in every other conceivable way: This was what she was supposed to be doing in the moment she was supposed to be doing it. There are so few times in one's life when this happens that she wished she could pause and enjoy it for a little while, but she had things to do and she couldn't put them off.

"Someone left the light on," Clare observed of the shed. When they got closer, Magpie could see one large white moth beating its wings against the glass pane of a high window, trying to get in.

Magpie moved her body in front of the padlock so Clare wouldn't see the impossible way it slid off into her hand, the way it opened without being opened, the way it responded to Magpie's unspoken command.

She pulled open the door, and it did not creak or otherwise protest.

She could see the two worlds contained in the shed, and a glance back at Clare revealed that Clare, too, was seeing something impossible, the doubleness of the shed, the way the shed was both here and someplace else.

"Mags," Clare whispered, and her voice sounded scared, but she didn't run away.

"It's okay," Magpie said. "I've been here before."

And in that moment she remembered everything, and she had really done it, and Near was real, and she would show them all now—she would show them just what she was capable of.

FOUR FOR A BOY

If you give a name to an impossible thing, does it make the impossible thing any less impossible?

Magpie thought so, and she had named this place before she had even come here, and she had called it Near and wrote down its details in a bright-yellow notebook, and it was real, and it was right in front of them, spreading out so far in every direction that there was no room left for doubt in her mind that she had left her neighborhood in Farther, New England, the World, and traveled somewhere else entirely. Somewhere near. Somewhere Near.

Another world, another place, another plane of existence, she couldn't say for sure. It also didn't seem that important.

Next to her, Clare vomited noisily into the plush lime-green grass that covered the hillside they'd found themselves on.

They'd taken a few steps away from the shed, and they were entirely in Near, on a grassy hillside, but Magpie could still see pieces of her world in a shed that was translucent and both there and not there: an old pair of roller skates, a wicker chair, a crack of darkness that she thought might be the door of the shed left ajar and open to the nighttime of her world.

This world was bright and sunny, a cheerful yellow sun high and floating in a blue sky. Puffs of clean white clouds. Down the hillside, a half hour's walk or so, Magpie could see a small town. Blue and white and yellow houses all surrounded by a clean line of fencing.

Picturesque, Magpie thought. That was the only word for it.

"Are you okay?" she asked Clare, meaning something closer to *Are you almost done?* Because she could not stand the wet, sloppy sound of vomit hitting grass. It reminded her too much of her mother, and this place could not be tarnished with the memory of Ann Marie.

Clare sat back, kneeling, and wiped her mouth with her sleeve.

"What the fuck just happened?" she asked, her voice shaky and cold. "What is this place? Where's your backyard? Where's the shed?"

But then she saw it, and she sat up straighter, and Magpie knew Clare was trying to explain the existence of the shed in this world, how it clearly didn't belong here and yet was so obviously *there*. The thereness of it was unmistakable. And everything else was inside of it. An entire world tumbling out of it. Clare's eyes looked wildly around at the sky, at the grass, at the not-there-but-there shed and finally landed on Magpie, holding on to the only thing she knew.

"I've been here before, but I didn't remember," Magpie said. Her own voice was calm and even. "I remember now."

"You've been here? What is this place?" Clare asked, hugging her own body with her arms, pulling herself together in a tight embrace.

"Can't you see?" Magpie asked, and nodded her head in the direction of the town, the only small cluster of buildings within sight, surrounded on every side by miles and miles and miles of undisturbed grass stretching unblemished to the horizon.

Clare looked. She shielded her eyes with her hand.

"See what?" she asked after a moment. "It's just a town."

"I know," Magpie said.

"I don't want to go down there."

"But can't you see what it is?"

"I don't know what you mean. I don't want to go down there," Clare repeated softly. Her breathing was ragged, uneven. Her eyes grew wider.

Magpie softened; she realized she was being a jerk. Her own smug excitement at being back in Near—at remembering! at it being real!—was so overwhelming to her that she'd forgotten feeling *exactly* like Clare did now the first time she'd stepped foot in the shed.

Through the shed.

Clare sat on the grass again, her legs bent, and placed her head between her knees. She took deep, gulping breaths that shook the air around her. She started to cry.

Magpie knelt in front of her. "Clare, are you okay? Are you okay? I'm so sorry. I would have warned you, but I didn't remember. I promise I didn't remember until now. I've been here, but it's like... It's like I lost it all. Are you hurt?"

Clare composed herself enough to lift her head a little. Her mascara was smeared down her cheeks; she was crying hard now, her shoulders heaving in time to her ragged breaths.

"Anxiety," she whispered, the word thin and scratchy. "Anxiety attack. Just... give me a minute."

Magpie put her hands on Clare's knees as Clare lowered her head again.

They stayed like that for a long time, Clare crying and breathing, and Magpie with her hands on Clare's knees, squeezing and rubbing them, hoping she was doing enough.

Eventually, Clare's breathing evened out. She raised her head and wiped at her cheeks with the backs of her hands.

"I haven't had one of those in a long time."

"I'm sorry," Magpie said.

"You didn't remember? You didn't remember this was here?"

"No. Not until I got here."

"Okay," Clare replied. "I believe you."

Clare ran her hands through her hair, took a few more

deep breaths, then looked around again at the world they'd entered.

"It's still here," she said. "I thought I might be dreaming, but I've never had a panic attack in my dreams."

"It's real," Magpie said. "I've been here before. The shed, it's some kind of...doorway."

Clare looked back at the shed, transparent and strange in the bright sun of this new place. She nodded her head slowly. "So what's that town?"

"I haven't gone down yet. I couldn't work up my nerve to get any closer," Magpie admitted. Then, as if she were revealing the biggest secret she had ever locked away inside her heart (and she was, she was), she added, "It's called Near."

"Near," Clare said, trying the word out on her tongue. "Wait—if you've never been down there, how do you know what it's called?"

"I just know," she whispered.

"What do you mean, you just know?"

"I can't explain it," Magpie said. It was easier than telling Clare about the notebook. It was easier than trying to explain that she had *made* this place. That she had *named* it. She had probably said too much already. She watched Clare carefully, studied her, and that's how she saw the moment Clare decided that she didn't really have any choice but to trust Magpie. Clare was a trusting individual, kind and eager to believe the best in people. Magpie put a hand on her knee again.

"How are you feeling?" she asked.

"Better," Clare said, nodding slowly. She pulled herself to her feet, then offered Magpie a hand.

When they were both standing, Clare turned to look at the place where the garden shed still stood, still translucent, still impossible.

"We should go back," she said.

"I think we should get a closer look. Now that there are two of us."

Clare looked down at the town. "There's something about it."

"What do you mean?"

"Something... familiar."

Magpie knew the answer, of course; she had known it because she had *made* it, but it had slithered to someplace deep in her brain, someplace hidden and dark, and she could only remember it now, as if being here again had dug the truth out of her.

"We could just go a *little* closer," she suggested. "Just to see."

Clare's eyes darted to the shed. "Do you think it will stay there? Or do you think it will go away?"

"If we go down there?"

"Yeah," Clare said, and she looked back to the town, to the place that lived both inside Magpie's heart and now, somehow, all around them.

"I think it will. Don't you just... feel like it will?"

Clare considered. She took a long, slow breath. "Are you sure?"

"We've come all this way," Magpie said, even though *all this way* was only one single step into a shed that unlocked itself at Magpie's touch. "I think it will stay."

"Should we test it?"

"How do you think we should test it?"

"Here," Clare said. She took Magpie's hand and led her away from the shed: five feet, now ten feet, now fifteen. They kept their eyes trained on the not-shed, and although it glimmered and flickered in the bright streaming sunlight, it remained *there*. That is to say—both there and not there. It didn't disappear.

"I think it's okay," Magpie said.

"I think I know what you mean now," Clare said. "How you can feel it."

"That the shed won't disappear?"

"Yes," Clare said. "I don't know how to explain it."

"So should we go down there?"

"I think we should, maybe," Clare agreed. "Just to see it a little closer."

Magpie took one inhale of one breath to imagine what this moment might look like if it were Allison, not Clare, standing before her. Allison would not have had a panic attack. She would not have permitted it. Allison would have stepped through the doorway in the shed and not cried or thrown up; she would have raised her head to the bright,

bright sun and laughed. She would have considered herself deserving of this world so spread out and open in front of her. She would have made herself its queen.

"Let's go," Magpie said, and she took Clare's hand in hers and squeezed it once and let herself feel thankful, for just a moment, that Clare was Clare and not anybody else in the world, especially not Allison. This place did not deserve Allison. And Allison did not deserve Magpie. And Magpie did not need Allison. No—not anymore.

They set off down the hill.

The sun of Near was high in the sky, and there was a soft breeze that blew in over the top of the hill and gently swept around them as they made their way toward the town.

When they had walked for about fifteen minutes, the shed finally winked out of eyeshot. But they knew it was still there, just too far away now to see properly. They could *feel* it, as if it were some strong magnet set atop the hill, some beacon that was broadcasting its existence and making them feel calmer.

They were closer to the town now, closer to Near, and the buildings were coming into focus, growing larger in their sight, like in the final descent of an airplane, when the world at first looks dollhouse-size and then gradually becomes real again.

Finally, just a stone's throw away now, Clare stopped. Magpie watched her squint. Magpie watched her trying to make sense of it.

"That playground," Clare said, and pointed.

Magpie looked. There was a small complex of buildings on the outer edge of the town, and in between two of them was a playground. There was a bright-red slide, a merry-go-round, a jungle gym shaped like a pirate ship, complete with a flag and ship's wheel.

"That's just like the one at the elementary school," Clare said. "I take Teddy to the playground on the weekends sometimes. I mean, that's...that's exactly like it."

"Huh," Magpie said. She already knew, of course. But she felt it would be better if she let Clare reach her own conclusion.

"And that building on the other side of it," Clare said. "That's our high school. The whole complex. The high school, the middle school, the elementary school, the playground. Do you see it?"

Clare looked around. Magpie watched her eyes follow the road that led out of the education complex down to a stop sign with a gas station on the corner.

"And there," Clare said, pointing. "That gas station."

"Yeah?"

"Don't you see? This is *Farther*. Except...it's not. There's something different about it."

"Well, it's cleaner, for one thing."

Clare turned to Magpie. "Oh. You already knew."

"I wanted you to see it for yourself."

Clare turned back to the town and pointed out more

landmarks. "The mall. The pharmacy. The old mill. Mags, this is *crazy*."

"I know."

The town itself—Near—was perfect. As if nothing blemished or faded or worn had ever been let into it. It was unlike Farther in that respect. It couldn't be anything less like Farther. And yet it was unmistakable. It *was* and it *wasn't* Farther, just like the shed *was* and *wasn't* in Near. Just like so many things in Magpie's life that both *were* and *weren't*. She had a sister and she didn't. She had parents and she didn't.

They walked closer.

The cars parked curbside at local businesses were spotless, not one slap of bird shit to be seen. The garbage cans on the corners of the busier streets were immaculate, not a single pressed circle of gum on any of their lids.

Everything was clean, and the air smelled sweet, and the sky above them was as blue as a jaybird, and when they reached the white picket fence that surrounded the entire town, Magpie reached a hand out to open the latch that kept it shut, but Clare stopped her just before she could.

"Wait," Clare said, and Magpie waited, and Clare looked back at the hill, which was just a hill now, as plain a hill as you could hope for, with not even the smallest hint of a magical portal on top of it.

"What?" Magpie asked.

"Maybe this isn't a good idea."

"We've come this far."

"Have you noticed that there aren't any people?" Clare asked.

Magpie had. And it was one of the best things about it.

Not a single car was being driven. Not a single person was out walking a dog or checking the mail or finishing up an afternoon jog. The town was as still and silent as Magpie's own heart. And because it was so familiar to her, she felt at ease, peaceful. She had dreamed and written for six long months of a place where the things that had happened to her had never happened to her—a place where she could decide her own history and her own future. And here it was: Near, a town where she could finally be free.

"They're probably all at work," Magpie said. "Or school. Or sleeping."

"It's the middle of the day."

Magpie's heart fluttered with the sudden realization that if Clare did not come with her, if Clare decided to retreat back up the hill to step into the translucent not-shed that would lead her back to Magpie's own backyard, Magpie would have to go with her. Because, when Clare stepped back into their world, she wouldn't remember any of this, and she wouldn't know where Magpie had gone, and what would she do then? And what if Magpie forgot again, too?

No—they couldn't leave yet. She had to see more of it.

"Would it make you feel better if there were people here?" Magpie asked. Then, lighter: "Even though people are terrible?"

Clare nodded, a small frightened nod that reminded Magpie of a bunny. Then she said, "People aren't terrible," and Magpie was about to argue with her when they both heard it at the same time: the faintest shuffling of feet.

There, just on the other side of the fence, was a small boy holding a red ball.

He wore shorts the color of salmon, a white collared polo shirt, a pair of clean white tennis sneakers. The ball he held in his hand looked brand-new, as if his mother had just taken him to the store that morning to get it. He didn't bounce it, just held it, and he looked at Magpie and Clare as if he was surprised to find himself there. He even looked down at his feet, at his arms, at the ball in his hands, as if he'd only now noticed that he had a body to begin with.

Magpie did not immediately realize who the boy was, but Clare did, and she wrenched open the gate and threw herself at him before Magpie could even put a hand out to stop her, and she grabbed the boy by the shoulders and shook him hard, her voice panicky.

"Teddy? Teddy?" she shrieked, shaking him every time she said his name.

The boy just looked at her, as if maybe he didn't know his own name, and Clare pulled the ball from him and threw it away and then cupped his face in her hands, and said, "Ringo?"

The boy relaxed at once, as if his chosen nickname

released him from some invisible spell. He smiled, then tried to take a step toward his ball, but Clare held him firmly.

"Ow, Clare! Lemme go!" he complained.

"What are you doing here?" Clare demanded, her voice rising to a fever pitch. "How did you get here?"

"Lemme go!" he yelped again. "Lemme go, Clare, you're hurting me!"

"How did you get here?" Clare yelled, squeezing his arms so hard that Magpie could see his skin turning red.

Teddy narrowed his eyes at her, wrenched himself away so fiercely that he fell backward, landing hard on his bottom, scrabbling away like a human crab.

"I said, LET ME GO," he shouted, jumping to his feet.

Clare made to go after him, but Magpie was ready that time, and she grabbed Clare's arm and held on tightly. Ringo made it five or six feet, then paused. His arms where Clare had gripped him were red and angry. They would bruise. There were tears in his eyes, and he kept glancing at the ball frantically, as if he needed it back, as if it were somehow more than a ball, somehow imperative that he reach it.

"What are you doing here?" Clare asked, her voice panicky again, her breathing jagged. She turned to Magpie. "What is he doing here?"

"How should I know?" Magpie asked, and when she was sure Clare wouldn't go after him again, she released her arm and watched Clare crumble a bit into herself, folding up smaller, hunching and scared.

"You're not supposed to be here," she said.

He shrugged, and said, "What do you mean, Clare? I live here."

"You don't live here, Teddy; you live somewhere else."

Ringo laughed a short, easy laugh that echoed strangely through the otherwise quiet town. "Who's Teddy?"

"Ringo," Clare corrected herself. "Ringo, fine. Just come with me, okay? We need to leave."

"I'm not going anywhere," Ringo said. "You can't make me go anywhere."

"Ringo—" she said, and Clare took a step toward him and he took a step back, the perfect mirror image, just a half second out of time.

"I'm hungry, Clare," he said. "Are you coming home for dinner? Daddy made spaghetti."

And the word hung on the air.

Daddy...

And Clare took a breath that did not end.

And the boy flashed a quick smile. A mean smile. And then he darted forward and grabbed his ball, clutching it to his chest as if he could finally breathe again. "You know what I think?" he said. "I think I don't want you to come home at all. I think I want to eat all the spaghetti myself."

And he stuck his tongue out at her.

Quick, like a snake.

And he turned and ran and disappeared between two houses.

And Clare sat down in the grass and put her head between her knees again.

———————

Magpie let Clare cry and shake on the grass; this panic attack lasted longer than the one on the hill. Or perhaps it was a continuation of the first one. Perhaps all panic attacks were connected, never-ending, just ebbing and flowing for all eternity.

Magpie waited.

Clare howled and sobbed, and Magpie understood her howls and sobs to be the kind that stemmed from loss—the loss of a father who had not, as it were, shot himself in the family garage but who had had the decency to do it somewhere just ever so slightly out of reach.

Magpie had experienced plenty of loss, but her losses were still alive and walking around—Allison and Eryn and Magpie's own father, who had broken the secret code and showed up to a house where he was no longer welcome.

And Ann Marie.

Not gone but gone anyway.

Not there but there at the same time, moving through the house with veins clumsy with alcohol. Refusing to eat Jell-O in a hospital room and sending grown-ups to check on Magpie, as if Magpie had ever needed checking up on.

And then Clare stopped crying. She leaned back on the

grass and wiped snot from her upper lip and flattened her short hair against her scalp, and as Magpie realized she would just a moment or two before she did, she left.

Out the gate.

Away from Near.

Up the hill.

"Clare!" Magpie said, and ran after her, pausing only for a second to make sure the gate was closed behind her. "Clare, wait!"

Clare was fast when she wanted to be, and Magpie had to run to catch up with her, and by the time she did, they were both out of breath, and Clare's face was dry and red and resolved.

"This place isn't real," she said. "You put something in my pizza."

"I put something in your—what? Clare, we didn't even get the pizza yet."

"You drugged me. You're real fucked-up, you know that? Everything they say about you is true," Clare said. "Even the stuff about your father. Allison told everyone. He fucked your aunt and you walked in on them and you're so sick you probably *liked it*." Her mouth was filled with venom in the shape of words. She spit them out at Magpie one by one. She pulled her arm away when Magpie tried to grab her, then she took off running up the hill, and Magpie struggled to catch up to her, but the distance between them grew bigger and bigger as they went.

Clare kept going up and up, and Magpie kept going up

and up, albeit a lot slower, and when she finally reached the shed, Clare had already gone through.

Magpie turned to survey the small town again. *Her* town. Her Near.

It was still there, and Magpie knew that it would be there for her whenever she needed it, and she knew, somehow she knew, that this time she'd remember it. And she knew she would come back. Again and again and maybe—maybe one of those times she wouldn't leave.

She took a deep breath and stepped into the shed that was and wasn't there. And with every step forward she took, the shed became more *there* than *not there* until finally it was fully there, and the grassy green hill was almost fully not there, and Magpie put her hand on the door of the shed and pushed through to her own dark cricket-chirping backyard.

Clare stood in front of the shed, bathing suit on, eating a piece of pizza.

"Took you long enough," she said. "Did you get them?"

"Get what?" Magpie asked. She was feeling a bit light-headed; it was hard work to hold on to a memory that was doing its best to flit away from you.

"The chemicals, duh," Clare said, and rolled her eyes and laughed and had another bite of pizza. "You said you were getting the chemicals for the pool, remember?"

"Right," Magpie said, smiling because—she had done it. She had remembered Near. And Clare hadn't. And everything was fine. "I think they're actually in the garage. I just realized."

"Well, hurry up! And have some pizza. I want to go swimming," Clare said.

Magpie remembered the things Clare had said to her as they ran up the hill.

They were terrible things.

Allison had told everyone what Magpie's father had done.

You're real fucked-up, you know that?

But that wasn't Clare now.

Clare now was eating a piece of pizza so quickly she kept dropping bits of cheese down the front of her bathing suit, yelping and laughing when they burned her skin, fishing them out and flicking them on the grass. Clare now would never remember what she had said to Magpie in Near because Magpie would never let her into Near again. She understood now that it was for her. It was for her and no one else.

And her heart sang and her feet hardly touched the grass and she went inside to get herself something to eat.

FIVE FOR SILVER

Clare woke up early the next morning and called her mother to come pick her up.

"We're going to the outlets," she explained, running Magpie's comb through her hair. "Otherwise I'd stay later. Thanks for the pizza."

"Thanks for coming over. You really saved me with my dad," Magpie said.

"Anytime. Go back to sleep! Text me later."

Magpie let Clare outside and locked the door behind her, then she went back into her bedroom and got her yellow notebook and sat cross-legged on her bed holding it.

The things Clare had said to her in Near echoed somewhere in the back of her mind. She opened up the notebook and removed a pen she had tucked into its spiral edge and wrote on a blank page: *Nobody will be mean to me, and I will*

have someone who knows me as I know myself and who wishes
me only happiness and who will never betray me.

She tucked the notebook under her pillow, leaned back, and closed her eyes.

Clare hadn't meant those things. Magpie knew that, she really believed it—Clare had just been scared and panicking and overwhelmed. But in that moment on the hill, Clare had been so much like her, like Allison. The way her face had contorted in anger. The way she had picked her words to do the most damage.

Magpie tried not to think about it, to make her mind blank, like a sheet of paper. She felt exhausted still, and after a few minutes, she fell back to sleep, and she spent most of Sunday in bed with her curtains drawn tightly and her door shut. Finally, in the late afternoon, she got out of bed and changed into her swimsuit and moved out to the backyard.

It was a muggy day. Magpie felt tired and lethargic, the kind of exhaustion that comes from spending too long lying in bed not sleeping, just wasting the hours till night.

She lowered herself into the pool all at once, ducking underneath the cool water and using the ladder to hold herself at the very bottom.

When they were younger, Magpie and Eryn would go into the pool after dinner when the heat from the day had settled thickly over the backyard and the sun was low enough to cast long shadows over the water. They would stay away from the black parts of the pool, irrationally afraid of what they couldn't see, invisible hands that would pull them underneath the water and trap them there to drown. They would stay in the pool until their fingers wrinkled and their eyes turned red from the chlorine and their heads sloshed so full of water that their mother would have to soak cotton balls in rubbing alcohol and squeeze them into their ears to evaporate it. They would stand shivering on the pool deck, sharing the same towel, their hair tangling together, and the whole world shrinking down to just the two of them, just this pool.

Those nights and those summers felt as if they lasted forever, but in reality Magpie knew that Eryn would have been quickly growing up and out of the novelty of playing with her much younger sister. Soon she brought friends over. Soon Magpie was not invited into the pool anymore. But Magpie could not blame her sister, who was so grown-up even at twelve, thirteen, her hair cut into a bob that hugged her chin, her legs so long that they came up to her eyes, her laugh so contagious that random people would stop to look. Her sister had been magical.

You're going to drown if you stay down there.

Magpie opened her eyes underwater. She was still sitting on the bottom of the pool, and her lungs were burning. She released her grip on the ladder and propelled herself upward. When her head broke the surface, she took a breath that physically hurt.

"Who said that?" she asked, and turned a wild circle in

the pool, expecting to see her father again, uninvited and looking down at her.

But there was no one in the backyard.

She spun around again, but there was no one in the pool, then she dragged herself onto the swim platform for a better view, and still she couldn't see anything.

Nothing was different at all. Except...

There was a folded towel on the swim platform.

Magpie hadn't brought a towel outside with her; she'd forgotten. She knelt down and picked it up, unfolding it and holding her arms open to spread it out.

It was her sister's old beach towel. The one she had dropped in Near. The one she hadn't remembered dropping because she hadn't remembered anything from her first visit until last night with Clare. The embroidered initials: *ERL.*

Magpie spun around a final time, slower.

The shed light was off.

The backyard was empty.

And a voice had spoken into her ear as clearly as...

But there hadn't been anyone, of course. If someone really *was* in the backyard, she wouldn't have been able to hear them underwater.

She let her arms fall. She considered the towel—how had it gotten here? Or maybe she hadn't dropped it in Near at all? Maybe it had always been on the pool platform, folded neatly, waiting for her. Was she losing her mind?

"Get a grip," she whispered to herself.

She looked at the shed. The light was off. In the late afternoon sun, it seemed ordinary, commonplace. But Magpie knew its secret. Magpie could open the door again. She could go back inside.

But not now. No, she couldn't put it off any longer—because the phone had been ringing every twenty or thirty minutes since eight that morning, and she knew it was her mother; she knew without even looking at the caller ID. So she wrapped the towel around herself and went inside and took a shower and braided her hair and then rode her bicycle to the hospital.

Ann Marie was sitting up in bed, eating a colorless lump of something that might have been meatloaf, might have been lasagna. Magpie stood in the doorway and tried to be invisible. And it worked for a minute, then, of course, it didn't.

"Magpie? Is that you?" her mother said. Her coloring had returned, her skin no longer the grayish-blue it had been when Magpie had last seen her. Her fingers shook as she lowered the fork to her tray and picked up a napkin to dab at the edges of her mouth. "Sweetheart?"

When was the last time her mother had called her *sweetheart*? When was the last time *anyone* had called her *sweetheart*?

Her sister, before she grew up and found yoga and stopped eating sugar, had called Magpie *Little* sometimes because she was so many years younger, because when she tried on her sister's dresses they dragged on the floor and covered up her hands.

Little.

Sweetheart.

Magpie.

How many names could one girl possibly carry?

"I'm sorry I didn't come yesterday," Magpie said, stepping into the room, letting the full, sick glow of the overhead lights wash over her.

"You don't have to apologize for anything," Ann Marie said. "You certainly don't have to apologize for not coming to this terrible place."

"It isn't so bad. Look. No Jell-O." Magpie pointed at her mother's tray where, in lieu of Jell-O for dessert, there was an unopened package of rice pudding.

"I made a formal complaint," Ann Marie said, and she tried to smile, but her smile turned quickly into a sort of grimace, and that turned quickly into a series of racking sobs that sent tremors through her thin body.

And Magpie made a decision to be the dutiful daughter, to do what she was supposed to (in case anybody was looking), so she rushed to her mother's side and put her arms around her while she cried, stroking her hair and whispering things she hoped would calm her down.

Eventually, Ann Marie stopped crying, but she still clung

to Magpie with a death grip, as if she knew Magpie was even then fighting everything in her body that was screaming at her to run, get out of there, crawl straight back to Near and never come back again.

(But could she? Could she go into another world and disappear forever?)

Magpie gently wiggled out of her mother's arms and looked at her. Ann Marie's face had gone all red and blotchy, and there were still stubborn tears leaking from the corners of her eyes.

Magpie almost felt bad for her, and then she didn't, and then she *tried* to, because this was her mother and she ought to want her to feel happy and safe and well. But she only wanted her to stop sniffling. Which it didn't seem like Ann Marie was going to manage in the foreseeable future.

"Here, finish your dinner," Magpie said, and helpfully speared whatever wiggling gunk was on her mother's plate with the fork. "You need to get your strength up."

This was something she had heard before, in movies and TV shows—*you need to get your strength up*—and it seemed like good advice, all things considered.

Ann Marie opened her mouth, and Magpie airplaned the food in and thought about the reversal of roles, of the caregiver becoming the cared-for, of her mother getting older and older until she was back in diapers or else dead from drink before she got the chance to age.

They worked together to clear the plate of food, then Magpie swiveled the tray away from the bed, and Ann Marie looked as if she might cry again. She reached her hand out to the bouquet of flowers Magpie had bought for her with Ann Marie's own money. Someone had put it into a vase. Ann Marie pressed a petal between her thumb and forefinger and hiccupped twice loudly.

"I'm so sorry for everything I've put you through," she said.

Magpie wanted to say something along the lines of *Hey, at least I didn't walk in on you boning my uncle*, but she didn't think it was the right time for that. So she sat on the edge of Ann Marie's hospital bed instead and tried to fix her face into something that resembled compassion.

"You don't have to apologize to me."

"Of course I do. I have so much to apologize for. I know that. I drove your father away and I drove your sister away and it's a miracle I haven't driven you away, too."

And this interested Magpie, because it was the first time Ann Marie had hinted that her husband's transgressions might be, in part, her fault.

"What do you mean, you drove Dad away?"

"Oh, there's no excuse for what he did, so don't think I'm giving him one," Ann Marie clarified. "I just mean, I know I'm not blameless for the dissolution of my marriage."

Magpie found herself wondering if this was the first time

in six-plus months that she'd had a sober conversation with her mother. She remembered that Ann Marie, when not four or five drinks deep, was smart and thoughtful, and took the time to examine things from multiple angles. It was just like her to explore her own part in her husband's adultery and ultimate betrayal.

But that word. "What do you mean *dissolution*?" Magpie asked.

Ann Marie withdrew her hand from the bouquet and tapped a manila folder of paperwork on her bedside table. "Apparently, six months of asking for forgiveness is about as much as your father can take. And I don't blame him, Magpie. I should have taken his call. I should have taken it if only to tell him I wasn't going to take it, if you know what I mean."

"What is that?"

"He came to see me. On Friday, then again this morning. We've had a long talk, and we both agree that it's time to make it official."

"To make what official?" Magpie asked, but she already knew, of course, and the icy feeling in the pit of her stomach confused her, because wasn't this was she wanted? For her father to go away, to disappear?

"Your father and I are getting a divorce," Ann Marie said.

There was silence for a number of heartbeats—at first Magpie counted, then she lost count, then she started counting again, then her mother had taken her hand and was squeezing it gently. "Magpie…do you know how to get in touch with your sister? There are things I need to say to her. To both of you."

At the mention of her sister, Magpie looked up sharply, then shook her head. "Eryn changed her number. I've told you that."

"I know, but I also know that she isn't all that far away. I thought maybe you might have gone to the campus. I thought you might have tried to track her down. Your father—he says we need to give Eryn her space. And I agree with him, but… she's my daughter. I should have tried to find her before now. I should have driven to the campus and looked in every open classroom until I found her."

Magpie had never gone to Fairview College, not even before Eryn had left, not even though it was so close, not even though there was a bus that went right from Farther to the center of the campus. Eryn had always been too busy. Even before she had left, there had always been a million reasons why that weekend wouldn't work, why that month was out of the question.

After Eryn had left, Magpie hadn't even considered it. It would have felt so humiliating to beg her to come back.

Or because Magpie knew—she *knew*—that it would make no difference.

Eryn *wouldn't* come back.

"It's all right," Ann Marie said after Magpie didn't reply.

"I just figured I'd check. She's your sister, I never would have thought..."

That she'd leave me here to drown?

That was what Magpie wanted to say, but she didn't get a chance to say it, but it was said anyway, in a breathless little voice that seemed to come from just behind her shoulder and from all around her at the same time. Magpie turned her head quickly—expecting Dr. Cho, maybe, or one of the nurses playing a practical joke—but there was no one there. Just like there had been no one there in the pool.

"Sweetheart?" Ann Marie asked, retightening her grip on Magpie's hand.

"I didn't—sorry—did you hear something?"

Ann Marie's mouth settled into a thin line of annoyance. She looked past her daughter at the open door of the hallway. "The man across from me turns his TV up so loud. I've made several complaints."

The relief of the easy explanation spread over Magpie, and she felt herself relax. "Yeah. It must have been the TV. Anyway, no—I haven't heard from Eryn since she left. I don't have any way of reaching her."

Ann Marie nodded, as if that's what she'd been expecting. "I'll call the college. They must be able to get her a message. I'm her mother."

But as Magpie stayed sitting on her mother's hospital bed, she couldn't help but wonder what Ann Marie thought should be afforded just because she happened to be someone's mother. The selection of egg and sperm and soul and heart and brain were so random that it was a mystery why Magpie hadn't been born to a family living on the damp coast of Scotland, spending her days spray-painting sheep so they'd know which furry bundles belonged to whom. It was an unknowable, inexplicable wrinkle in fate that had landed her here in Farther, to Ann Marie and Gabriel Lewis, younger sister of Eryn Rachel, niece to a woman who, some sixteen years later, would ruin everything by crawling into her own sister's bed.

Ann Marie's declaration—*I'm her mother*—meant nothing in the grand scheme of things when the grand scheme of things meant that humans were an impossibility of a billion different things happening in just the correct order, leading to a habitable planet, leading to the evolution of (wo)mankind, leading to the final push and the wail of Margaret Lucy Lewis as she was placed for the first time in the red sweaty arms of *her mother*, who could have been Ann Marie or who could just as easily have been a hundred million other women across the very big planet of Earth.

"Magpie? You do know how sorry I am, right? I'm going to do so much better. I'm going to get some help. Finally, I'm going to get some help."

And Magpie had heard that before. The daughter or sister or brother or husband or mom or dad or cousin or friend of every alcoholic in the world has heard that before.

And every time you heard it . . .

You believed it.

To avoid another house visit from her soon-to-be-ex-father (she knew that was not how divorces worked, but she preferred to think of it that way, all things considered), Magpie promised Ann Marie that Clare would be sleeping over again.

"I'll call her as soon as I get outside," Magpie had said over her shoulder as she waved a final good-bye at the depleted, stick-thin vodka shell of her mother. "They don't like you to use phones in here."

But she hadn't called her. She'd gotten on her bike and pedaled to Kent's, and maybe it was the pizza last night or maybe it had been Linda's stew, the memory of which still caused Magpie's mouth to fill up with saliva, but at any rate, she decided to try something new for dinner.

She stood in the frozen-meal aisle, taking her time, reading each brightly colored box.

And then she heard it.

A sound she would recognize anywhere. A sound she could pick out of a lineup.

A high squeal of laughter.

Allison.

Despite the goose bumps on Magpie's skin and the low-ered temperature of the aisle, she felt the prickling of sweat in the hollows of her armpits. The grocery store wasn't busy. They were playing some unidentifiable soft jazz over the speakers. There was one other person in the aisle, a younger mother with bright-red lipstick and a toddler on one hip. She kept asking the toddler what he wanted for dinner, and he kept changing his mind.

Magpie took a few steps closer to the end of the aisle. Another peal of laughter. That was Allison, always laughing, always loud, always announcing her existence to whomever happened to be in the same place she was.

Another step and then Magpie paused because she heard a new voice, a lower voice, a guy's voice.

"Just pick something. I swear, if we're late to this movie, I'm going to lose my shit," he was saying.

And Magpie recognized that voice, too. Magpie heard that voice when she didn't want to, in the corners of her brain that didn't take orders, that didn't shut up when she wanted them to.

"I will not be rushed," Allison responded.

Magpie took another step, then they were in full view—Allison, of course Allison, and Brandon Phipp. He had his arms crossed, an annoyed expression on his face. Allison was studying the open refrigerated shelf in front of her.

"You're the only weirdo on the planet who brings chocolate

milk into a movie theater," Brandon said. "Just get some Reese's Pieces like the rest of the universe."

"Would you love me if I was just like the rest of the boring universe?" Allison retorted. She found what she was looking for. Magpie knew what she would grab before her hand closed around it. It was the chocolate almond milk sold in liter bottles. Allison would stick the entire thing in her purse and drink it over the course of the movie. By the time the credits rolled, she would be bouncing in her seat in an effort to not pee herself.

"Are you ready now?" Brandon asked.

"Yes, but let's stop in the candy aisle, because now I want Reese's Pieces, too," Allison said. As Magpie watched, Allison pecked Brandon on the cheek. He grabbed her ass when she pulled away. She swatted at his hand and missed.

Magpie pressed herself against a freezer door.

They walked right past the aisle without looking in her direction.

It used to be her in Brandon's place.

Allison liked romantic comedies, and she would drag Magpie to see whatever new one was playing that weekend. It would always be Allison's turn to pay, but somehow Magpie would end up being the one scraping around for enough to cover their tickets. Allison would sit sipping her chocolate milk in the darkness, sighing at all the romantic parts, fidgeting around happily when the two leads finally kissed for the first time.

Afterward, if there was something else playing, they would sneak into another theater. They'd sit in the back for this one because it was usually something they didn't even want to see. A kid's movie or an action or horror film.

"Why do you make us sneak in if you don't even want to watch it?" Magpie had asked her once.

What Allison had said was "What, like you have something better to do?"

But what she meant, Magpie thought, had been something more unpleasant. Because lately she had always been asking to sleep over at Magpie's. She had always been thinking of activities that would keep them occupied and away from the Leffertses' house for as long as possible. Allison went to the mall most days after school. She'd spend full weekends at Magpie's.

Allison's family lived in the rich part of town in a big house with five bedrooms and four bathrooms and a three-car garage. But one of the last times she'd seen it, there'd been a for-sale sign stuck into the front lawn.

"Oh, that?" Allison had said, laughing. "We're looking for something even bigger. I want my own walk-in closet. I have nowhere to put my shoes."

But there'd been a whisper later in the hallways of Farther High: Mr. Lefferts had lost his job. They'd stopped paying their mortgage. The house was in foreclosure. They had to be out by the end of the month.

Magpie had asked her about it one night. Sitting in the

back of the theater as a scary movie played on the screen, screechy music in the background as the murderer stalked his next victim.

"Who told you that?" Allison had snapped, her eyes flashing white in the darkness.

"I don't remember. I just heard it."

"Well, who did you hear it *from*?"

"I don't remember!"

"Oh, it just, like, appeared in your brain one day?"

"In the lunchroom, I think. I think...Elisabeth might have said something."

"Elisabeth? Okay. Thanks for telling me. It's not fucking true, obviously. The only people richer than my parents in this town are the Phipps."

The next day at lunch, Elisabeth, who usually sat at Allison and Magpie's table, was sitting clear across the cafeteria.

The rumors died down abruptly.

Magpie never mentioned it again.

Magpie had believed Allison. She had believed Elisabeth had made the entire thing up to get back at Allison for borrowing and ruining one of Elisabeth's favorite dresses.

But now, in Kent's, her heart pounding, her head spinning, it all came rushing back.

She stood motionless, counting.

She counted to one hundred.

Then she grabbed the first frozen meal her hand landed on—something with rice and quinoa and corn and halved cherry tomatoes and baby spinach—and paid for it at the self-checkout with her mother's credit card. She was out of the store and on her bike less than a minute later, pedaling furiously, her heart hammering in her ears. Why would Allison shop at Kent's instead of Baker Farms where she worked? But the movie theater was closer to Kent's. It made sense for them to stop there on their way.

Magpie was sweating by the time she reached her driveway, and just the sight of the darkened windows helped calm her down. It was one of those things she had gotten used to since her father had left and her mother had started drinking again: arriving home to an empty house. Usually, she didn't know where her mother was, but now Ann Marie was accounted for, safely tucked into her hospital bed where she would watch *Jeopardy!* until she fell asleep with the remote still clutched in her hand, a line of drool making its way sedately down her chin. It was okay. Magpie was alone. Allison hadn't seen her. Brandon hadn't seen her.

She rolled her bike into the driveway and let herself in the house.

Twilight was her favorite time to be alone because the light that made its way through the windows was soft and gentle, and if she kept the lamps off in the house, the whole place was lit in the last rays of daylight. She put her dinner in the microwave and poured herself what was left of the lemonade and added some ice and vodka to it, then she stood at the kitchen sink, letting her breathing slowly return to normal, taking small sips of the drink, letting the ice clink against her teeth.

And then—in the indescribable way people sometimes have of knowing they are suddenly not alone—she froze.

And many things happened at once.

The short feather-soft hairs on the back of her neck stood up, and the skin on her arms erupted into goose bumps, and her breath caught somewhere in the middle of her throat, stubbornly refusing to dislodge.

And it was the culmination of all of these things, but also something not so easily pinpointed, something quieter and stranger and more dangerous and more terrifying, that made her pick up the kitchen knife currently sitting in the drying rack.

And turn around.

There was no one there.

But maybe, to be more accurate, there was *nothing* there.

Except there was.

There was something. Both something *and* nothing.

And as Magpie watched, it seemed to solidify.

Something impossible took shape in front of her. Something she did not have a word for. Something there and not there, as the shed in Near had been both there and not there. So she wasn't scared of this thing before her because it was obviously from Near, and Near was obviously a fierce and burning part of her, and being part of her, it could not hurt her, could never hurt her, and she breathed a sigh of relief and clutched the knife to her chest.

You're going to poke your eye out.

How to describe what it sounded like?

When it talked, it was as if its words were both drilled directly into Magpie's heart and whispered into her ear while also somehow reverberating from every angle of the kitchen. She was *filled* with its words although she could not say if the voice was more female or more male because it seemed to be somewhere between the two polarities, a happy medium that reminded her of the way her own voice sounded when she internally monologued. Much like she was doing now: *Oh my God; oh my God; ohmyGod.*

She put the knife down on the counter, understanding that its warning had been a good one, that her hand was shaking too much to be trusted with something so sharp.

And then—how to describe what it looked like?

That was a little trickier.

Because the thing before her had both shape and didn't, had both form and was see-through, stood both before her and floated, looked both solid and ephemeral, elusive and ambiguous. And the more Magpie tried to focus on whatever it was, the harder it became to see. It had an almost human shape. An almost bestial shape. It was a hundred almost things without being any of them at all.

You're going to wear me out if you keep staring, it said.

For that's how Magpie had begun to think about it. As an it.

Because that's not offensive at all.

And then she realized it could read her mind.

And then she realized it probably *was* her mind. And—

You're both right and not right. Plus, you're being rude. Say something.

So Magpie said, "Hello?"

And the thing before her smiled a smile that was a million teeth and the darkest shadow on a winter's night and the sharp flash of tongue that beasts do to taste the air that surrounds them.

And it said:

It's nice to finally meet you.

SIX FOR GOLD

Both the thing and Magpie did not move for a solid minute.

A minute is a very long time to not move.

Try it now. Stand up. Are you in your bed? In a café? On a train, a plane?

Stand up and look at your watch and do not move for sixty seconds.

And while you're not moving, pretend that you're standing in a darkened kitchen with your frozen dinner burning in the microwave behind you, wishing suddenly you hadn't put down the kitchen knife, wishing suddenly you had called Clare after all, wishing suddenly a whole slew of things, probably none of which would actually help you now had they been what you did instead of coming home alone to the empty house on Pine Street and pouring yourself a glass of vodka lemonade.

The safeness inside Magpie, the assurance that this thing, this *it* could not hurt her because it so clearly came from Near, and Near so clearly came from inside her own body, crafted out of her own mind and flesh and blood, was slowly leaving her. Your own mind *could* hurt you. She knew this. And so—when it came right down to it—so could *it*.

Will you stop calling me that?

"What should I call you?" Magpie asked, not missing how strange it was to stand in one's own kitchen and have a conversation with a thing that probably wasn't real but that *seemed* so real that it made everything else seem somehow less than real. The fridge—a laughable make-believe thing. The countertops—how could she have ever considered them to be solid? The only real thing in the entire world was this shadow in front of her and, perhaps, Magpie (although just barely).

Something clever. Something deserving.

And then the name leaped to the tip of her tongue with such sudden force that it almost knocked her over. The thing laughed. (Because it could read her mind, remember.) (Because it *was* her mind, remember.)

Hither. I like that. You have this whole directional thing going on.

"Can you stop doing that? Stop answering me before I've said anything?"

Sorry. But you made me this way. You wrote me down in your little notebook. What was it? Oh, yes—"and I will have someone who knows me as I know myself and who wishes me only happiness and who will never betray me." Well—one life-long friend at your service.

"But you don't . . . I mean, you aren't . . ."

You should have specified human *if it's bothering you that much. But you didn't, so here I am, as wishy-washy as you wrote me to be.*

As if to demonstrate, it shifted lazily into something like a dog, then into something like a giant, then into something like a wolf.

All the better to eat your enemies, my dear.

"What? I don't want you to eat anyone!"

Well, that's awfully boring.

It shifted back into something like a human. But not a human. As if you described to an alien what a human looked like and they managed to get it almost right. Mostly right. Teeth too big, eyes too close, ears too pointy. Skin too pale.

"You're from Near?"

Of course I am. The most perfect place in the world. I have to thank you for rendering it so completely even if you failed to do so for me.

"But I've been writing about Near for six months. Why has it taken me this long to find it?"

It was waiting for a sacrifice. It was waiting to see if you were really, really ready.

"A sacrifice?"

A sacrifice, a promise, a test, a tear.

"A tear? My tear?"

The night Ann Marie had gone to the hospital. The night she'd almost drank herself to death. Magpie had cried on the notebook, one single tear blotting out the word *ME*.

You don't cry that much for such a sad girl. It's a pity, really. I liked it when you cried. It made you smell like rain.

"You're a little creepy, do you know that?"

That's because you're *a little creepy, Magpie. Do* you *know that?*

And she did, and she let this word into her heart, *creepy*; she opened up a tiny door for it to crawl in and settle among the blood; she felt it pumping in time with the little chambers there, settling in to the rhythm of her body.

"Near is real," she whispered.

Of course it is. You've been there.

"And I can go back?"

Whenever you'd like. The door will always be open to you.

She looked out the kitchen window now, and as she looked, the light in the shed turned on. She found that by simply thinking it she could turn it on and off. She could open or close the doorway. She was the maker and the ruler of an entire world.

Don't let it go to your head.

She blushed. Hither shook with something like laughter.

"I still don't understand—why would me crying have anything to do with it?"

You crafted my home out of your own sadness. You peeled it out of you and shaped it into trees and grass and houses and hills.

Your despair made *Near. You felt so deeply, and for so long, that your very sadness grew limbs and walked away from you. You have moved mountains, Magpie Lewis, and you are only just getting started.*

Magpie could not deny that she liked the sound of that. And she liked the sound of her voice, the way it echoed pleasantly in the small kitchen, the way it bounced against the cabinets and walls, and made her sound bigger than she actually was when she said, "What do we do first?"

And she liked the hissing, quiet way Hither looked at her with its not-quite eyes and its not-quite mouth and its bloodless skin, when it replied:

My dear. We do exactly what you want to do.

So Magpie went back to Near.

Hither stayed close to her, always in the corners of her eyes, always dancing around her periphery just out of reach.

Not that she *wanted* to reach out to it, really, because she imagined its body would turn to smoke in her hands, running through her fingers like murky water dredged out of some haunted fairy-tale swamp.

She led the way through the not-shed to the bright high spot on the hill. The perfect hill, the perfect day, all blue and cloudless, warm and soft.

She remembered—suddenly—the hospital waiting room, the way her hand had shook with cold as she'd pulled out the notebook and written *I am always warm.*

And she *was* warm now, and happy and peaceful, and there was her world in front of her, her world of Near spread out before her.

And anything she wrote in the yellow notebook would come true.

Oh, but you needn't waste your time with writing now.

"What do you mean?"

Writing is so tedious. And plus, you didn't even bring a pen with you. Although . . . you could *just make one . . .*

"Make a pen?"

Wish one up. Go on, give it a try. Wish up a pen. Wish up anything you like.

So Magpie held out her hand, flat, palm up to the perfect Near sky, and she wished for a pen.

And nothing happened.

You've already done it, so you already know you can *do it.*

"I've already done it?"

With the little kid. What's-his-name. Lennon?

"Ringo?" Clare's brother. He was here in Near, and Magpie definitely hadn't written him down in her notebook. She hadn't even really wanted him here in the first place but . . .

Clare had. Clare had said, *Have you noticed that there aren't any people?* and Magpie had said, *Would it make you feel better if there were people here?* and then there *had* been a person there. Ringo. He had appeared in an instant, and what had he said about their father? That he was here and alive?

Now you have it.

"So I just...wished him into being? I wished an entire person into being?"

Don't get ahead of yourself. You wished a copy of a person into being. A temporary copy. The little twerp disappeared as soon as he was out of your sight. His sole purpose was to put your friend at ease. Not your fault that it didn't really work, though. You tried your best, and it was very kind of you. And I've seen your mind, Magpie. There isn't room for many kind thoughts in there.

"That's a little rude," Magpie said.

You'll live. Now go on; try again. Practice makes perfect.

So Magpie held up her hand again. And she closed her eyes to block out a bit of the sunshine, to concentrate a little harder. And she thought of a pen.

Or rather—the pen leaped, fully formed, into her brain.

It was a pen she'd never seen before. A bright shining silver. And instead of a normal clip, there was a pen roll shaped like a snake that slithered around the cap three times before coming to a rest. It had eyes of bloodred, and Magpie knew somehow that they were two little rubies. In her mind, she uncapped it, and it was a fountain pen with a nib the color of coal, a deep, vibrant black that shone with spots of ink that matched the rubies. Bloodred and glistening.

And then she became aware of a weight in her hand, a delicate line of coolness that started at the tips of her fingers and ended where her wrist began.

She opened her eyes and there it was—the pen of her mind. Perfect in its beauty, so shiny that it caught the sun and burned her eyes.

That's not bad for a second try. If a bit pretentious.

Magpie ignored this, uncapped the pen, and looked at the nib. It seemed made out of something impossible, a heavy black that couldn't have been from this world.

"But will this exist only in here? Or can I . . . take it home?"

You are *home. But if you mean can you take it back to Farther, then I think the answer depends on how much you want it.*

Magpie wanted it very much. She slipped the pen into her pocket and felt its weight press reassuringly against her hip. She wondered what else she would be able to make. She had only the limitations of her own mind to contend with.

Don't get too *ahead of yourself. These things are made from you. And you are not limitless.*

There had been a blood drive at her high school last year—before it had all happened. Magpie had just turned sixteen, and with her mother's signature, she had been allowed to give blood for the first time. She remembered the experience now in stark detail: the peanut butter crackers they had put into her hands; the gymnasium all neat and orderly with cots and tubes and intravenous infusion poles; the people who drew the blood, their hair in neat little buns or clipped back into ponytails; the quirky cartooned scrubs they wore. The way they had lifted her arm above her head when the flow of blood hadn't immediately started. The way the red leaked slowly from her veins and filled up such a large bag. Did she really have that much to spare?

She had expected to feel something as the blood was siphoned out of her, but aside from a slight burning at the needle's entry point, a gentle tug around the tiny wound, there had been nothing.

Except afterward when she had sat nibbling at the peanut butter crackers, dutifully eating one after another until the package was gone.

She stood up. She kept a hand on the cot. She felt a gentle rushing of blood to her head, a sensation she couldn't exactly call unpleasant, more like... different. One pint lighter. She began to see stars across her vision, a general lightening. She sat back down and took a deep breath. Someone handed her a cookie. Chocolate chip. She ate it.

The next time she stood up, she felt stronger. She felt her body recovering. But still... the sensation of being lighter... the sensation of having given something, of having something removed from her... it was at once impossible to describe but also impossible to ignore. She had felt less than. *Slightly* less than. But still less than.

You are not limitless, Hither had said.

Magpie thought she knew exactly what it meant. But she patted her pocket where the silver pen now rested. *Maybe not,*

136

but you'd be amazed at what a little rest and a little sugar can do for a person, she thought.

Right, but the effort needed to wish up a chocolate chip cookie negates the restorative properties of said cookie.

"Maybe I can wish up you not reading my mind all the time," Magpie snapped, and Hither fell into an irritable silence and became even more transparent than it had been a moment before.

Magpie began to walk down the hill to the town of Near.

She let herself be impressed by what a stunning job she had done.

She let herself look around, to notice things that she had either not noticed before or that had not *been* there before. Like—the grass around the town was not endless as she had thought it was. Instead, it stretched very, very far in every single direction, but it stopped just before the horizon, where Magpie could see, clearly, the sharp reflective surface of a great body of water. So Near was an island.

"Did I do that?" Magpie asked, but Hither was apparently not done being offended and did not answer her.

She tried to remember if she had ever written anything in the yellow notebook about an island.

I told you, *not everything has to be written down.*

"Oh, are you speaking to me now?"

It didn't reply.

She continued down the hill.

The town of Near grew larger and larger before her. She wished it wasn't *quite* so long a walk to reach the bottom.

And her next step brought her right to the front of the white gate.

She was so surprised that she couldn't stop in time, and she slammed right into it.

"Ow!"

Be careful what you wish for.

And Hither seemed so tickled with itself that it grew a few sizes bigger and a few shades darker and laughed again, a strange full-body shudder that seemed a cross between a seizure and a shiver.

Magpie had wished the walk wasn't quite so long, so her magical world had deposited her on its doorstep.

Right. So maybe Hither had a point. She *did* need to be careful what she wished for.

She opened the gate and stepped inside the town. Since her first visit was still a little fuzzy in her mind and her second visit, with Clare, hadn't really allowed for any exploring, this was almost like her first time here. She made a point of paying attention. To how things looked. To how things smelled (like cotton candy, like caramel apples). To how things felt (she knelt to the ground and touched her finger to the concrete of a sidewalk; it was essentially the same as concrete back in Farther except springier, more forgiving).

She walked to the high school first.

It should have been a ten- or fifteen-minute walk, but she managed it in just a few seconds.

It was hard to understand how it happened. She was standing in front of one of the two gas stations in town, and with her next step, she was in front of the middle school, and with her next, she was in front of the high school. It was like a dream, where time and travel pass in the blink of an eye and it seems completely normal. Only afterward, when you think back, do you realize the impossibility of it.

If there had been any doubts before that Near was a perfect replica of Farther, they melted away when Magpie pulled open the front doors of the high school and let herself inside.

The halls were empty, but if she *wanted* to, if she stood and thought about it, she could hear classes in session. Distant voices shouting out answers to questions, pencils and pens being dragged along paper.

And there—walking toward her. Who was that? Elisabeth? Yes, it was—she walked clutching a stack of books to her chest, and when she saw Magpie, an enormous grin spread across her face.

"Hey, girl!" she said.

Magpie almost turned around. A force of habit: assuming no one would ever greet her, assuming no one would ever be talking to *her*, especially one of Allison's friends.

But this wasn't Farther. And Magpie wasn't ostracized here.

But still—it felt a little strange. Smiling back. Making herself speak: "Hi, Elisabeth."

"Such a beautiful day, isn't it?" Elisabeth asked. Still smiling. Still happy to see Magpie.

"It is . . . yeah."

"You should get out of here. Go to the mall or something. I'll come with you if you want!"

"Oh, no. No, that's okay. You should stay here," Magpie said.

"Whatever you want!"

For a moment—just a split second—a shadow crossed over Elisabeth's face. She was a girl, but she was also something else. She was also an impossible thing, a thing that could shape-shift and swirl into something else.

But then she was just a girl again. And she smiled— endlessly smiling, smiling—and disappeared down the hallway.

Magpie turned around.

Hither was still there. Or had it left and come back? Or was it in two places at once? Or three or four?

"Have you been here the whole time?"

I have, indeed.

"But right there? Right there the whole time?"

Here and other places.

Magpie rolled her eyes.

She left the high school.

She started walking down one street, then another, aimlessly letting her feet decide where to go.

And perhaps because humans are such creatures of obvious habit, she found herself, after ten or so minutes, at the beginning of Pine Street. *Her* street. And there—just a few houses in—her house.

Or rather—the perfect version of her house. With a lawn freshly mowed and devoid of brown spots and crabgrass, curtains open to let the sunshine stream in through the spotless windows, three clean shiny cars in the driveway.

Three cars.

Her mother's station wagon and her father's truck.

Which meant—she quickly realized—that in this world she had chosen to erase what had happened. She had brought her father back and cleansed the past six months of the echo of his one fatal sin. In this world her parents weren't getting a divorce, because her father hadn't cheated on her mother with her mother's only sister. In this world they were still invited around for Christmas dinner. In this world her grandparents took her out to breakfast on Sundays and slipped five-dollar bills into her pocket when she left.

And the third car.

In this world Eryn hadn't left, because Ann Marie hadn't started drinking again. In this world their perfect nuclear family was still contained in this small house. The lights were on in the finished basement—in Eryn's bedroom—and Magpie had crossed the lawn and was pulling open the front door before she even realized she had moved.

Her parents were watching TV in the living room.

Everything was clean, neat, freshly vacuumed and dusted. To her left, the kitchen was spotless. A rack full of clean dishes set out on the counter to dry. A smell of the disinfectant spray her mother used: Fabuloso. To her right, the hallway that led to her and her parents' bedrooms. And to the right of that, the stairway that led down to where her sister still lived with them.

"Sweetheart!" Ann Marie called from the couch. She stretched her arms backward over the top of the couch, reaching blindly for her daughter.

Magpie went.

She walked into her mother's arms, and Ann Marie hugged her awkwardly, laughing at how much she had to contort her arms.

Gabriel Lewis reached a hand back and squeezed his daughter's wrist. "Dinner's in the oven, Magpie," he said. And once he'd mentioned it, she could smell it—some kind of lasagna, her favorite, melting cheese and warming vegetables filling the house with their mouthwatering aroma.

Her mother let her go, and Magpie asked—cautiously, as if her words might break—"Is Eryn home?"

"She's downstairs, honey. Let her know dinner is almost ready, will you?" Ann Marie said.

Magpie moved toward the top of the stairs, looking down at the basement. She knew her sister would not be like the sister of her real life—the sister who had to be paid to take Magpie to the movies, the sister who left Magpie on the front steps with no skills with which to take care of herself.

This Eryn would be perfect, the Eryn of Magpie's treasured imagination, the older sister who had waited and hoped and wished for a younger sister to love and look after and stay with.

This Eryn hadn't left.

Magpie paused at the top of the stairs.

She looked around the living room and realized that Hither was not with her. Had it stayed outside? Had it not followed her into the house?

She glanced at her parents—smiling, content, watching TV. Her father saw her staring and winked at her. A quick shadow across his face.

But no—only her father.

Magpie walked downstairs.

The door to Eryn's bedroom was open.

Magpie could see her—her beloved and perfect and needed sister—who was lying across her bed on her stomach with her legs bent at the knees and crossed at the ankles. She was reading a book, but when she heard Magpie at the door, she flipped it closed and beamed up at her. Her smile lit up her whole face. She was so happy to see Magpie that the entire room grew brighter.

"Gosh, where have you *been?*" Eryn asked. She flipped herself over on the bed, let her legs fall over the side, let her feet swing back and forth. "I've been waiting for you all *day*. I thought we could go swimming."

And Magpie wanted this so much—she wanted to go

swimming with her sister more than she had ever wanted anything in her entire life—that they were suddenly there, in the backyard, in the pool, their suits on, and their hair knotted up in buns, and Eryn with a little turquoise-blue pool donut around her waist and Magpie lying on the pizza float, her hands dipping into the water, the sun shining so brightly, ignoring their mother calling them in for dinner.

"Let her wait a minute," Eryn said, paddling over to her sister, dumping a cupful of cool water onto Magpie's stomach. "Couldn't you just stay in here forever?"

And she could, she could, she could, she could.

Magpie propped her arms behind her head and drifted along on the pool float, Eryn bouncing around beside her, an endless ball of energy, until finally she lunged and tipped Magpie off the float.

"I'm bored," she said. "Let's play a game."

"What game?" Magpie asked.

"Close your eyes."

"Marco Polo?"

"*Close* them," Eryn insisted.

Magpie closed them. "Marco," she said.

"Polo."

"Marco."

"Polo."

Magpie dove and missed. Eryn's laughter sounded like it came from a million miles away. Eryn always won Marco

Polo; she swam faster than Magpie; she seemed always to be in a dozen places at once.

"Marco."

"Polo."

Magpie crept forward, her hands spread in front of her, listening closely for any noise Eryn made, any ripples in the water, any breathing. Surely she should have reached the edge of the pool by now. She walked slower, more cautiously, waving her hands around. There was no way she hadn't reached the side yet. Was she walking in circles?

"Marco."

"Polo—"

From right behind her: a whisper in Magpie's ears. Magpie whirled around and reached out wildly but came up with only air.

"I don't want to play anymore," she whined softly.

"You can't quit in the middle of game" was Eryn's reply—at once next to her and far away from her and all around her.

Magpie couldn't help but feel a little hurt, a little confused. Wasn't Near supposed to be exactly how she wanted it? Well, she didn't want to be in the pool anymore. She wanted Eryn to be nicer. She wanted to feel safe.

She opened her eyes.

And the pool stretched on forever, an impossible expanse of bright-blue chlorinated water covering an entire world. An entire world of cerulean.

And then she blinked, and she was standing on the pool platform, and Eryn was squeezing out her hair, hopping up on one leg to get the water out of her ear.

"You won," Eryn said, her eyes flashing dark for just the briefest of moments. "You won, are you happy?"

"But I didn't catch you."

"You did," she argued. "Look."

She held out her arm. There was an angry red mark there, even now beginning to fade away, the unmistakable print of a palm and five fingers wrapped around the skin.

"I did that?" Magpie asked.

"Be careful what you wish for," Eryn echoed.

"I'm sorry."

"You better not let it happen again," Eryn threatened, but then she smiled so wide and so big that Magpie couldn't tell if she was joking about all of it, about the entire thing. The red mark was gone. They were dry and clothed and sitting around the table for dinner. Their father was in the middle of a story about something funny that had happened to him at work. Their mother was laughing hysterically, the glass of iced tea in her hand shaking, the liquid slopping up the sides, almost spilling out. Eryn caught Magpie's eye as she raised a bite of lasagna to her mouth. She winked.

This had always been Magpie's favorite time with her family. If nothing interesting had happened to her father on any given day, he would make something up, spinning elaborate yarns that never failed to leave Magpie and her mother in stitches. Sometimes his family couldn't tell the difference between fact and fiction; they would go around the table and take votes. Winner would get an extra helping of dessert.

Eryn had grown up and out of these dinners, and more often than not, she didn't bother showing up anymore—but the Eryn of Near sat next to Magpie and kicked her feet playfully underneath the table and ate the lasagna even though it contained cheese and gluten, two of the things she'd sworn off forever.

And then they were finished with dinner and sitting cross-legged around the coffee table playing a game of Monopoly. Magpie was winning, and then she had won, and it was only after the sun had long gone down and her parents and sister had trundled sleepily off to bed that Magpie remembered that this wasn't the real world. In the real world Ann Marie was in the hospital and Gabriel had filed for divorce and Eryn was probably doing yoga at the tail end of a three-day juice fast and Magpie had to be at school tomorrow.

"Wait—*do* I have to be at school tomorrow?" she asked Hither, who had appeared and draped itself lazily over an armchair in the living room, its feet propped up on the coffee table in a way Magpie didn't like.

It removed its feet.

Do you mean do you have to go back? Or can you live here forever?

"Yeah. I guess that's what I mean."

Hither considered.

147

I suppose you could stay here. For a time.

"But what's happening out there? While I'm in here? Is time moving? Or is this like in the books where the kids go into the cupboard and time freezes while they grow old?"

Are you asking if this is like a fantasy story? A fairy tale for good little Christian children?

"Well, when you put it like that..."

Let me try to explain it. Time is certainly not frozen, no. That would be impossible. The more accurate explanation is that time is moving here *in the blink of an eye. So when you return to your home—to that place—it will appear as if no time has passed. But the two times—here and there—they are really just moving at very different speeds.*

"The blink of an eye," Magpie repeated.

So if you stayed here for a very long time, it would be like several blinks of an eye. So really, like no time at all.

"But Clare was able to get the pizza," Magpie said. "When she left before me—it took me a little while to get up the hill but not *that* long. And it would have taken her more than the blink of an eye to pay for the pizza and get a slice and get back to the shed to wait for me."

It gets tricky when people enter and leave at different times. It messes things up. It's best to keep all parties together, keep hands and feet inside at all times, and follow all proper signage.

Magpie rolled her eyes. "That seems like a convenient answer."

Convenient or not, it's the truth. You've opened up a portal in a garden shed in your backyard that leads to a land that is at once inside you and outside of you. You've created a universe, and you want the rules to be simple and easy and tied up in a bow? Well, sorry to disappoint you. Nothing about this place is simple.

"It could be simple if I wanted it to be simple."

Already getting full of yourself. Well, if you're asking, my recommendation is that you leave. For now. Like I said before—you aren't limitless, and it's taken a considerable amount of energy to hold yourself here for as long as you have. You need some rest.

Even as Hither said that, Magpie felt something like fatigue settle over her body. The strange emptiness she'd felt after giving blood. The same rush to the head, the same gentle wooziness, like a series of small waves that kept crashing over her, gradually becoming more intense in their momentum.

"I guess I could get some rest. As long as—"

Near will not go anywhere. Whenever you want to come back, you may. Now that you have created it, it is in no danger of disappearing.

Comforted, Magpie nodded.

She pulled herself to her feet with some difficulty, some resistance fighting in her bones. She didn't want to go, but she saw the logic in what Hither said; she felt her own strength failing as she walked out of the house on Pine Street and through the twilight-purple streets of the town she had made.

She met not another soul—and there was a strange comfort in that. How often could a girl walk alone through dark streets at night and not be anxious, not constantly casting backward glances over her shoulder, not constantly worrying about meeting someone she didn't want to meet.

Well, you're not exactly alone.

And there was a hint of something in Hither's voice— hurt feelings, maybe? But how could it possibly have hurt feelings when it was an extension of Magpie, a reflecting board for her to basically have conversations with herself.

I am not *a reflecting board, and I'm beginning to feel like you don't listen to anything I say.*

Huffing, Hither dematerialized and left her fully alone.

She didn't mind.

If she wanted to call it back, she could.

Magpie was too tired to consider the trick she'd used before to skip the miles between the shed and the town, so she walked slowly, lazily, enjoying the solitude of a town without people. Or rather—a town without people at the present. But if she wanted people, she could have people. Anyone in the world she wanted to walk with, and they would appear, ready and willing.

But she would rather be alone. For now.

The closer she got to the shed, the more she thought about the world she was about to return to. The world of Ann Marie being released from the hospital tomorrow. The world of Mr. James wanting to help her not fail sophomore year. The world of Brandon Phipp's party. The world of Ben and the project about Amelia Earhart. The world of Clare and her dead father. The world of Eryn leaving and Magpie's father leaving and everyone leaving. The world of leaving.

By the time she reached the not-shed, she was so tired that her vision was beginning to blur. But before she went through, she took the pen out of her pocket and held it in her hand and concentrated with everything she had inside her.

And when she reached the other side—the backyard of her real house on the real Pine Street, the real pool and the real pizza float half-on, half-off the small swim platform, the real moon glowing above her, just a faint echo of the way the moon had glowed in Near—she looked down at her hand.

And she was still holding the pen.

SEVEN FOR A SECRET

Magpie slept like the dead, collapsing onto her bed with a belly full of Near-dinner and waking ravenous and weak in the early morning. She ate leftover pizza over the kitchen sink—had it really been only two days since she and Clare had stumbled into Near together?—and then took a hot shower, washing her hair and letting the water turn her skin red.

She sat with the yellow notebook and the Near-pen after her shower, letting her hair drip dry against the back of the couch, feeling the weight of the things in her hand as she wrote a new sentence on an empty page.

And they all lived happily ever after.

She placed the notebook in the bottom drawer of her bureau among the winter sweaters she wouldn't wear for months and months, or maybe never—because Near would not have winter snowstorms. Or if it did, the snow would be warm. Like cotton. Or spun sugar.

Hither made a noise in the back of its throat.

Wasting all your energy on warm snow. The uselessness.

Magpie thought that was the point, that not everything had to be useful.

She felt better after the shower and the pizza. She packed a bag for Ann Marie, a change of clothes and a pair of socks and sneakers, then she started walking to the hospital. It was three miles away, but they would take a cab home together.

As she walked, Hither sometimes floated alongside her and sometimes fell behind and sometimes disappeared entirely and sometimes turned into a many-winged bird-like creature and flew above her, casting a wide shadow that shielded Magpie from the sun.

It did not escape Magpie that a thing casting a shadow must be a thing with some degree of realness to it.

It was a warm day, and Magpie was happy to have an excuse not to be in school. Even though there were only three weeks left until summer, those three weeks felt like their own eternity. It was inconceivable that they would ever pass. And yet here she was, forced to live through them, to slog through the endless minutes contained within each set of night and day.

At least she had her own place to return to now. Her own Near.

She wanted to go back to it—and she would, just as soon as she got Ann Marie home and into bed.

She wondered more about how time worked between Near and Farther. If she spent years and years in Near, would she return to sixteen when she decided to come out again?

Are you back on that silly fantasy stuff? You're not a rubber band; you can't snap back and forth.

But she *could* decide never to come back again. Once she had practiced enough, once she had built up her strength, she could sustain herself within Near for an entire lifetime. Everything would be just how she wanted it. A perfect life.

"But if I die in Near, what happens? Does my body just appear here again?"

You ask the most asinine questions.

But Hither didn't say anything else, so Magpie thought maybe it didn't know the answer.

Asinine or not, her entire life had settled around a new point of gravity. She revolved now, not around the Earth, not around the sun, but around Near and the new place she had created for herself.

She reached the hospital after almost an hour of walking. Hither became as small as something like a butterfly or a crab (or some cross between the two, because it had both wings and claws) and alighted on her shoulder. She bypassed the front desk and went straight to her mother's room. Ann Marie was signing paperwork and listening to a nurse's instructions. She gave a happy little wave when she saw Magpie standing in the doorway but then returned her attention to the forms on her lap.

Magpie waited until the nurse had left, then she took Ann Marie's clothes and shoes from her backpack and placed them neatly on the end of the bed.

"Thank you so much for coming. You took tired," Ann Marie said.

Magpie didn't want to say what her mother looked like (a person who had brushed a little too close to the cold jaws of death, for starters), so instead she just smiled and shrugged. "I guess I didn't sleep well last night. Just excited to get you home."

This was the exact right thing to say; Ann Marie's eyes grew wet with immediate tears, and Magpie averted her gaze. She always thought it was best to pretend not to notice when other people cried, and her mother was no exception to this rule. If anything, her mother was the *reason* for this rule.

"Pull the curtain, will you, Magpie?" Ann Marie asked.

So Magpie pulled the curtain shut around the bed to give her mother privacy, and she did her best not to watch as Ann Marie stood up slowly. In the hospital gown, her mother looked the skinniest Magpie had ever seen her. She looked as if she had lost half of herself sometime during the past six months, as if, when Magpie's father had left, he had scooped up pieces of his wife and carted them away, never to be seen again. She slipped the gown down over her shoulders, and Magpie couldn't help but look at her mother's breasts to make sure they weren't the same sick blue they'd been when she had found her, half-dead, on the bedroom floor.

As Ann Marie raised her shirt over her head and gingerly slipped into it, as she pulled on a fresh pair of underwear and stepped into the khaki shorts Magpie had brought her, Magpie couldn't help but feel a rush of affection for her mother. Maybe this was what Ann Marie needed to never drink again. Maybe this brush with death was the final straw. Maybe Ann Marie would blanch at the smell of vodka now. Maybe she would get sick just thinking about the medicinal sting of it sliding down her throat.

Should Magpie have poured all of the half-full bottles down the sink before she'd left the house? What were you supposed to do when you went to the hospital to pick up an alcoholic from a particularly gnarly binge? Were you supposed to destroy all the evidence? Were you supposed to burn down the house? Were you supposed to create a new life for them, one devoid of the memories of all their many, many fuckups? Was Magpie singularly responsible now for her mother's new, sober life? Was she required to build a world that did not revolve so heavily around the alcoholic-beverage industry?

"Sweetheart, I asked if you could pass me those sneakers," Ann Marie said.

Magpie passed her mother the sneakers, and Ann Marie slipped them on and began to lace them.

Bunny ears, bunny ears, playing by a tree…

That was how Ann Marie had taught Magpie to tie her

own shoes. Magpie had a vivid memory of being in kindergarten. The teacher, a woman with short curly hair, had a sneaker made out of wood. Laces the color of Granny Smith apples. One by one, the students came up and tied a bow. After every success, Magpie felt her inevitable failure settle on her shoulders. She had always worn Velcro. What sense did it make to perform the complicated loop and swoops required for tying laces when she could simply slip her foot into the shoe and place one Velcroed section on top of the other and—voilà—done.

But she was sent home with a note, and although Magpie couldn't read the note, she imagined now that it said something like *Your underachieving daughter must learn how to tie her shoes before entering the first grade* because that night Ann Marie sat her down on the living-room carpet and handed her a sneaker, and said, "Bunny ears, bunny ears, playing by a tree…"

Magpie couldn't remember the rest of the rhyme.

Had Ann Marie been drinking that night? When had she stopped drinking the first time? Magpie had always had a terrible memory for unpleasant things; her brain erased the past in bits and chunks.

Except for now.

Because she could remember the past six months in excruciating detail. Every minute of every day.

"I swear, Magpie, you look like you're in a different world," Ann Marie said. She placed a cool hand on Magpie's cheek. Then she frowned. "It's Monday, isn't it? Oh no. I've made you miss school."

"It doesn't matter. It's basically over."

"I can't believe you're going to be a junior. My little girl."

"Let's get going."

"We should make an appointment to get your learner's permit. I can teach you how to drive. When I was your age, I loved to drive. Your father and I would go driving for hours."

"Do you have everything?" Magpie asked. "We need to call a taxi."

She led her mother out of the room to the elevators, and when they reached the front lobby, she pulled out her cell phone and dialed the number of the local cab company. She had quickly memorized it that morning because it was the same digit seven times.

They waited outside on a bench.

It was a sunny bright-blue day, and Hither was scrounging around in the dirt for something—was it eating *bugs*?—and Ann Marie had her head turned up to the sky, letting the sunshine fall onto her open face, warming her skin, so when she placed her hand on her daughter's hand Magpie almost recoiled, it was that hot.

"Don't you just love summer?" Ann Marie asked.

And Magpie did, or she *used* to when summer smelled of chlorine, of vinyl pool floats, of a time before—

"Mags?"

A shadow and a voice were thrown over Magpie as someone familiarly shaped walked up to the bench. Magpie shook her hand out from under her mother's hand and shielded her face from the sun. Her breath caught in her throat as she saw Ben standing in front of her dressed in pale-blue hospital scrub pants with a scrub top covered in rainbows.

"Ben?"

"Mags! It's you. I thought it was you."

But then, inevitably, Ben saw Ann Marie, and his expression clouded over with something like worry—for just the briefest of moments—before he caught himself.

"Do you...Are you...?" Magpie could not seem to finish her sentence.

"I volunteer here on Mondays and Wednesdays," Ben supplied. "During my study periods. My parents are big on volunteering."

And because Ann Marie was staring, and because it was becoming more awkward *not* to introduce her than it would be *to* introduce her, Magpie put her hand on her mother's knee, and said, "This is my mom. Mom, this is Ben. We go to school together."

"Ben. It's so nice to meet you," Ann Marie said, and when she raised her hand to shake Ben's, Magpie noticed that it shook a little, as the body often shakes whenever you deprive it of something it is very used to getting. She hoped Ben didn't notice.

"Likewise, Mrs. Lewis," Ben said. "We missed you at lunch today, Mags."

"She's my escort," Ann Marie said proudly, patting her daughter on the arm. And that one word—*escort*—lingered on just a beat too long for some reason, floating around in the air like fog.

And then the taxi pulled up, and the moment was over.

Magpie helped Ann Marie into the car, then she dipped her head into the back seat, and whispered, "Just give me a sec, okay?"

Ann Marie winked and nodded, and said, "Don't mind me, sweetheart. Don't mind me, *Mags*." And Magpie wanted to both punch her in the face and kiss her at the same time.

She straightened up and swung the door closed, not quite latching it, just enough so Ann Marie couldn't eavesdrop. Then she turned back to Ben.

"I'm sorry about that," she said, just as he said, "I'm sorry."

And then they both paused for a minute and laughed nervously and didn't know what to do with their hands.

Barf.

Magpie had almost forgotten about Hither. She spotted it now, shaped something like a human, strutting back and forth behind Ben as if it were putting on a show.

She did her best to ignore it.

"You don't have anything to be sorry for," Magpie said. "This is a free country. Or at least a free hospital. You know."

"Still, I just ... I wouldn't want you to think ..."

"Think what?"

"I dunno. That I was following you or something."

Magpie laughed. "I don't think you followed me to the hospital, Ben."

"Well, good. Then my plan is working."

The most delicately awkward silence.

If it had been weird seeing Ben outside of school the first time, it was definitely weird seeing him now, in those scrubs, with a pair of Ray-Ban sunglasses pushed up onto his hair, with the certain swagger of someone who is confident in this space. Magpie never wanted to feel confident in a hospital. That sounded awful.

And she knew she had to tell him the truth. She had already told Clare, and it would be too risky to try to lie now. So she said, in a voice hardly above a whisper, "She was admitted. For—"

"It's none of my business," Ben said quickly. "I'm actually late. I'll just . . . see you tomorrow?"

"For alcohol poisoning," Magpie added quickly, in the vein of someone pulling a bandage off a deep wound. She winced as her blood spilled and pooled by her feet. Or was that Hither? Turned red and imitating a puddle?

"I'm sorry," Ben said.

"She's getting help," Magpie assured him. "It was an accident."

"Of course."

"She's not, like . . ."

"Of course not."

"Well. I should probably go. To get her home."

"Yeah, yeah. I'll see you tomorrow, though? Or I could, you know, get your homework for you if you're not going to be in."

Magpie had to exert a certain amount of effort not to laugh. She had not done homework in such a very long time.

"It's fine," she said. "I'll see you tomorrow. I'll be there."

Ben smiled, then he hugged her, a quick hug with no real advance warning so Magpie was left ambushed and unsure of what to do with her arms.

You could try hugging him back.

Right. That made sense.

She hugged him back.

It was nice hugging Ben. He smelled like spearmint. Gum or mouthwash, maybe.

Did you just say he smells like mouthwash?

When they pulled away, Ben gave her a funny salute, then walked into the hospital. Magpie opened the door to the back seat of the cab and slid in next to her mom. She closed the door quickly behind her because she did not want to share a car with Hither.

It turned into a dragon and spit fire at the windows.

The cab driver pulled away from the curb, unaware of this.

"So," Ann Marie began, attempting and failing to sound only moderately interested. "Ben, huh?"

"He's just a friend," Magpie said.

"He's pretty cute."

"I guess so. I hadn't really noticed."

"I'm glad you're meeting new people, sweetheart. You know how much I love Allison, but it's good to have more than just one friend."

Because Allison had been it for years. The beginning and end of Magpie's social circle. The only person Magpie went to the movies with, ate lunch with, did her homework with, invited over for sleepovers. The only person *period*.

Well.

Not anymore.

Magpie wondered if she should tell Ann Marie that, if now was the time to let her mother in on the little secret that Allison and Magpie had not spoken for six months after the Big Terrible Thing That Magpie Did.

And she almost did tell her.

But then she looked at her mother and saw how frail and tired she looked. The big dark circles underneath her eyes. The blacks and blues at the crook of her arms where the IVs had been inserted. The broken nail on the ring finger of her right hand. When had she broken that nail? When she'd fallen? When she'd vomited down the front of herself? Before or after that?

So Magpie bit her tongue instead, and said, "Ben's pretty nice."

"And Clare," Ann Marie remembered. "I've never met Clare, either."

"Clare and Ben are friends," Magpie said. "We sit together at lunch."

"Sweetheart, that's so nice. We'll have to have the two of them over for dinner sometime. I could make something, or we could order in. Do you know if they like Chinese food?"

"I dunno. Probably."

And as if the thought of ordering Chinese food had exhausted her, Ann Marie let her head rest against the seatback and closed her eyes.

And a thump from the roof let Magpie know that Hither had landed on top of the car.

Can't get rid of me so easily.

———————

The next morning Magpie found her mother awake before her and cooking breakfast, humming to herself as she flipped an omelet at the stove.

This was so shocking to Magpie as to be confusing—was she dreaming? Was she hallucinating? Had she crossed into Near without realizing it? But upon closer inspection, it really *was* Ann Marie, not Near–Ann Marie, complete with blacks and blues and dark circles still painted underneath her eyes.

But there hadn't been an egg to speak of in the refrigerator, not to mention orange juice and sliced cantaloupe, both of which now sat on the kitchen table.

"Mom?"

Ann Marie jumped a little, then laughed and turned off the burner. She slid the omelet onto a plate where another one already sat waiting. "I hope I didn't wake you. I was up early and thought I'd do a little grocery shopping. I hope you're in the mood for eggs."

Was Magpie in the mood for eggs? She honestly couldn't

say. She couldn't even remember the last time she'd *had* eggs, and here was Ann Marie crossing to the table and sliding the newer, piping-hot omelet onto a plate with three slices of melon and a golden-brown piece of toast.

"If you want jam, it's in the fridge. I got strawberry and blackberry," Ann Marie said, as if this were a normal morning, as if she'd been making breakfast every day for the past six months, as if it were perfectly reasonable for her to be awake before Magpie, *and* dressed *and* sober.

Magpie sat down without getting the jam, and her mother sat across from her and cut into her omelet.

"It's beautiful outside," Ann Marie said, placing a square of omelet onto her toast and biting into it. All Magpie could see was the perfect dental cast her mother's teeth had made in the slice of sourdough. Ann Marie chewed and swallowed. "I thought we could do something after school? Go to the mall, maybe? I'm sure you could use some summer clothes. You haven't had anything new for a while."

Ann Marie's credit cards were maxed out within an inch of their life, so Magpie was a little confused about where her mother thought the money to buy her daughter something *new* would come from.

Ann Marie had a job—sort of. She worked at the perfume counter in the only department store in Farther's pathetic mall. But she had been demoted from full-time to part-time in March because she called in sick (drunk) too much, and Magpie hadn't seen a paycheck delivered to their mailbox in a while.

As if Ann Marie had guessed what her daughter was thinking about, she said quietly, "I called the store this morning. They're letting me have a few shifts this week. I told them...I told them that things have been a little rough around here. But that I'm ready to pick up the pieces. I can't sit and wallow forever, can I?"

Magpie had actually thought that this was *exactly* what her mother was planning on doing, but she didn't say that aloud. Instead, she said, "Sure, Mom. We can go to the mall. If you want to."

"I would love that so much," Ann Marie said.

At school Magpie concentrated on being a ghost. Hither was sometimes there and sometimes not there, and Magpie thought it somehow used itself as a cloak to hide her from prying eyes. At any rate, Mr. James didn't talk to her before English, and none of her teachers called on her, and nobody called her a slut in the hallways, and at lunch not even Clare or Ben seemed to notice her. Except Ben slid his coffee over to her and she drank it gladly, and when they walked to history together afterward, the cloak was lifted, and Ben nudged her arm with his.

"How's your mom?" he asked.

"She's much better," Magpie said. "I'm sorry that you..."

But she didn't know what she was sorry for. That he saw them? That he had yet another glimpse into the mess that was Magpie's life? First the rumors at school and now this, her mother drinking so much she had to be carted away with flashing lights and sirens.

"I didn't know if I should bring it up," Ben admitted. "But I was worried about you, of course. I almost texted you last night, but...I don't know. I'm just here for you. If you ever want to talk about anything. Okay?"

"Thanks. Honestly, I'm okay."

Magpie was thankful that they had reached history by then, and she settled into her seat and let the cloak settle over her once again. She took out the yellow notebook, the one Hither said she didn't need anymore, the one she had pulled out of her bureau drawer that morning because she couldn't bear the thought of being away from it, and she uncapped the impossible pen and—just to be safe—she wrote:

My mother never drinks until she almost dies. She never ends up in the hospital with blue skin and bruises from IV needles. She holds a job. She takes me shopping. Everything is fine.

She closed the notebook and placed her hand palm up on the desk.

A tiny, impossible thing crawled into it.

Hither looked up at her and winked.

What a curious feeling.

Magpie hadn't felt it in so long that she almost didn't recognize it for what it was.

The feeling of safety.

Now it was something she could pick up and hold.

NEVER TO BE TOLD

On Friday Mr. James sat at the desk across from Magpie and folded his hands in front of him, and she realized that she had not done what he'd asked. She hadn't written an essay.

Instead, every day she had practiced becoming invisible, and every night she had gone into Near and had dinner with her Near-parents, her Near-sister, and then she had come back to the real world exhausted with the effort of keeping her world-size secret.

She had gone to the mall with Ann Marie on Tuesday.

They had not bought anything.

Ann Marie had, true to her word, gone in for shifts at the perfume counter on Wednesday and Thursday, and would go again that night.

They gave her the shitty shifts, she said, because she had a shitty track record as an employee.

And then she had laughed, as people laugh when they say something hard that is also the truth.

Magpie felt herself shrinking underneath the glare of Mr. James even though he hadn't said anything yet, even though he only stared at her with the disapproving stare all teachers must be taught in graduate school before they're allowed inside a classroom.

"Margaret," he said, then he employed a dramatic pause. This, too, was taught. Magpie was very familiar with the dramatic pause. She had learned to zip herself up against it. She was immune to its power.

"My mother was in the hospital," she said. "That's why I was out on Monday."

Mr. James softened only the tiniest smidge. "I'm so sorry to hear that, Margaret. Is everything okay now?"

"She's a diabetic," Magpie said, not knowing exactly where the lie had come from, only that it had sprung fully formed to the tip of her tongue.

"That must have been very hard for you."

"Well, yeah," Magpie said. "It was."

"If you had come to talk to me about it, I certainly would have given you some leeway."

"It's not easy to talk about."

"I can understand that. Of course I can understand that. But given your situation, and given the fact that it has been *months* since you have done anything resembling schoolwork—"

"I read that story," Magpie interrupted. "The one about Connie and Arnold Friend."

"Right, and we had agreed that you were to write a paper on it."

"But my mother..."

"I am not an unforgiving person, Margaret. I apologize if it seems like I am. I am not without sympathy. But I cannot let you continue to sit in my classroom day after day doing nothing. So your last chance is this: The paper is on my desk on Friday, a week from today, and it's a *good* paper. It has a word count now. Two thousand. Double-spaced. The whole nine yards. It's on my desk on Friday, or you fail English. I want to be very clear here, Margaret. Do you understand what I'm saying?"

"I understand."

"I am giving you a full week. I know this hasn't been an easy year for you, Margaret. I understand that. But it's time to show up."

It's time to show up? Who does he think he is?

Hither juggled English textbooks in a corner of the classroom. It wore—for some reason—an overlarge dunce's cap. Magpie watched it out of the corner of her eye, then she remembered it was her turn to speak.

"I understand," she repeated. "I'll write the paper. I promise."

Another withering, quiet stare, and he left her—finally—alone.

At lunch Clare suggested that they do something fun that night, the three of them: Magpie, Ben, and her.

"It's been a shitty week," she declared, setting her tray down heavily on the table. It consisted of a bowl of apple slices and a chopped salad that actually didn't look half bad.

"What happened?" Ben asked.

"Just a load of homework. Like—there are two weeks of school left. If I don't know how to figure out a compounded interest rate by now, I'm probably never going to."

"It's actually not that hard," Ben said.

"Shut up, math nerd," Clare retorted, rolling her eyes. She threw one of her apple slices at Ben; it bounced off his shoulder and landed on the floor.

"What kind of something fun?" Magpie asked.

"Like—okay, hear me out—but the bowling alley does this thing called Galactic Bowling every Friday night. They have disco balls and super-loud music. Sounds just weird enough to be amazing."

"Sounds like you've been there before," Ben said. "Wait— are you a bowling nerd? Are you a bowling nerd who's calling me a math nerd? When bowling has no practical application in life and math *does*?"

"I hate you," Clare said. "You're uninvited. Mags?"

Magpie shrugged. She didn't have any plans. She didn't have anything against bowling. And three nights of going into Near had left her tired. Worn out in that confused way she felt after giving blood. Plus, she could always go there after if she wanted to. "Sure, I could do that."

"Wow, don't fall over yourselves," Clare said, rolling her eyes.

"Somebody's in a mood," Ben said.

"I told you, it's been a shitty week! And I just want to throw a heavy ball down an aisle at some pins, okay?"

"I believe it's called an *alley*," Ben said.

"You really are a jerk," Clare snapped.

"I'm sorry, I'm sorry. I'd love to go bowling with you, Clare."

"Great. Galactic Bowling starts at ten. We can meet there."

"Do you have your own ball?" Ben asked, needling her.

"Yes," Clare admitted. "And I'm going to use it to bash your face in."

In history Ms. Peel gave the class some time to work in their pairs for the final project. Ben and Magpie pulled their desks together, and Ben spread out some notes. He waited a minute, but Magpie produced nothing; she hadn't done the research they'd both set out for each other at the beginning of the week.

It wasn't that she hadn't meant to. Because she *had*. And she felt terrible watching Ben shuffle his papers around, pages

and pages full of handwritten notes and printouts and arti-
cles diligently highlighted with neon-yellow ink. She felt so
terrible that she couldn't think of what to say—what was that
thing you said when you did something you shouldn't have
done? What was that word for when you'd spent an entire
week disappearing into a secret world instead of doing even
the barest minimum of work on a group project?

"I'm sorry," she said, coming up with it at last, the words
tumbling out of her in one quick bunch, spilling on the desk
in front of her, dirtying Ben's perfectly white papers with their
guilt.

For one horrible minute she thought he would imitate
the disappointed silence of Mr. James. She shrank smaller in
her chair as Ben's face melted into an expression of concern.

"Mags. It's completely fine. I know what you've had to
deal with this week."

"I swear I meant to," Magpie said quickly. "I was going
to, I *promise*—"

"Don't even mention it; I completely understand. I
should have offered to do your part."

"No, Ben, that's not what I want at all."

"I know you're not tricking me into doing more work,
Mags. It's really fine."

Ben looked earnest. Magpie searched his face for a hint of
resentment, but she couldn't find any. She felt an uncomfortable writhing within her; it wasn't his job to be there for her.
It wasn't anybody's job.

It's sort of my job, Hither corrected, walking by their desks while balancing a stack of history books on its head.

"I'll work on it this weekend," Magpie replied. "This week just got away from me."

"I'll do some extra work over the weekend to get us back on track. You just be there for your mom and take care of yourself, okay? Do you even want to go to this bowling thing tonight? You can totally bail; I'll deal with Clare."

"No—I want to," she said. "It sounds kind of fun."

Ben looked relieved. He reached his hand across the desks and touched Magpie's fingers. A part of her liked it; another part of her felt nothing much at all.

———

The bowling alley was in the next town over; Magpie left her house at nine thirty and rode her bike through the dark streets while Hither bounded alongside her, ignoring all rules of gravity, flying through the air like a giant shadowy bird.

She reached the building—a big neon sign on the roof proclaimed STRIKEOUT LANES—just as Ben was locking up his bike at the bike rack. Magpie noted again what nice things the helmet did to Ben's hair, especially when he ran a hand through it.

She was feeling all right—the bike ride had been nice, invigorating, and now here was Ben with his funny half smile and his funny stuck-up hair and his funny way of watching her as she locked up her bike next to his, as if it were the most interesting thing he'd seen all day.

When she straightened and turned to face him, he looked away quickly, and if it had been lighter out, perhaps she would have seen him blush.

"After you," he said, gesturing to the front door.

What a gentleman.

Clare had gotten there before them and rented the lane already. She had changed from school; she wore a very short black skirt and a midnight-blue sparkly top. The three of them exchanged their shoes for the clownish rentals they had to wear, then they headed to lane thirteen.

"Teddy keeps asking about you, by the way," Clare told Magpie.

"Really?" Magpie said. She had a vision of Ringo, in Near, holding a red ball.

"Where's the pretty girl, Clare; I want to see the pretty girl again." Clare laughed, rolling her eyes. "You *are* pretty, don't get me wrong, but he's such a little twerp."

"Speaking of twerps, you invited Jeremy, right?" Ben asked.

"Yeah, he should be here any minute," Clare confirmed.

"Who's Jeremy?" Magpie asked.

"My boyfriend. Didn't I tell you? He goes to Edgewood High." Clare frowned. "I didn't tell you? At my house? Gosh, I'm such a space cadet."

Double date, Hither whispered in Magpie's ear; she turned around quickly, but it was already gone.

175

"No, I didn't know you had a boyfriend," Magpie said.

"God, you're lucky. For the past three months and twenty-seven days it's all I've had to hear about," Ben said.

"I don't talk about him that much," Clare said, swiping at him. "Look, Mags didn't even know!" Clare let a dreamy expression take over her face. "But yeah, you'll meet him tonight. He's pretty great. Like, okay, he's *really* pretty great."

A double date.

Magpie had prepared herself for her date with Ben at the movies a week from today. She had even prepared herself for the required one hour Clare insisted they spend at Brandon Phipp's party beforehand. But she had *not* prepared herself for tonight being a double date. She had not even considered it, and now she felt tricked.

Clare stood up and began fiddling with the computer. She put Ben's name in as *Shitbrain*.

Ben sat next to Magpie. He seemed sheepish, a little guilty.

"She only told me she was inviting him after school," he whispered, so Clare wouldn't hear. "I didn't mean for this to be—"

"I'm not mad," Magpie said quickly.

"It's not the *worst* thing if he's here, right? I mean, it's not like...Well, it wasn't totally out of the question, right? Because we'd talked about going to see a movie...?"

"I just wasn't expecting it, but it's totally fine."

Ben looked crestfallen, unsure of how to respond.

You're being a big bitch.

"I'm being a big bitch," Magpie repeated.

"No, not at all," Ben said.

Like, it's totally fine. I just would have worn a nicer shirt.

"It's totally fine. I would have... It's fine. I'm sorry if I seem weird."

"Not any more weird than usual," Ben said, smiling.

Clare entered Magpie's name as *Prettygirl*. She entered her own name as *Queenface*. She entered a fourth name, Jeremy's, as *Hunkbutt*.

As if called into being by such an embarrassing moniker, a boy Magpie could only assume was Hunkbutt himself waltzed into her line of sight. He snuck up behind Clare and threw his arms around her, kissing her neck a mile a minute.

"This is what they're like," Ben said, rolling his eyes. "Welcome to the Claremy show."

"Claremy!" Jeremy exclaimed, pulling away from Clare. "That's amazing. That's the funniest thing I've ever heard. You must be Mags." He high-fived Ben, then stuck his hand out for Magpie to shake. She did. "Claremy! That's very funny."

"It's not *that* funny," Clare said. "Did you meet Mags?"

"I just met Mags. She seems very nice. I'm hoping she's Prettygirl or Queenface as opposed to Shitbrain," Jeremy said.

"Ben is Shitbrain, duh," Clare said. "I'm Queenface, duh."

"I'm sorry she's so mean to you," Jeremy told Ben.

"I've adapted," Ben said, shrugging.

"All right, let me just go get a pair of these terrible shoes and then prepare to be seriously crushed in Galactic Bowling, cool?" Jeremy said. He pecked Clare on the cheek again, and she looked positively starry-eyed as he skipped to the shoe-rental desk.

Hither mimed vomiting into a rack of neon-pink bowling balls, but Magpie thought it was sort of nice. She'd mostly gotten over her shock of being thrust into a double-date scenario, and now she concentrated on finding a ball that fit her fingers. She settled on an orange one, nine pounds, and lugged it back to the ball return. Ben had picked a green ball; Clare had picked purple; Jeremy came back with one of the neon-pink ones held precariously over his shoulder.

"Pretty sure somebody peed in these shoes," he declared, tossing the rentals on the floor and sitting down to lace them up.

"You're first, Shitbrain," Clare said sweetly. Ben made a face, and she blew him a kiss.

Magpie had never gone bowling with Allison—she wouldn't have worn the shoes; she wouldn't have liked how the ball made your fingers smell like sweat and grease sometimes. She also didn't like to lose, so she generally stayed away from anything that required keeping score: too much of a risk.

"Image is everything," she'd told Magpie once, her legs shin-deep in pedicure water. Magpie's own water had been too hot, but she hadn't wanted to complain. "Ow! That *hurts*," Allison had snapped at her nail technician.

The memory made Magpie feel a little queasy.

Ben bowled a strike and the crowd went wild.

"You're up, Prettygirl," he said to Magpie, trying not to look pleased, trying not to blush, not quite making eye contact when he called her that.

Magpie got up, found her ball, and hit a lackluster three pins. The crowd went wild again. She quickly realized that the crowd went wild no matter whose turn it was, no matter what sort of score they ended up with. The nonbowling three of them acted as personal cheering brigade for whichever name was up on the screen.

Magpie sat next to Ben, and Clare hopped up to take her turn.

"Nice job," Ben said.

"I only got three pins," Magpie replied, rolling her eyes. Her second ball had gone straight in the gutter.

"You're turning your hand," he said. "Right when you let the ball go. That's why it went crooked."

"Wow, Ben, I didn't know you were such an expert bowler; you'll have to give me a lesson," Jeremy said, winking as he got up to congratulate Clare on a spare.

"He's a good guy," Ben whispered, pointing his chin at Jeremy, who had bent down to retie his shoelaces. "He has a trans aunt; she took me to my first pride parade."

"Oh, really?"

"Yeah, she's cool. And Jeremy's not from Farther, you know, so he didn't know me before," Ben said. "I was kind of nervous. To tell him. But he was totally normal; he just launched into this really funny story about his aunt spraying him in the face with a garden hose." Ben laughed. "It had nothing to do with her being trans; he's just really random."

Clare erupted into applause, and Magpie and Ben looked up to see that Jeremy had gotten a strike. After three games, everyone had won except Magpie, but they were all tired, and their time was up, and losing a bowling game against friends didn't seem like that much of a loss to Magpie anyway.

It was after midnight by the time they made their way out to the parking lot. Clare was giving Jeremy a ride home, and Ben insisted on biking back to Magpie's house with her to make sure she got home okay.

Très chivalrous.

"You guys could probably just stick your bikes in the back of my mom's SUV," Clare offered.

"We're fine. It's a nice night," Ben said.

"Mags? Last chance," Clare said.

"We're fine," Magpie echoed. Clare shrugged, then stepped forward and in one movement had wrapped her arms around Magpie's shoulders and squeezed her and then was gone again. Jeremy hugged her next, and then he and Ben did some funny guy hug, and he got in the passenger seat of the SUV, and they were gone. It was just the two remaining bowlers. Ben started off toward the bike rack and Magpie followed.

They unlocked their bikes and were on their way, Ben sometimes coming up beside Magpie, sometimes falling behind, sometimes talking, sometimes not. It *was* a nice night, he was right—the humidity of the day had burned off, but it was still warm, and the stars were out, and there was a smell in the air, as if it might start to rain soon. But a nice, welcome rain. A rain that would bring a cool morning with it.

When they reached Magpie's house, they both slid off their bikes in the driveway. There were no lights on inside, but Ann Marie's car was parked in the driveway. Was she already asleep? Magpie hoped so. She turned toward Ben, and he'd taken off his helmet and looped it around his handlebars. But he still held his bike; he didn't kickstand it—as if he knew this was as far as he was allowed to come.

"I had a really fun time tonight," he said, then he laughed and touched his hair. "Is that the most stereotypical thing I've ever said?"

"I had fun, too," Magpie said.

And she had a sudden, wild thought.

She should take him to Near.

Ben was one of her closest friends now. And in Near she could repay him for his friendship. His words echoed back to her—*he didn't know me from before.* She had heard the things people had said about him when he'd first come out. She had heard what *Allison* had said about him. But she hadn't known him then. And she hadn't done anything. But she could do something *now.* She could give him whatever he wanted. She could give him a car, a pile of money, a—

A pile of money.

I was wondering how long it was going to take you to think of that.

Magpie could bring *money* back from Near. She could *make money and bring it back.*

It's not quite that simple, actually. Money is complicated. Lots of little anticounterfeit bits.

"I should get inside," Magpie said. She could only think about the color green raining from the sky and filling up buckets like nothing.

You want to make it rain money? I hadn't realized you were such a little capitalist.

Ben nodded, then looked past Magpie and up at the house, suddenly concerned. "Your mom—I hope she's feeling better."

"She's fine," Magpie said. "Probably sleeping. Thanks for asking."

"I'll text you," Ben said. He did not make a move toward her. She stepped backward and nodded.

She did not want Ben to kiss her because if he did that, he might get the wrong impression: that she was the type of girl who should be kissed. And she wasn't. She was the type of girl who should be run from.

"Text me," she said. "Get home safely."

She angled the bike between them, so even if he suddenly thought he should get closer to her, he couldn't. There was a wall of metal, of rubber, between them.

"All right," he said. He fitted his helmet back on and swung a leg over his bike.

He seemed to know that she didn't want him to wait

for her to get inside. He started off down the street; Magpie dropped her bike on the grass and dug her keys out of her purse.

She was quiet going in the house. Ann Marie's bedroom door was closed, and Magpie could see a flickering light coming from underneath it. She had the TV on, muted, while she slept.

"Tell me why I can't make money?" Magpie whispered.

You made one pen and you think you're a wizard. Hither had taken up much of the couch, spreading an unnecessary amount of limbs over the cushions and pillows.

"I made one pen and it didn't kill me. So why should money be any different?"

You want to go into Near and bring a hundred bucks back? Be my guest.

"But why should I stop there?"

Because one pen is one pen. And one hundred-dollar bill is one hundred-dollar bill. It would take you months to create enough money to add up to anything substantial. And you haven't made anything since the pen, I've noticed, so clearly you're still feeling the effects.

Magpie wasn't necessarily still feeling the effects, no; she hadn't made anything since the pen because the way it had made her feel had *scared* her. There was the feeling that something had been taken from her, yes, but there was something else. There was the power she had felt—the power that she could both make and take whatever she wanted. And the desire to do it again, and again, and again . . . And the fear that once she gave into that desire, she wouldn't be able to stop.

But then—what was the point of creating a world that would answer to her every whim if she was too scared to take advantage of it?

So she went out to the backyard. And before she could really think about what she was doing, she had thrown open the shed door and strode through it to the bright, sunny hillside of Near.

It seemed to always be sunny in Near when she entered it. Always around four o'clock in the afternoon. Of course—she could make time speed up or slow down according to her whim. That was easy. She could make it nighttime with the blink of an eye, just as she could take one step and cover a mile of ground.

Hither had come through with her. It looked indignant; its almost-human arms were crossed over its almost-human chest.

What do you suppose you're doing?

"I'm proving you wrong. This is *my* world, and I can make anything I want. I can make enough money to do whatever I want."

But you don't need money in here. Everything is free for you. You are a god here.

"But you need money in the real world," Magpie said. "And I could buy my own house, a car, an entire town. I could buy the town of Farther and make it just like Near. I could do anything I wanted to."

And she raised her hand, palm up, and it happened much more quickly this time: a flutter of wind, a flash of light, and there was a perfectly real hundred-dollar bill resting in Magpie's fingers.

Not a counterfeit bill. A bill as real as the pen in her pocket, the pen she carried with her now wherever she went to remind herself that she had written her own destiny, that she was in control of everything.

I'd stop there. I warned you before; you are not limitless.

"But you're just a part of me," Magpie said. "You're just something I created. So if you're telling me I'm not limitless, that's just my *own* subconscious doubting what I can do. And I'm never going to break free of that unless I try."

Your logic sounds good and all, but that's not how it works. I'm telling you, you're going to hurt yourself if you try to do more.

"I'm going to hurt myself if I *don't*," she corrected.

And then . . .

There was . . .

A flash of light.

And another bill fluttered down.

And another . . .

And another . . .

And that was all Magpie could see: a green rain cloud of money.

And she felt triumphant and strong and powerful and huge.

Until she didn't feel any of those things.

And the world went dark.

EIGHT FOR A WISH

Magpie became aware, gradually, of two things: the sound of a bird singing from far, far away and the pounding headache that was beating against her temples, as if her brain had become too big for the skull that encased it.

She opened her eyes. Wherever she was, it was daytime, and the sunlight felt more like a knife slicing into her vision in a streak of white-hot flames. She groaned and covered her face with her hand.

She was lying on something soft. The grass in Near? What was the last thing she remembered? Hither was lecturing her about something. Hither was telling her not to do what she wanted to do. But she had done it anyway, because it was her world, and what was the point of having your own world if you couldn't do what you wanted in it?

And then nothing. She couldn't remember anything.

She groaned again and opened her eyes under the protection of her cupped palm.

The sunlight was much more bearable when filtered through the tiny cracks in her fingers, but still her skin glowed red with it and it hurt to blink and it hurt to not blink and it hurt to do anything.

So after a moment or two of feeling sorry for herself, she removed her hand from her eyes and attempted to let them adjust to the sunlight.

And she found that she was in her bedroom, although she couldn't immediately say whether it was her bedroom in Near or her bedroom in Farther because they looked very similar.

She groaned again. She couldn't help it. It felt as if somebody were actively sledgehammering her head. She turned to her left and saw a glass of water on her nightstand, two brick-red pills of ibuprofen lying next to it. And lying next to *them*—the size of a ladybug—was Hither, looking at her with I-told-you-so eyes.

"Where am I?" she asked. Her voice came out no louder than a whisper. She was trying very hard not to groan again, but it was a battle she thought she would end up losing.

Do you not remember?

"We were in Near . . ."

And you collapsed. Because you thought you were smarter than I am. Which means you're really the exact opposite.

"Are we still in Near?"

I dragged you back through the doorway. It wouldn't have

been good to stay there in your present condition. You need your rest. You need to replenish your strength. Although you wouldn't have needed either of those things if you had just listened to me in the first place.

"How long have I been sleeping?"

An annoyingly long time. You've been quite dramatic.

Memories were coming back to Magpie in strange flashes. Something pulling her bodily along a field of lime-green grass. Waking up two or three times before now, but falling almost immediately back into a deep, heavy sleep. Ann Marie standing over her holding a glass of something, fretting, wringing her hands, and saying Magpie's name over and over.

"Where is my mother?" Magpie asked. "Is it Saturday yet?"

Saturday is long gone, see you later, ancient history. It is Sunday, my little princess of the nonlistening.

"Sunday? I've been sleeping for more than a day?"

Lucky for you, you were blessed with a self-involved beast of a birther, or she might have hauled you right back to the hospital she just left. That's what any sensible mother would have done.

"What do you know about mothers?"

Only what you know.

Magpie would have answered, but Ann Marie chose that moment to walk briskly into the room.

"Magpie? I thought I heard you. My poor baby. Are you feeling better?"

Magpie was happy she hadn't been brought to the hospital, of course, but she couldn't help but feel a little bit... stung. What mother let her child sleep for an entire weekend without thinking something might be wrong?

Magpie did her best to look ignorant. "Mom? What happened? Was I asleep?"

"Oh, sweetheart, it was terrible. I found you in bed like this on Saturday morning. You were in a cold sweat; you wouldn't stir much when I tried to wake you, but I knew you were okay at least. You said your head was pounding. I'm sure this is the worst migraine I've ever seen. Do you remember when I used to get them? They started when I was about your age, but thank God, they seem to have stopped for me now. I was so happy neither of you had ever gotten one; I thought they'd skipped a generation. My poor baby."

But Magpie did feel just the slightest bit better. At least Ann Marie had checked on her. And if Magpie really had said her head was pounding (she had no memory of that conversation, but her head *was* pounding even now), then it made sense that Ann Marie thought it was just a bad migraine. Magpie remembered being younger and not being allowed into her parents' room because Ann Marie was sleeping off a migraine, a wet washcloth over her eyes to both block out the light and cool her sweaty face. Days of being shushed constantly because Ann Marie needed complete silence.

"It still hurts a lot," Magpie said.

"You're overworked and overtired, no doubt," Ann Marie

responded. "I always said those schools expect too much of you kids. You can forget about going tomorrow. Maybe Tuesday, too. You need your rest, Magpie, all right?"

"I have work to do—"

"Forget it. They can live without a few homework assignments. You're an excellent student; you aren't going to compromise your health for anyone."

And that was all it took to happily flick the idea of Amelia Earhart or Joyce Carol Oates out of Magpie's head. She stretched out a little in bed, and said, "I think I'm hungry. Is there anything to eat?"

"Of course. Just sit right here, and I'll bring you a plate of something."

Ann Marie leaned over the bed and kissed Magpie on the forehead.

The kiss felt more like a punch, an explosion of pain that sank deep into Magpie's head.

Ann Marie left the room.

I bet you listen to me from now on, huh?

"Get over yourself," Magpie hissed, putting her hand on her head again.

You could have died. The least you could do is thank me for getting you someplace safe.

"I'm safe in Near. I would have been safe. It's out here that worries me more."

Already not listening to me. Maybe next time I won't be so helpful.

Magpie did not go to school on Monday, and she didn't go to school on Tuesday, and on Wednesday Ann Marie was gone before Magpie even woke up, so she spent the day, mostly recovered, floating in the pool and enjoying hours on end without anyone around.

She did not look at the shed much.

She felt its presence as if it had its own gravity, as if it were doing its best to pull her toward it. But she still felt the weakness inside her own veins, the feeling that something had been taken from her, the feeling that she had exchanged a piece of herself for something. A trade gone wrong.

She tried not to admit to herself that Hither had been right because it was gloating enough as it was, and she didn't want to give it any more fuel for its fire.

She went back to school on Thursday, deliberately late so as to miss Mr. James's class, and nobody talked to her until lunchtime when Ben and Clare fell upon her as if she had just returned from a war.

"Mags! Where the hell have you been? I texted you, like, a billion times. I was going to show up at your house if you weren't here today. What's wrong?" Clare demanded in a frantic whisper. Magpie was grateful for that; the last thing she needed was the attention of the rest of the lunch table.

"I'm really sorry. I've been so sick. Honestly, I haven't even looked at my phone."

"We were really worried about you," Ben said, his voice even quieter than Clare's so Magpie had to lean in a little bit to hear him.

"Ben thought you weren't coming to school because you had such a terrible time at bowling," Clare said. "But I told him three days of classes are a lot to miss just because you didn't win." She paused, then added thoughtfully, "Wait... That's not why you were out, right?"

"No, honestly. I was just sick."

"That's what I said it must be, but when you didn't answer your phone, I was honestly like, is she maybe dead? I had Ben check the hospital computers for your name."

"Really?"

"She really did," Ben confirmed. "Which is a total invasion of privacy on, like, twelve different levels, but I was happy when I didn't find you."

"Or a Jane Doe," Clare added. "I told him to look for a Jane Doe, too."

"We don't get many Jane Does," Ben said, rolling his eyes. "This isn't *Grey's Anatomy*."

Luckily for Magpie, this comment sent Clare and Ben into a spiral of questions (from Clare) and answers (from Ben) about just how similar Ben's volunteer work at the hospital was to *Grey's Anatomy*, which was, so she professed, Clare's favorite show. (As it turned out, there were not many similarities at all.) Magpie took this reprieve from questioning to eat a few bites of her grilled cheese and listen in on the rest of the table.

Which was currently locked in a vicious debate about Brandon Phipp's party.

Which was—Magpie's stomach sank to find out—tomorrow night.

Tomorrow night?

Time flies when you're almost dying in a made-up fantasy world.

Magpie turned her head to see Hither standing on the table closest to hers. It was doing some sort of complicated Irish jig. She did her best to ignore it.

"Mags, are you still a no?" Luke asked.

"No, actually. I think I'm gonna go for a little bit," Magpie replied.

"Let's just do something else," Brianna suggested. "Literally anything else in the entire world. My dad is a dentist—we could all get root canals?"

"I've had a root canal," Clare piped in. "It was *awful*. The worst part is—"

"The smell. We know, girl. When are you going to retire this root-canal story?" Luke asked.

"The smell?" Brianna asked. "What does that even mean? What does it smell like?"

"Rotten flesh," Clare said seriously. "It's all rotten in there. My dentist said I was the youngest person she'd ever given a root canal to."

"You say that like it's something to be proud of," Ben said, shaking his head. "I love you, but you are so weird."

"Also, are we seriously back to debating this party?" Clare asked. "Do we ever talk about anything else? I mean— it's just a party. We're not all required to suck the dick of Brandon Phipp. Ha. That kind of rhymes. Suck the dick of Brandon—what?"

The entire table had come to a complete, eerie hush, exactly as if a light switch had been flicked off, muting the six of them so completely that you could have heard a pin drop. Well, all of them except Clare, who had continued talking right through the muting until she'd realized that all eyes were on her, and all eyes were doing their best to scream *Shut the eff up*.

And then she realized why. And her own eyes widened to roughly the size of dinner plates. She covered her mouth with one hand.

And then four pairs of eyes slid off Clare and moved over to Magpie.

Who was silently gathering up her things, a funny look on her face because, of course, out of everyone gathered here today, she was the only one who had, on the worst night of her life so far, sucked the dick of Brandon Phipp.

It does *kind of rhyme, doesn't it?* Hither asked as Magpie clumsily stood and left the lunch table, beelining toward the cafeteria doors with a single-mindedness only the truly mortified can produce.

It added, *What, are we going somewhere?*

And it followed her into the hall.

Magpie had not visited her locker in the middle of the day for six months and three weeks, but she felt oddly calm doing so now because it was lunchtime and Allison was eating in the cafeteria with all of the other sophomores.

She tried not to think about the way Clare had so easily made a joke—which would have been under other circumstances completely benign—about giving Brandon Phipp head.

If she thought too much about it, she was left with a funny taste in the back of her throat. Something hot and sticky sliding down her chin. The sensation of not being able to breathe. Tears stinging her eyes. Brandon Phipp's hands tangled up in her hair.

She dropped books into her locker with the intention of making noise to distract herself from the thoughts running wildly through her brain. She could sense Hither somewhere close but not immediately visible, somewhere lurking around the edges. Maybe it was scared of the way she felt right now, the rage that coursed through her veins and made her skin hot to the touch.

Good. Let it be scared. Let everyone be scared of the things Magpie could do to them.

She shoved book after book into her locker, then she slammed the locker shut with a satisfying crash that echoed through the hallways and echoed through her skull.

She was left holding her backpack, the yellow notebook inside, the yellow notebook that might as well have been a part of her, so closely was she linked with it. And the pen that she had made. And her phone, forgotten and out of power.

She was going to leave.

She didn't need this school; she didn't need this town; she didn't need this *world*, not when she had one of her own to return to.

So she spun around, ready to storm out, to escape the unbreathable air of this terrible place—

But there was someone blocking her way.

Two someones blocking her way.

Mrs. Henderson, the guidance counselor with the radar for eating disorders. She was with the vice principal of Farther High, a woman named Amanda Wood, with a face as hard as her name suggested, her mouth now set into a line so straight that you could set a ruler by it.

"Ms. Lewis," she said, and Magpie noted that it was never good when an adult called you by your last name. It was never followed by something pleasant, something easy, something like *I just wanted to tell you I love your shirt today. Wherever did you get it?*

As if to prove this point, Amanda Wood added, "If you could follow me, please. We'd like to have a bit of a chat."

Magpie had two options.

Option one, of course: She could follow them.

That seemed to be the obvious choice.

Option two was a little bit more slippery.

In short: She could turn and run.

Oh, here you are being all dramatic again. A little chat with these nice ladies won't kill you. Plus, the bell's about to ring. You don't want to cause a scene, do you? You never know who might be visiting her locker....

Which was enough to convince her.

Magpie put a smile on her face, a smile she hoped conveyed a message somewhere along the lines of *Everything is fine, and I am a happy and well-adjusted student.* Then she nodded, and said, "Of course," and followed the two women down the hall.

Magpie had been in the guidance counselor's office once before, last year, so she knew that's where they were headed. Mrs. Henderson made it a point to meet with the incoming freshman class individually, half-hour sessions to introduce herself and hand out some pamphlets about healthy eating. She'd done a little redecorating since then; there was a new plant in one corner of the room and a painting that took up much of one wall. It was a painting of the sea on a calm, sunny day. There was a single sailboat just far enough away so you couldn't tell if somebody was on it. The water looked actually wet, as if you could slip right into it and end up in another world. Magpie thought she had read about something like that happening. Before this, she wouldn't have believed it was possible. But now she understood that things like that actually happened.

"Do you like it?" Mrs. Henderson asked, mistaking Magpie's silence for admiration. "My daughter painted that."

Was it part of her therapy, Magpie wondered, part of the treatment for her anorexia? To paint the sea, to make it look as real as possible?

Just say yes, for goodness' sake.

"Yes. I like it very much," Magpie said.

Mrs. Henderson, the proud parent, nodded her head, as if something had been proved. Then she pointed at one of the three chairs set in a lopsided triangle in front of her desk, and said, "Please. Have a seat."

Magpie did.

The two women did.

And for a moment they all stared at one another, but if they wanted Magpie to be the first to talk, they would have to wait a long, long time, because Magpie could stay silent for years, subsisting on only macaroni and cheese and the occasional vodka lemonade.

"This isn't going to be an easy discussion, Margaret," Amanda Wood said. Ah, so she knew Ms. Lewis's first name. Magpie didn't know if it was Ms. Wood or Mrs. Wood or Miss Wood so she chose, in her mind, to refer to the vice principal by her full name because that is how the other students of Farther High did.

And no duh, it wasn't going to be an easy conversation.

No conversation that ever took place with a guidance counselor and vice principal present was ever *easy*.

"A number of your teachers have been in touch with us," Mrs. Henderson said. Her voice was exactly how a guidance counselor's voice should be: soft and lilting and sounding a little bit as if she might burst into tears at any moment.

"Oh?" Magpie said.

It was best to say as little as possible in these types of situations.

"Margaret, it would appear that you haven't been handing in many assignments at all," Amanda Wood said. "Your class participation has been almost nonexistent. You were out once last week, you've missed classes three times this week, you were late this morning, and there is only one week left of school. Truancy is something we take very seriously here, Margaret."

"It's only truancy if I don't have a good reason, right?" Magpie asked.

"*Do* you have a good reason, Margaret? Because if one does, they usually would have reported it to the office by now," Amanda Wood said.

"My mother was in the hospital," Magpie said.

"That was last week, correct? Mr. James informed us of that, yes. Has something happened to her more recently?"

"I had a migraine," Magpie said.

Every time she spoke, she heard her voice grow
softer
and
softer
and she hated herself for it.

"I see," Amanda Wood said.

"Margaret, we want to help you. We're just trying to get to the bottom of this," Mrs. Henderson said. She was clearly playing the role of good cop in this little play they were all in.

"I just missed a few days of school. I can get my mother to write a note if that would help," Magpie said.

"If it were just the issue of a few missed days, we wouldn't be here," Amanda Wood replied. "We understand that life can sometimes get in the way of school. We aren't without understanding."

"So what is it?"

"As of now, your algebra and science teachers inform me that you will fail their classes this year. History—Ms. Peel—is contingent upon the final project's completion. And Mr. James tells us that you have an assignment due tomorrow that will determine whether you pass or fail. Let me make this clear to you, Margaret—if you fail either history or English, you will not successfully complete sophomore year. You will have to retake classes during the summer, and your chances of graduating on time will be compromised."

Mrs. Henderson shifted in her seat. "Margaret—are you on track to complete these two assignments? Ms. Peel tells us the final project is done with a partner. Have you chosen yours?"

"Yes. It will be completed."

"And English?" she pressed. "What about the assignment that's due tomorrow?"

"It's done," Magpie lied. The lie was easy to tell, just as slippery and wet as the painting of the sea.

"Margaret," Mrs. Henderson continued. "If I may be frank...I've looked over your records from freshman year. You never quite made the honor roll, but you were a solid student. Bs and Cs. You missed a total of ten days last year. There was nothing like this. There's been a complete shift. I'd be remiss if I didn't ask you what was going on here."

"It's just...been a lot of stuff," Magpie said, fumbling over her words, feeling the heat start to build in her cheeks and her neck.

"You can talk to us," Amanda Wood said. "If there's something going on. If something happened."

"Nothing happened," Magpie said, perhaps a bit too quickly. Mrs. Henderson pursed her lips, as if she wanted to say more but couldn't decide on the words.

Amanda Wood, for her part, seemed eager to put the conversation to rest. She clapped her hands together softly, and said, "So we should have no further problems. Margaret, you are on an academic suspension that will carry into your junior year. You will have weekly check-ins with Mrs. Henderson and monthly check-ins with me. You will be given a worksheet that every teacher must sign at the beginning and end of every class. Every assignment you hand in must be logged on that sheet. We will be getting in touch with your parents, to keep them informed about what's going on. Since school is out next week, we are taking it on good faith that you will hand in the two discussed assignments. I don't expect you to need a follow-up meeting next week, but if you do, I'm sure we can arrange it. Mrs. Henderson will be able to explain things more completely. Do you have any questions?"

Magpie had a lot of questions. But one question was more pressing at the moment than all the others.

Because more than anything else, she wished she could disappear.

Whenever she wanted. Wherever she wanted.

Like now. In this moment. Just slip away into another world.

So—why the garden shed?

Could she open a door to Near somewhere else?

Or was it tied to that specific place?

What are you up to?

Oh, dear friend.

Everything. She was up to everything.

———

Magpie went through the motions.

She went to all her classes that afternoon.

She went home and made dinner and ate it and unplugged the phone so if Amanda Wood called later, when Ann Marie was there, she would get a busy signal.

And then she left the house, slipping out as soon as the sun had disappeared below the horizon line, pushing her bike fast down Pine Street, putting miles between her and the garden shed.

She ended up in a field of Christmas trees.

A little farm that would chop them down in December and sell them to the people of Farther to decorate with tinsel and lights, to shove presents underneath, to pretend Santa was proof of some real magic in the world.

She used to come here twice a season every year. Once with her own family to pick out a tiny tree to go in their tiny living room and once with Allison and her parents. When they had been younger, she and Allison would play hide-and-seek, darting between rows of evergreens and jumping out to scare each other.

She hadn't come at all this past winter.

Ann Marie hadn't mentioned it.

They'd eaten Chinese food on Christmas Eve and leftover Chinese food on Christmas Day.

Magpie slipped off her bike and let it fall to the ground with a muted thud.

Hither had been following her the whole way, of course, first a dragon, then a bird of prey, then something that might have been a panther stalking behind her bike with great fluid strides.

It watched her now with interest as she pulled the yellow notebook from her backpack and uncapped the Near-pen and held both of them, one in each hand, and closed her eyes.

Didn't I say you don't need that anymore?

"I like it. It helps me concentrate."

What are you trying to do here?

"Shouldn't you already know?"

But she smiled because she had been practicing keeping her thoughts to herself, and it had worked, and as she raised the pen to the notebook, Hither watched her intently because it had no idea what she was going to write.

Which was this:

I am able to get to Near no matter where I am. I can open a doorway with this pen. I can draw one into existence. I can make one out of thin air.

She closed the notebook and held it to her chest.

I see.

"You can't talk me out of it."

On the contrary. I'm surprised it took you this long to consider the possibility.

"So it can be done?"

I suppose you're about to find out.

Magpie held the pen in her right hand.

Though it was made of metal, it was warm on her skin, and she imagined that it pulsed with some impossible energy from some impossible world.

She raised the tip of the pen and touched it to the air.

And she felt—somehow—the most delicate pressure against it. As if it had found some purchase in the night molecules.

Slowly, she dragged it downward.

And before her eyes the thinnest glowing line appeared.

She drew another line, then a third, then a little doorknob to finish off her creation.

204

She had a drawn a door. Out of thin air. Out of the very night. Out of nothing.

And she reached her hand out and clasped the knob...

And pulled.

———————

Magpie stepped through a row of Christmas trees into another world.

The waters that surrounded the island of Near were closer now than they had ever been before. A mile away, two at the most. She thought of the painting in Mrs. Henderson's office. She thought of her swimming pool. She squinted at the horizon line; the water of Near was so calm and expansive and serene that Magpie almost wished she was at its edge—but then she caught herself and didn't. There would be time for that later.

The new doorway disappeared behind her as soon as she had stepped through, the glowing line fading into nothingness as she turned and watched. And in its place—the not-shed. So she could open a doorway anywhere in Farther and always end up here, back where she started, in her own not-backyard.

The town of Near sat as perfect and quiet as she had left it. In a breath she was there at the gate, and in another breath she was walking into her own house on Near–Pine Street, the smell of chocolate in the air, the sound of laughter from the kitchen where her mother and father stood baking an enormous three-tiered cake.

"There she is," Ann Marie said, when she saw her daughter. "Are you hungry, sweetheart?"

"Of course she's hungry!" Gabriel answered. Magpie set the yellow notebook down on the kitchen table as Gabriel cut a piece of cake, a thick triangle of brown, heavy with icing. He stuck a fork into it—the cake was so dense that it supported the utensil's weight and propped it up so it looked like a flagpole—and handed it to Magpie. Then he cut another piece and gave it to her, and said, "Give this one to your sister, will you?"

Balancing the two plates in her hands, Magpie headed downstairs. Her sister's door was open, and Eryn was on her bed like last time, waiting for Magpie.

"Cake!" she exclaimed. "Yum, gimme!"

Magpie sat next to her on the bed, and they ate forkful after forkful of the cake, which was the richest cake Magpie had ever put into her mouth. When they had finished their slices, they dropped the plates and forks onto the carpet, and they disappeared, as if whisked away by some unseen maid. Magpie realized that Hither wasn't here; had she gone through the doorway too quickly for it to follow? But she didn't need it now. It would only try to convince her of her own limitations, and she needed the exact opposite. She needed someone to show her she could do *more*.

"Why are you looking at me like that?" Eryn asked, raising her eyebrows, leaning back on the bed. "You look like you're hatching some evil little plan."

"And if I am?" Magpie asked, her voice falling to something like a hiss, like a noise made in the back of some animal's throat.

Eryn raised her eyebrows even higher, then smiled slowly, and said, "Great. Things were getting a little boring around here."

———————

Magpie stayed in Near until she was tired enough to want to return to Farther. She'd eaten two more slices of cake in Near, but stepping through to her own backyard made her suddenly hungry, as if she hadn't eaten a thing, so she made herself macaroni and cheese and ate it over the kitchen sink as Hither, a long black snake, slithered around her ankles and over her bare feet. She was relieved her mother wasn't home so she wouldn't have to talk to anyone.

She slept well that night, and when she woke up in the early afternoon to an empty house and not so much as a note from Ann Marie, she stretched luxuriantly in her bed and stayed there until she got bored.

She checked the messages on her phone. Only three, from Clare.

I'm so sorry about what I said.

I didn't even think.

I feel like such an asshole.

It was just after two.

Magpie had missed almost the entire day of school.

Almost.

She didn't reply.

She ran herself a shower so hot that it left her skin tingling and red.

She took her time getting dressed, then she took her time biking to school, and when she finally arrived, the halls of Farther High were empty after the last bell and Magpie's footsteps echoed off the walls as she walked to the English department wing and stood outside Mr. James's classroom.

I don't like the look on your face.

"Get used to it," she replied, but her voice revealed just the tiniest bit of shakiness. Just the slightest little quiver to it.

Have you thought this through?

Had she thought this through?

No.

But there had been this spark that ran through her when she had woken up and remembered it was the day of the party.

This little jolt of an idea.

And it had grown and grown inside her.

And it had led her here.

And she felt just a little bit guilty for what she was about to do.

For what she was about to *try* to do.

But she had to see if she *could*.

So she took a deep breath, a breath meant to fill up her lungs with courage and resolve instead of air, then she pushed the door of the classroom open and stepped inside as if she owned the place, as if everyone else were just paying rent.

Mr. James was at his desk, hunched over a stack of papers, and when he heard the door open, he raised his head, then immediately shook it, disappointed.

"I don't accept late work," he said.

"What do you mean?" Magpie asked.

"Your assignment was due today. Class is over. School is over. I don't accept late work."

He bent over the papers again.

Magpie did not like the way he so easily ignored her.

"I wasn't coming here to give you the assignment," she said. Her voice was strong and unquavering. Good.

Mr. James sighed and looked up again. He seemed tired, the specific kind of tired that affected teachers at the tail end of a long school year. The same tired that affected the students of Farther High. The same glassy-eyed, wild stare.

"Margaret, there is nothing left to discuss between us," Mr. James said. "I have given you every conceivable opportunity to improve your grade. I have no choice but to fail you."

Magpie shut the door behind her.

"I have something to show you," she said.

"I've made it clear that I don't accept late assignments—"

"And *I've* made it clear that I'm not here to give you a

fucking assignment!" she snapped, and the force of her words took both her and Mr. James by surprise. He half stood, then faltered, sat again, then clasped his hands on his desk.

"What would you like to show me?" he asked, his voice taking on a new tenor, a careful, controlled tone that made Magpie's teeth ache.

"I think you're really gonna like it," she replied.

She swung her backpack around and reached into it, and out of the corner of her eye, she saw Mr. James flinch. Did he think she had a gun? How funny.

But she only pulled out a pen, just an innocent little pen, and he visibly relaxed.

"What's this about?" he asked.

"Just watch. Have some patience."

"Margaret, you're being highly—"

But he shut up. Because Magpie had uncapped the pen, and she had made the first slice of light in the air.

She paused.

Mr. James got up from his desk. The line of light was between them; if Magpie moved just so, she could make it look as if it was cutting his body in two.

"What is this?" he asked.

"I said you would like it," she replied, and she made another line. The top of the door.

"How are you doing that?"

"It's the special pen," she said, wiggling it. "Watch what else it can do."

And she made another slash. The outline of a door glowed in the classroom. She stepped around the rectangle of light to stand on the same side as Mr. James, then she drew a little doorknob.

"That's a..." Mr. James paused.

"Open it."

"What is it?"

"You know what it is; just open it."

Mr. James's face was lit up by the light of the impossible door. Magpie saw his hand twitch; she knew English teachers in particular understood how many different forms a door to elsewhere could take. When presented with a doorknob made out of light, not a single one of them would be able to resist.

Mr. James took a step toward the door. Magpie bounced on her heels; the suspense was killing her.

Do you know what you're doing?

Magpie ignored Hither. All of her attention was focused on Mr. James, who was turning the knob...

And turning it...

And pulling the door open.

For a moment there were two worlds in the ordinary English classroom. There was the world of Farther, where Magpie and Mr. James now stood. And through a doorway lined in bright white light, there was the world of Near. A rolling expanse of green. A sky as blue as lapis.

And for just another moment Magpie thought she would have to push him.

But then he was stepping through the threshold.

And she followed him inside.

———————

Mr. James did not puke like Clare had, but he did fall to his knees, and his breathing became ragged and heavy, like a thing that clawed and ripped at his chest.

Magpie stepped neatly around him.

The doorway zippered itself up.

The not-shed was just a few feet away.

The ocean was even closer.

Are you paying attention?

"To what? To the water? Why would I care about that?" Magpie said aloud, and at the sound of her voice, Mr. James pulled himself back onto his shins and looked at her.

"Where are we?" he asked, and she gave him a few points because his voice did not shake like Clare's had. "Who were you talking to?"

"We're in Near," Magpie replied. Then she pointed her chin in the direction of the town, at a solitary figure that was making its way up the long and sloping hill. "And I was talking to her." Well, she had been talking to Hither. But Hither had melted away now, and she supposed it was all the same. Hither, Near, her Near-sister. It wasn't necessary to differentiate.

"Is there someone else here?" he asked, and followed Magpie's gaze down the hill.

Magpie didn't think he would recognize her sister. Eryn had graduated before he'd started teaching at Farther High.

For that's who it was, of course, solemnly making her way up the hill to greet them. Eryn, wearing jean cut-off shorts and a lavender tank top, her hair in its familiar messy bob and her arms swinging by her sides.

"That's my sister," Magpie said proudly, because in this world having a sister like Eryn was something to be proud of, not something to try your hardest to forget.

"Where are we?" Mr. James asked again. "This place, it looks like... Did you call it *Near*?"

"Clever, right?" Magpie replied happily. "I made this whole thing. While you were living your boring life, I was making a *universe.*"

"I don't understand."

Mr. James had turned pale. His breathing had quieted but came now in little spurts and catches.

"I wouldn't expect you to," she replied.

"Is this because... Is this because I was going to fail you?"

Magpie rolled her eyes. "No. Do you think I care about school anymore? About *grades*? Honestly, this isn't even personal. Maybe it's like the girl in that story. You never answered my question—why did she go with him? Why did she just let that happen to her? But I was thinking about it... and haven't I been just like her? Just letting all this shit happen to me? Well, not anymore. I'm not Connie anymore; I'm Arnold Friend."

"I don't...I don't understand," he said.

"I'm not going to be led anymore; I'm the one who's going to be doing the leading," Magpie said softly.

A beat and then—

You don't have to do this. You can change your mind.

Hither's voice—but where was it?

"Leave me alone!" Magpie demanded, whirling around, trying to catch sight of it.

"Who are you... Who's there?" Mr. James asked, because he had figured out that Magpie's sister was still too far away for Magpie to be talking to her.

You can bring him home. He won't remember anything.

"He could have just left me alone!" Magpie protested, still turning in circles, still yelling at nothing. "Everyone could just have left me alone, but they didn't, and that's not my fault, and it's not my fault what happens to them now!"

"Margaret..."

But Eryn had reached the top of the hill. She smiled sweetly at Mr. James, who was still resting on his knees, then she moved over and squeezed her younger sister around the shoulders.

"I always miss you so much when you go away," she whined.

"Pretty soon I'll never have to go away," Magpie promised.

"Can you do that?" Eryn asked.

"I guess we'll see," Magpie said, and shrugged. "Hey, Mr. James, do you want to know what happens if you die

214

in Near? Because I was thinking about it, and I really have no idea. Do you just, like, wink out of existence? Do they never find your body back home? Is it like you were never even born?"

Mr. James scrabbled, crab-style, sideways, away from Magpie and her sister.

Eryn removed her arm from around Magpie's shoulders.

Magpie took a careful step back.

For a single blink of an eye, Eryn was just a girl.

Just a girl in cut-off shorts and a tank top and messy hair and a sloppy grin.

Just a girl who looked like how Magpie might look in six years. The same color hair. The same color eyes. The same color skin.

Just a girl with a funny grin on her face. A grin that didn't seem nice at all.

And then, in the next moment, in the next blink, she was slightly bigger than just a girl.

And then bigger.

And then bigger.

And as Magpie and Mr. James watched, Eryn's teeth grew more and more fanglike.

And her limbs grew longer and longer.

And when she opened her mouth, her jaw unhinged.

And her open throat was like a cave.

And she snarled.

And then you really couldn't say she was much like a girl at all.

NINE FOR A KISS

The thing that had swallowed Mr. James shrank down to the size and shape of a girl again, and that girl hugged Magpie tightly and pecked her on the cheek and then turned and walked back down the grassy hill to the town of Near.

Magpie watched her go for a minute or two, then she turned to see if Hither had shown up again, but it wasn't anywhere to be found. Or—yes, it was, just over there, but it had shrunk to the size of a mouse, and it was dark and heavy, like a mouse's shadow.

Near was quiet and still, an overwhelming kind of silence that felt like a blanket. Magpie's ears rang. She tried to decide if she regretted it, feeding Mr. James to her sister, to Hither, to the world.

But she didn't regret it, not really. Because she had proved something.

She became aware of a sharp pain in the back of her neck. A blossoming headache. She was tired and hungry, and the night was not over. The night was far from over.

Magpie stepped through the not-shed and emerged in her own backyard again.

As far as she could see, the one fatal flaw in her plan was that her bike was still at the school. But she wouldn't need it. She could walk to Brandon Phipp's party. Or, hell, she could go back into Near and make a car for herself.

But the pain in her head was now shooting bluntly upward. She needed to rest and eat and bide her time.

It was almost four.

Magpie made a box of macaroni and cheese, and she sat eating it on the couch in the living room. Her mother had made some attempts to clean the house since her hospital stay, but they were surface tricks only: a rag run over a shelf, a passing attempt at vacuuming. At its core, the house was dirty enough now that it was easy to imagine it might never be fully clean again. The coffee table was ruined with rings from sweating glasses of vodka; the carpet was stained with the daily trek of mud from front door to kitchen to bedrooms to bathroom; the couch Magpie sat on smelled faintly of mildew, as if someone had once spilled a glass of something and it had never properly dried.

Magpie had spent every day of the past six months in this house, moving through these rooms, but it was only now that she saw it properly, that she saw what it had become. It was a shame, maybe—to some people it might have felt like a shame—although Magpie couldn't seem to bring herself to care.

The noise of a car door slamming broke her reverie. She looked down at her bowl of macaroni and cheese and found it empty. She was still hungry, as if the effort it had taken to change her Near-sister into something capable of swallowing a person whole had depleted everything inside her. She looked up from the bowl and stared at the front door, waiting for it to open.

Someone fumbled with the doorknob, then Ann Marie burst sloppily into the house, midlaugh, her hair unwashed and greasy, and her shirt unbuttoned just one button too many to be decent.

She saw her daughter, and her grin erupted into something so wide and big that Magpie knew, as if she hadn't known the moment she'd seen her, that Ann Marie was drunk.

Drunk and driving at four in the afternoon.

Magpie had hoped the near-death-inspired sobriety would have lasted longer than two weeks, but what could one do?

One took what one could get.

"Sweetheart! It feels like I haven't seen you in *weeks*," Ann Marie said, throwing her coat at the peg rack on the wall, missing, ignoring it.

"I've been around," Magpie said.

"Is school done yet? It is, isn't it?"

"Yes, it's done," Magpie said, because as far as she was

concerned, school *was* over—at least, she didn't plan on ever setting foot in those hallways again.

"Oh, it's such a beautiful day outside," Ann Marie declared, throwing herself into the armchair that sat across from the couch. This version of Ann Marie was the one not drunk enough to be sad or mean, just drunk enough to fail a sobriety test if pulled over, just drunk enough to smell lightly of alcohol, just drunk enough to forget that her own life was inarguably just as ruined as Magpie's was.

No—as Magpie's *used* to be.

That all ended today. It ended with the party tonight.

"Where were you?" Magpie asked, if only because it was her turn to speak, and Ann Marie was staring at her, waiting, her grin lessening ever so slightly with every second that passed.

"I was at work," Ann Marie replied, and the lie was so big that Magpie had to force herself not to laugh, had to shove the empty spoon into her mouth and bite down on it for something to do with her tongue.

Ann Marie frowned, as if trying to decide whether Magpie was being rude or not.

Magpie withdrew the spoon and stood up.

"Are you still hungry?" Ann Marie asked. "There's Chinese. From the other night. It should still be good."

"I'm fine," Magpie said, because the thought of eating her mother's leftovers turned her stomach in an unpleasant way.

She went into the kitchen.

The mouse's shadow that was Hither sat on the faucet of the kitchen sink looking at her.

"What do you want?" she whispered.

"What, sweetheart?" Ann Marie called from the living room.

"Nothing!" Magpie shouted. Then, lowering her voice again, she asked, "Are you just going to stare at me for the rest of the night, or are you going to make yourself useful?"

How would you propose I make myself useful? I only want to make sure I do exactly as you wish, otherwise you might feed me to an impossible thing, too.

Magpie narrowed her eyebrows. "If it was an impossible thing, I wouldn't have been able to feed him to it."

"Magpie?" Ann Marie said, her voice closer now.

Magpie whirled around to find Ann Marie standing in the doorway of the kitchen, swaying a bit, holding on to the doorjamb for balance.

"What, Mom?" Magpie snapped. "What could you possibly want?"

Ann Marie looked stricken. She raised her hand to her chest and started to open her mouth but couldn't seem to think of anything to say.

"Go to sleep," Magpie continued. "Take a drink with you. Do whatever you want. Just leave me alone."

"Were you talking to someone?" Ann Marie asked hesitantly, peering behind Magpie into the kitchen as if she might find something hiding there.

"I was talking to myself, okay? Maybe if you had been here at any point in the past six months, I could have talked to you and I wouldn't have had to invent a fucking imaginary friend!"

The word *fucking*, when spoken in front of one's mother, has a curious way of inflating. Each letter acts like a balloon, and together the seven of them floated up to the ceiling, expanding and thriving and sucking all the air out of the room.

Ann Marie, for her part, looked less stricken this time and more like she was dipping into the territory of dangerous. A quick glance at the sink told Magpie that Hither was gone, and she was on her own.

Fine. She was used to being on her own.

She went to push past Ann Marie, but her mother moved as quickly as a whip to block Magpie's path.

"Get out of my way," Magpie said.

"Don't you *ever*—"

"GET OUT OF MY FUCKING WAY!"

And there was a movement of a hand so quick it was only a flesh-colored blur.

And Ann Marie slapped Magpie across the face.

Hard.

Magpie took a staggered step backward and raised her hand to her cheek. The pain took a few heartbeats to settle in, and then there was a rush of warmth to her face, a burning sting that brought tears to her eyes more out of surprise than anything else.

Ann Marie began again: "Don't you *ever* talk to me that way again, do you understand me? I don't give a *shit* what you think you've been through or what you think you're entitled to; you are still my daughter, and I am still your mother, and you will show me the respect I deserve. Do you understand?"

Magpie blinked slowly—and while her eyes were closed, she saw her Near-sister's jaw unhinging. She saw the look on Mr. James's face in the exact moment he realized what was about to happen. She saw the way the sun glinted off the spit that had collected on her sister's enormous teeth.

She could make that happen again.

She could lead this version of her mother into the garden shed.

She could call Eryn up the hill, and she could feed her mother to one of her own daughters.

Wouldn't that be something?

But she took a deep breath instead, and she let it out slowly, and she said, "I need to go. Excuse me."

But Ann Marie didn't move from the doorway. "Did you hear what I just said?"

"I need to go," Magpie repeated.

"You are not leaving this house until you acknowledge me, young lady," Ann Marie said.

Magpie took a moment to look at her mother.

Ann Marie's face was as red as Magpie imagined her own cheek was. Her eyes were wide and wild, some combination of empowered and frightened. She looked as if she might hit

Magpie again—or as if she might turn and run away. She looked as if she was deciding between the two.

"Do you realize that if I told Dad you hit me, he would be here in ten minutes to pick me up? What makes you think I'll stay with you forever? You'd be all alone."

"I hardly hit you," Ann Marie said, but her voice tipped a note or two away from where it had been a minute ago, and now she sounded just a little bit scared.

"Please get out of my way," Magpie said. "I have somewhere to be."

This time Ann Marie took a step to the side, and Magpie pushed past her so violently that her mother was thrown back. Her shoulder collided with the doorjamb, and Magpie wondered idly whether she'd even felt it. Vodka had a tendency to do that to a person; it made the pain go away. Sometimes it made the hard things easier, the necessary things doable.

But Magpie didn't need any help.

Any hesitancy she had felt when she'd led Mr. James into Near was gone.

She had decided what she would do, and she would do it.

She didn't need vodka. She didn't need anything.

Just a little silver pen.

———————————

Magpie took the long way on an already long walk to Clare's, arriving at the house nearly an hour after leaving her own.

Her stomach was growling painfully at that point, and she was happy to reach Clare's driveway just as the pizza delivery guy was pulling out of it. Clare hadn't even shut the front door yet; she saw Magpie and squealed and hopped up and down, almost dropping the four boxes she held in her arms. Lucky for Clare, Jeremy appeared behind her and, laughing, relieved her of her pizza burden.

Hither, who until that moment had been no larger than a fly buzzing annoyingly against Magpie's ear, was suddenly as big as a lion and blocking her way into the house.

"Move," Magpie hissed.

Just what do you have planned? And why can't I hear you anymore?

It seemed worried.

Good.

Let it be worried.

Let the whole town be worried.

If they knew what was good for them, they *would* be.

"Move," Magpie repeated, and something in her voice this time turned Hither from a lion into the tiniest little cat, no bigger than a football all curled up on the grass.

Magpie resisted the urge to kick it.

"Mags, *hellooo*, do you need a written invitation?" Clare called from the front door.

Magpie did *not* kick the imaginary cat.

She plastered a smile on her face and skipped up to Clare,

letting herself be hugged and even, although it went against everything in her current nature, hugging in return.

"I was worried you weren't going to show," Clare said, pulling away. "You still aren't answering your texts and…" Clare glanced nervously back into the house, where Jeremy had disappeared with the pizzas. She reached back and pulled the door shut so they were alone on the front stoop. "I'm so sorry. About what I said yesterday. I was a complete shithead."

It took Magpie a moment to remember.

A lot had happened since then.

But then it came floating back to her, what Clare had said.

We're not all required to suck the dick of Brandon Phipp.

It had stung in the moment, how easily Clare had made the joke. How she hadn't realized what she'd said, what it meant. It had stung, but now…

"Oh, that," Magpie said. "Honestly, I hadn't even thought about it."

"I know it was insensitive and rude and…The way you just got up and left, then you didn't answer any of my texts…"

"It's been a weird week. I've just been a little all over the place."

"I wish I hadn't said it. I'm so sorry."

"It's fine," Magpie said. She tried to sound reassuring, and she thought she mostly succeeded. Clare visibly relaxed, took a deep breath, smiled.

"Okay. So we're okay?"

"We're okay. I mean, aside from you insisting I go to this party," Magpie joked.

"It will be fun!"

"I'll believe it when I see it. Let's go inside—I'm starving."

Magpie found a full house crammed into Clare's living room: Luke and Brianna were already digging into the pizza, Jeremy and Ben were arguing over the stereo, and Teddy was putting on a finger-puppet show for a couch full of stuffed animals. Magpie waved a general hello to everyone and made herself a paper plate with two slices of mushroom pizza. She started eating it at the counter.

"Damn, girl. I've never seen you eat this much in my life," Brianna said appreciatively.

"She knows that's the best pregame strategy," Luke chimed in. "The more you eat now, the more you can *driiiiiink*."

"Guys, ixnay on the drinking stuff," Clare said, materializing next to them. "My mom's upstairs. And speaking of upstairs—Teddy, scram, will you?"

"I thought your name was Ringo," Brianna said.

Teddy shrugged, managed to load up an impressive amount of finger puppets and stuffed animals in his arms, and disappeared in the direction of the stairway.

"Mags," Ben said, brushing her arm lightly as he moved to stand next to her. "Hey. I didn't know if you were going to come."

Magpie, her mouth full of pizza, shrugged her answer, then gestured around the room as if to say, *Well, here I am!*

226

Ben laughed softly. "I'm glad you're here. Do you still want to leave early and see a movie?"

Magpie swallowed. "I think that sounds great. I won't need much time at the party."

"You won't need much time?"

"To get the gist of how boring it is," Magpie added, winking.

The wink meant that this wasn't what she'd meant at all.

Box by box, the pizza vanished until only a solitary slice of cheese was left. Magpie had eaten four pieces herself—although *inhaled* might be a more accurate word for it. There was now a plastic water bottle being passed around the living room, the contents of which was, of course, not water at all but a vodka so cheap that Magpie's eyes watered just smelling it. She declined and passed it on to Ben, who also declined and passed it on to Jeremy.

"I'll stay sober," Ben said. "I borrowed my mom's car so I can drive to the movies."

"I don't feel like drinking anyway," Magpie replied. "So if you end up wanting to, that's fine. I can drive."

You don't have your license.

Hither had appeared as a tiny bee perched on the top of Ben's hair. Magpie resisted the urge to swat it away or reply out loud. Instead, she thought, very purposefully and carefully, *I made you up and I can* un*make you, too.*

And Hither was quiet after that.

"Thanks," Ben said. "Maybe I'll take you up on that."

Magpie grabbed the last slice of pizza and put it into her mouth so she wouldn't have to think of anything else to say.

———————

The group walked to Brandon Phipp's house at ten o'clock.

The darkness of the night reminded Magpie of ink, and ink reminded her of her Near-pen, and she patted her pocket to make sure it was safe, and just feeling it made her swell with a sense of security she had never quite felt before.

Was this what it was like to be in control of one's own destiny? To be so meticulously sure of every step that needed to be followed, of every box that needed to be checked?

Magpie liked it.

She felt the night hanging around her like something she had to slice through, and she pictured the shining door that would lead her to Near wherever and whenever she wanted to go, and she saw this night lit up with it, with a door that was her own private portal to her one true home.

"You're being quiet," Ben said. He walked behind her as the rest of the group danced around in the empty streets, tripping over themselves and laughing and skipping and holding hands. In the end, Ben had taken a few swigs from the water bottle full of vodka, but unlike everyone else's, his tipsiness seemed to present itself quietly, steadying his hands, mellowing his already pretty mellow demeanor. Magpie looked over at him and smiled.

"Just thinking," she replied.

"Thinking about what?"

"This party. A couple months ago—even *one* month ago—I never would have gone."

"Because of..."

He didn't finish his sentence, but he didn't have to. There were a million possible endings and each one was right.

Because of what happened that night?

Because of Allison Lefferts?

Because of the way Brandon Phipp's dick smelled, like something salty and unwashed?

Because of the way Allison had burst into the room laughing?

Because of the way her laughter had died on the tip of her tongue, only the echo of it surviving as Brandon pulled away so violently that Magpie fell sideways onto the floor, choking on her own spit and something that did not belong to her?

And there it was. The moment Magpie had spent six months trying her hardest not to think about.

The moment her best friend had walked in on Magpie sucking the dick of Brandon Phipp—as Clare had so succinctly put it.

And Magpie had tried to explain, of course.

But Allison wouldn't listen to any of it. Allison wanted nothing to do with it at all.

Now, in this inky-black darkness, beside Ben, who swayed only slightly but did not otherwise give any indication that he was under the influence, it seemed to Magpie that she could see that night more clearly that she had ever been able to see it. She saw it more clearly now, so many months removed, than in the days or weeks after it happened. She saw it so clearly now that it was almost as if she were reliving it over and over. And although she had almost believed Allison's version of the story, there had always been a little kernel of the truth inside her. There had always been the knowledge, somewhere deep down, that what Allison said happened did not happen at all. Did not even touch upon what had happened. Did not even resemble it.

She was ready, finally, to put the blame where the blame belonged.

Ben was still waiting for her to respond, so she smiled, and said, "I have something now that I didn't have before."

She would let him try to figure out what that meant. It could be any number of things.

Friends.

Confidence.

A magical pen.

A magical world.

They walked a moment in silence, then Ben cleared his throat, and said, "I know this is a weird time to bring it up, but I just wanted to let you know that I finished the history assignment."

"You did?"

"I just figured...you've been under a lot of stress. You

haven't really answered my texts. Which I totally under-stand, I just—I didn't want to put it off until the last minute. I thought I might as well just get it out of the way."

"It's fine, I understand, I'll tell Ms. Peel that I didn't have anything to do with it."

"No, no, I mean—I finished it for both of us." Magpie turned and studied his face. His cheeks were a little pink, but she couldn't tell whether that was from the vodka or some-thing else. "I put your name on it. I already handed it in, actually. I hope that's okay with you, I just... I know you've been having... Well, I know you've been having a really shitty year, okay? It doesn't have to be a big deal."

Something cracked against Magpie's heart—or maybe it was her heart itself that was cracking, one long dark line from the left atrioventricular valve right down to the right ventri-cle. For just one second she saw Mr. James's face again at the moment he realized what was about to happen. The crack felt like a heavy, solid thing within her chest.

"I'm sorry," she said. "I kept meaning to do it. I really did. I just—"

"It's honestly fine. I knew I didn't *have* to do it. I knew you'd do it eventually. I just... I wanted to do it. For you."

When all of this was over, Magpie could bring Ben into Near. She could give him whatever he wanted—literally any-thing. But tonight, in this moment, she couldn't give him much at all. So she gave him one small thing: her hand.

And when she felt his fingers close around hers, she thought, *In another lifetime, in another version of me, this would have been all I ever wanted.*

But in this lifetime, in this version, she felt his fingers, the warmth of his hand, the way he stood a little taller when she touched him, and she felt only a void. The absence of a feeling—something that should have been there but wasn't. As if something that had once been inside her had been scooped clean out, leaving nothing but space in its wake.

Did you not listen to me? When I told you these things were made from you? Of you? And you are so very far from limitless, little Magpie. So very, very far.

Magpie turned her head to catch a glimpse of Hither.

But if it was there, it was too small now to be seen.

And in that moment, even with Ben's hand in hers, even with these people she could comfortably call *friends* dancing drunkenly around her, even in that inky night that seemed to her more comforting than this world had been in such a very long time, Magpie knew.

She was completely alone.

Not even an imaginary friend to keep her company.

But that wouldn't matter for much longer.

Pretty soon she would have an entire world full of people at her side.

Ready to do anything she asked.

Anything.

Starting tonight.

TEN FOR A BIRD

Brandon Phipp lived in a ridiculously large house in the middle of several ridiculously large fields that was surrounded by a number of ridiculously enormous barns where his parents kept the many prize-winning horses they raised for the racing circuits. These were not the dull brick-red barns that stored drying lines of tobacco, nor were they the long rectangular barns where the various livestock of Farther spent their nights; these barns were octagonal and ostentatious, and each one looked more like an interestingly shaped house than anything you might think of when you heard the word *barn*.

One of the Phipps' racing horses sold for four hundred thousand dollars. And one of their biggest winners—of the ones they hadn't sold—had, at last count, won them more than three million. And at current count, they were raising thirty-seven horses.

So no matter how you sliced it, the Phipp family was loaded.

The small group came to a stop near the end of the driveway where the fences that circled the entire hundred-plus-acre property came to meet at an overlarge iron gate that looked more than a little out of place in the middle of farm country. The gate was so big, in fact, that there was another regular-size door set into it, and this door had a little call box next to it, and after she regained her nerve, Clare marched deliberately up to it, punched in some numbers, and was met with a satisfying buzz as the door unlocked.

"You know the code?" Luke asked.

"Brandon put it on a private Facebook page for the party," Clare responded.

"Of course Brandon made a private page for his party," Brianna grumbled.

"How else would he let people know how to make it through his totally inconspicuous private gate?" Jeremy replied, laughing. He took Clare's hand, and they walked through the door. Brianna and Luke followed them, with Magpie and Ben bringing up the rear. Magpie let the door close behind her, shutting the group inside the Phipp property.

The main house sat a good half a mile down the driveway, and as they got closer and closer, Magpie's memory of that night six months ago—well, almost seven now, wasn't it?—grew sharper and sharper until it was so clear in her mind that it might as well have happened yesterday.

Magpie had been so drunk that the walk from the front

gate to the house had felt like an eternity, every step her own personal punishment for ever daring to have been born. The memory of her father's and her aunt's naked bodies had been so fresh in her mind that it was as if she were still seeing the burn of them, like when you look at something too bright and its shadow crowds your vision for minutes afterward. No matter where she looked, there they were: her father, naked and paralyzed with shame, her aunt covering herself with her arms.

Magpie had wanted to say, *Don't bother. There is nothing either of you can do to erase what I have seen.* But she couldn't say anything. She couldn't back out of the room. She couldn't look away. She couldn't even blink.

The moment had lasted forever. The moment was consuming her even now, a black hole that was sucking everything backward, gobbling up her entire universe, changing the landscape of her brain.

"Having second thoughts?" Ben asked her.

She realized she had stopped walking. Ben had paused a few steps in front of her. At some point they had let go of each other's hands. The rest of the group was forty, fifty feet in front of them. They'd have to jog to catch up.

Magpie blinked until the past had faded enough that she could finally see Ben clearly. She tried to smile, and when that didn't work, she tried to at least not grimace. And when that didn't work either, she nodded.

"There are a few people at this party who aren't going to be very happy to see me," she said.

"Who—Brandon? Allison? They can fuck off."

"This is their territory, though. I'm the intruder here."

"It's a party. That Facebook page Clare mentioned—it said, *All are welcome*. We fall under the umbrella of *all*, don't we? Plus, have you seen the size of this house? Chances are you won't even run into them."

Yes, Magpie had seen the size of this house. Magpie had been *in* this house. She had seen parts of this house she wasn't supposed to see, all the shadowy dark bits that were off-limits on nights like this.

Like Brandon Phipp's bedroom.

Like the quiet hallways that had led them there.

What had he said?

I just want to talk.

That was it. He had just wanted to talk.

Where's Allison? Magpie had asked.

She had needed to find Allison.

She was very, very drunk, and the house wouldn't stop spinning, and the hallway wouldn't stop spinning, and Brandon Phipp's bedroom wouldn't stop spinning.

Allison would be able to fix things; Allison would know what to do.

Allison always knew what to do.

Except tonight.

Tonight Magpie was the one who knew what to do, and Allison would be the one with the rug swept out from underneath her.

Two times on the walk from the front gate to the front door Ben had asked Magpie if she wanted to turn around and ditch, go to the movies, go *wherever*, do whatever in the world she wanted besides attend this party.

"Really," he said the second time, when the door was so close to them that even now Clare was reaching her hand out to open it. "We can do whatever you want. I don't mind. I don't even like parties."

"We're here," Magpie said flatly. "And I have to pee."

"You can pee in the bushes. I'll block you."

The offer was kind of charming, but Magpie shook her head, and in one decisive movement that occurred with so much forward momentum that she couldn't possibly change her mind, she let herself be consumed by Brandon Phipp's front door, and she was deposited, quite suddenly, in his enormous foyer.

The house felt alive.

It had a pulse and heartbeat in the form of loud music thumping relentlessly from somewhere farther in. The foyer was relatively empty, but through an archway to their left, Magpie could see what could only accurately be described as a swarm of bodies. She picked out some people she knew, but there were far more people she had never seen before.

"I know that kid," Jeremy said, pointing. "He's from Edgewood."

"Brandon knows a lot of people," Clare said, nodding knowingly. Like she and Brandon had ever once had a conversation, least of all one about the people he knew.

"Is the music going to be this loud the *whole* time?" Brianna complained.

"I'm hungry again. Is there food?" Luke added.

Magpie took a step toward the living room (or rather she took a step toward *this* living room, for Brandon Phipp's house was the kind that had multiples of everything).

"Where do we get drinks?" Jeremy asked.

And Magpie took another step toward the living room.

"Is it hot in here?" Clare asked, and sniffed her armpit.

"I *love* this song!" Luke squealed.

And Magpie took another step toward the living room.

And then, without anyone seeing, she pressed herself against a wall of bodies.

And let herself be sucked inside.

Magpie felt relief as soon as she was out of sight from Ben and Clare and the others because she had to do this part herself, and every moment spent with them was a wasted one. She couldn't have anyone watching her. She had only herself to rely on, and it was time to accept that and get on with it.

So she got on with it.

There were strobe lights set up in the Phipp household

that flashed in time to the music. Brandon's parents traveled out of town often, and he and his older brother took advantage of that to throw these ridiculous parties. When it was over, they would pay people to clean up everything and fix everything that had been broken and fish all the empty beer cans out of the pool and that would be the end of that— until the next time Mr. and Mrs. Phipp went to the south of France or wherever very rich people went on vacation.

The bodies around Magpie stank of cheap alcohol and beer as she diligently made her way through them, searching each of their faces for the face she most wanted to see. Which felt a little funny, because for the past six months she'd been trying her best *not* to see it.

But the situation was different now, and here she was, and she searched and searched and searched.

The party and the house were endless.

Room after room was filled with sweaty people dancing and drinking and making out on couches or standing in the corner trying to work up the nerve to do any of the above.

Hither stayed as small as a flea, nestled somewhere in her hair. She couldn't see it, but she felt it, and it made her feel as if she wasn't alone.

She made her way to the kitchen and slipped out though a pair of French doors to the backyard patio. She was surprised no one had jumped fully clothed into the pool yet, but if history was any indication, it was only a matter of time.

The music was just as loud out here, pumping over the

outdoor speakers and amplified by the surface of the still water.

And it was there, by the line of kegs, bent over the spigot of one trying to see why it wasn't working, that Magpie saw the person she'd been searching for.

Brandon Phipp.

And even better, Allison wasn't with him.

Magpie found the shadows in the backyard, and she stayed in them, getting closer and closer to the kegs while remaining invisible to anyone who might glance her way.

Brandon was arguing with someone. Magpie recognized the kid but couldn't quite recall his name.

"Jesus, I said *hold* it, asshole," Brandon said, and shoved his friend roughly.

Magpie would never understand these machismo male friendships, the kind where physical abuse and name-calling were exchanged in a violent attempt to prove you were not gay. The harder you hit, the straighter you were. And Brandon hit hard. The kid grabbed his shoulder and rubbed, then held up his middle finger. "Fuck off, shithead, this thing is heavy."

"You're a pussy," Brandon retorted.

"Not one, but I've seen your mom's."

And then they both laughed, two loud, heavy laughs that set Magpie on edge.

"This isn't gonna work. Somebody jammed this shit. What asshole put this together? Go inside and look under the kitchen sink; I need a hammer, something to get it moving."

The kid with the name Magpie couldn't remember got to his feet obediently and passed within two feet of her on his way to fulfill Brandon's orders.

Magpie stepped out of the shadows, and for a moment, she was still invisible. It was just she and Brandon; Hither, who was as small as a bug; this night; and this music, and then—

He turned around.

"Jesus Christ! You fucking scared me. What the fuck are you doing here?" he asked, actually jumping.

Magpie liked that. She wanted to see him jump again.

"Your Facebook post said all are welcome," Magpie said, and she smiled.

"Yeah, well, you're lucky Allison isn't here yet. But she's on her way, so I'd run back home if I were you."

"I'm not worried about Allison," Magpie said. "Are you going to offer me something to drink?"

Brandon smirked. "I can't believe you had the balls to show up here, Mags. Or wait—what did Allison call you? Magpie? Yeah, I have to give you credit for that." He looked her up and down. Not in a nice way. "So why are you *really* here?"

"I have something fun I want to show you."

"Something you want to show me?"

Magpie reached up to her shirt. She'd worn a button-up shirt knotted at the waist for just this purpose. She had given this moment a lot of thought, and everything was working out exactly the way she'd imagined it would.

She undid the top button.

"Something *really* fun," she said.

Brandon looked behind her. "Are you serious?" he asked. "I just said that Allison is on her way."

"So she's not here yet, right?"

There was a long moment.

A long moment in which Magpie wondered idly whether Brandon Phipp had grown into the sort of boy who would not take advantage of any warm body he could get alone. She supposed it was possible, insomuch as everything is possible. It was also possible that he would sprout wings and begin to fly.

But was it likely?

"Come this way," he said, and gestured to her. When she got close enough, he grabbed her arm, not gently, and led her around the back of the house away from the kitchen, away from the party noises, to another set of French doors that were shut and locked. He removed a key from his pocket and opened them, and they slipped inside.

A long hallway. A staircase.

A staircase that Magpie had been led up once before.

She let herself be led again.

But she wasn't like the girl in the story. She just had to pretend for a little while longer.

And it was so deliriously satisfying to let someone think they were in control when in reality they were so very much anything but.

A door at the end of the hallway was closed, and Brandon

opened it and pushed Magpie inside and then slipped in after her. He glanced down the hallway to make sure they hadn't been followed, then quickly shut the door.

The closet light was on, enough light to bathe Brandon Phipp's bedroom in a pale-yellow glow.

Before she could stop him, he pushed her against the wall.

And in the next moment he leaned in to kiss her.

And in the next, she pushed him back, hard, and said, "I told you I had something to show you."

"I am not interested in having a fucking conversation with you," Brandon replied. His voice had gone all husky and breathless, and Magpie rolled her eyes.

"Trust me, you're going to want to see this," she said, and before he could respond again, she had slid the pen out of her pocket and uncapped it in one single second, and in the next second, she had swiped through the air three times and made a perfect, glowing door.

"What the fuck?" Brandon said. He pushed Magpie away even though she was up against the wall and couldn't actually go anywhere. "What the fuck is this?"

A flick of her wrist and there was a doorknob.

Another flick and the door was open.

And one enormous shove and Brandon Phipp had fallen into Near.

And Magpie stepped daintily in after him and shut the door behind her.

Brandon Phipp—to Magpie's exceptional delight—puked. Long and hard and loud, gasping on his hands and knees as he choked and vomited into the grass.

"Not such a tough guy now, are you, Brandy?" Magpie teased, kicking him with her shoe, then kicking him even harder because she liked how it felt.

"What did you fucking give me? What happened?"

"You think I drugged you? Damn. I *should* have drugged you. That would have been some grade-A karma, right? I mean, I know you didn't have to drug *me*, but I also know you're not shy when it comes to the shit you put into girls' drinks. Right, Brandy?"

"Stop calling me that."

"Get off the grass. You look pathetic."

And maybe Brandon Phipp had lived his entire sheltered life without once being called pathetic, but that word seemed to spark a small recovery in him, and he got to his feet slowly and wiped chunks of sick off his chin.

"Where are we?" he asked. His voice had gotten smaller. *He* had gotten smaller. It was either Magpie's imagination or Near had made Brandon Phipp shrink two full inches.

"Welcome to Near. Pretty cool, huh?"

"We were...in my bedroom..."

"And now we're here, yup; speed up the adjustment period if you can—it gets a little repetitive."

"You're fucking with me," Brandon said. He put one hand on the back of his neck and rubbed it.

"Not any more than *you* fucked with *me*," Magpie said.

And Brandon's eyes grew wide, and Magpie knew he was remembering the same night she was remembering, the same night she had remembered—both *tried* and *tried not* to remember—every single night since it had happened.

The same night that changed and slithered in her memory, that warped and mutated and was sometimes clear and sometimes not clear.

But not anymore.

Now she finally knew.

Or—she finally *let* herself know.

She finally let herself remember what had happened the night Brandon Phipp led her to his bedroom and wouldn't let her leave.

"You know what I've thought an awful lot about, Brandon?" Magpie asked. She looked down to Near, to where a far-off figure was just stepping through the little white gate that kept the town safe and sound. "I've thought an awful lot about how many times a girl has to say no before a guy really believes her. You ask a girl to suck your dick, and she says yes, well—great, right? But she says *no*? Suddenly she needs convincing."

"You didn't do anything you didn't want to do."

"What I *wanted* was to find my best friend. And you told me you'd help me, remember? You told me you knew where she was."

"Look—*you* started kissing me," Brandon said. "No amount of psycho-girl logic is going to change that."

"Yeah," Magpie said, nodding. "I did. I kissed you, Brandon. It was the worst night of my life, and I thought I could change that by kissing you. But I remember now. I remember that I pulled away. And I said I was sorry. And I tried to leave to find Allison."

"I don't have to listen to this shit," Brandon said, but he didn't move. Maybe he *couldn't* move. He seemed rooted to the spot, swaying lightly in some imagined breeze.

"And you grabbed my arm and…I don't know why I'm telling you all this. You already know."

He had grabbed her arm. So hard she woke up the next day with bruises.

And he'd pushed her to her knees. So hard she woke up the next day with bruises.

And he gripped her by the hair.

So she couldn't turn her head from side to side.

And he'd said:

Open up, or I'll put it somewhere else.

Magpie squeezed her eyes shut, so the bright day of Near became a red glow filtered through the skin of her eyelids.

How many times had she said no?

Before she'd finally done it.

"Do you know what else I've thought a lot about?" she asked, opening her eyes again. Brandon was still stuck in the same spot. The figure walking up the hill was making impressive time.

"What?" he asked.

"Why a girl would believe her boyfriend over her best friend." Magpie paused. Her heart, when she thought of Allison, felt squeezed two sizes too small. Stuck into a space it wouldn't fit. "I guess that means she probably wasn't my best friend anymore. I thought it happened after that, but it must have been before, right? Otherwise...why wouldn't she believe me when I told her you made me?"

"I didn't MAKE you do ANYTHING!" Brandon shouted, and his voice echoed even though there wasn't anything for it to echo against. It just kept repeating and repeating until it got too far away for them to hear.

"That's what I used to tell myself," Magpie admitted. "It was easier to get to sleep at night if I believed it. But now it's easier if I just tell the truth and we all get on with our lives. Isn't that right, Ally?"

Brandon's eyes grew wide. He turned around so quickly that he almost fell over, and there was Allison right behind him, just as pretty and mean and hard as Magpie remembered her.

"This is kinda sick," the Near-Allison said.

"Babe? Babe, where are we?" Brandon asked, and he lunged for Allison, but she deftly avoided him, stepping to the side so he missed her and fell to his knees.

"I mean, you could have conjured up anyone," Allison continued. "But me? That's totally sick, Magpie. I like it."

"I thought you would," Magpie said.

Allison turned back to Brandon, who had scrambled to

his feet again and was looking back and forth between the girls, worry spreading over his face as he realized something wasn't right. "Well, let's get this over with, shall we? You're lucky I didn't eat a big lunch."

And the growing.

And the unhinging.

And the screaming.

And the blood.

Magpie took a seat on the grass, stretching her legs out in front of her and crossing them at the ankles, leaning back on her arms, feeling the warmth of the Near-sun on her face. She couldn't have written it more perfectly. While Mr. James had slid neatly down his monster's throat, Brandon struggled and flailed. It was almost as if Allison was playing with him, crunching down on the bones of his legs and then letting him almost get away, crawling across the grass on his arms, pulling himself forward before she knelt down and scooped him up again.

A neat spray of blood shot across Magpie's tennis sneakers.

There was considerably more blood this time.

Magpie found that she preferred that.

When it was over, and Near-Allison had retreated down the hill, dabbing at a spot of red at the corner of her mouth, Magpie turned around to take the doorway back to her own backyard—oh, how soon it was until she would never have to take that doorway again!—and found Hither, almost a human now, blocking her way.

Have you noticed the water?

Magpie hadn't, but she looked around her now and saw that the water—the vast dark ocean of Near—was closer now than it had ever been. If it got much closer, it would reach the town.

Magpie frowned. "Why is it doing that? I didn't tell it to do that."

Are you under the impression that you can tell your subconscious what to do and it will always listen?

"Jesus, are you just around to spout cryptic nonsense while I try to get actual, useful things accomplished?"

Hither considered.

Are you suggesting it was useful *for you to swallow up your English teacher and a boy who once shoved his penis down your throat?*

"Maybe *useful* isn't the right word. But it sure feels appropriate."

Are you finished now?

"Finished with what?"

Exacting this revenge.

"You make it sound so serious."

You make it sound so negligible.

"Well, the answer is no. I have a few more people in mind."

And you aren't worried about the consequences?

"What consequences?"

How is your head, Magpie?

Magpie touched the back of her neck, only now noticing the dull throb that had returned to it in the moments following Brandon Phipp's final exit.

"It's fine. I'm getting stronger."

You're getting weaker. You can't keep this up.

"Watch me."

She tried to step around Hither to reach the garden shed, but the creature grew in size to that of an elephant, complete with several sets of enormous ivory tusks.

I have substance here, Magpie. I have solidity. I wouldn't try your luck.

"I don't need luck," Magpie retorted. "Not when I have so much more."

And in a motion she was beginning to get pretty good at, she uncapped the pen and drew a doorway.

She hadn't tried it before, drawing a doorway in Near.

She had always used the shed to get back to Farther.

But everything was going so well.

And everything she wanted to happen was happening.

So she thought she would try.

And, sure enough, she did it.

The doorway led her right back to Brandon's bedroom. Right back to the party. Right back to—

Allison.

Magpie had no sooner stepped through the doorway and left Near behind her than the door to Brandon's own bedroom burst open, and there she was, the real Allison, all silky blond hair and flawless skin and cheekbones and arms and legs and mouth set in an angry little line Magpie had once been so familiar with that, against all odds, it felt a little like coming home.

"Ally," Magpie said.

"What the *fuck* are you doing here, Magpie?" Allison said. Her voice was just like Magpie had remembered: an angry, sharp thing that could twist in an instant to something sweet and sugary. Magpie had never met anyone more in control of their voice than Allison. It could be a thousand different things. A close friend or a dreaded enemy. A whispered tickle or a shout to rival storms. Something like a butterfly or something like a dragon.

When Magpie didn't answer right away, Allison moved like a force into the room, crossing to Brandon's closet, the light still on within, and violently wrenched open the door. "Where is he?"

Magpie had to catch a laugh, ball it up, and toss it away. "You think Brandon's hiding in the closet?"

Allison didn't answer, but she dropped to her hands and knees and looked under the bed.

This time Magpie couldn't help it; she burst into laughter so loud that it cut the room in two. "You think Brandon's under the *bed*? C'mon, Ally, this isn't a Lifetime movie."

"Elisabeth and Brittany saw you walking around the back of the house together. I *know* he's here somewhere."

"Behind the curtains, maybe? You could turn on the light; that might make things a bit easier."

Allison did turn on the light, and she did look behind the curtains, and then she hesitated, because although Brandon's room was bigger than your average high schooler's, there weren't that many more places where he could be hiding. Still standing next to one of the windows, she cupped her hands to the glass and peeked out into the night.

"You think Brandon jumped out of a second-story window? Jesus, Allison, if he didn't care that much to avoid being caught the first time, why do you think this time would be any different?"

"*This* time? So you admit that he was here?" Allison said, twirling around so fast that her hair flew out around her head like a fan.

"He *was* here. He had to go. He sends his regards."

"What are you talking about? Why are you even here?"

"Here like Brandon's bedroom? Or here like this party?"

"Both."

"Well. It's a party. You know how much I love parties."

"I swear to God, Magpie..." Allison had begun to pace

small circles in Brandon's carpet. "Will you just tell me where he is?"

"It would be hard for me to explain. But I can show you."

"Show me? Is this some kind of fucking game to you? I ruined your life once before, Magpie, and I barely even had to *try*. Imagine what I could do if I really put my mind to it."

"I'm shaking in my boots—really," Magpie said dryly. "Do you want me to take you to him or not?"

"Yes. I want to see Brandon."

"All right, then. Follow me."

YOU MUST NOT MISS

Allison did not fall to her knees when she stepped through the doorway into the bright day of Near because Allison did not let herself show weakness. She did not vomit or hold her stomach or do much more than clasp her hands together in front of her belly button. Magpie detected a slight increase in her breathing, but other than that, her ex–best friend acted as if it were a perfectly normal thing to walk through a doorway in a bedroom and end up in an entirely new world.

"What is this place?" Allison asked.

"Do you like it? I made it myself. It's called Near."

Magpie watched as Allison took it all in. Her eyes swept over the tiny town at the bottom of the hill and the waters that had grown even closer in such a short time, that were even now lapping at the base of the white picket fence that surrounded the picture-perfect copy of Farther.

Allison's eyes landed, finally, at a little patch of grass not five or six feet in front of them.

A little patch of grass that was covered in something that looked a lot like—

"Is that..." But Allison could not complete her sentence.

In the golden sunlight of Near, the patch of Brandon Phipp's blood shone like something made of a thousand little lights. It was so bright that it hurt Magpie's eyes to look at it, but at the same time, she made herself do it because there was something so comforting in the physical proof that Brandon Phipp had been here, had been alive, and was now—look! blood!—undeniably dead.

"What did you do to him?" Allison asked, her voice quiet but even.

"I didn't touch him," Magpie responded, and she was delighted to find that this was actually true.

"Where are we?"

"Near. I told you that."

"There's no place called Near."

"No place *you've* ever been."

"You said you made it. What did you mean by that?"

"I meant exactly what I said. It wasn't a trick."

"You made a...town?"

"A *world*," Magpie corrected.

Allison nodded her head. "Near," she repeated, and when she said the word, she made it sound like something much more than it was. Like a curse. Like a memory. "Where is Brandon?"

"Indisposed."

"Okay, can you cut the shit, Magpie? For once in your life, can you try to be normal? Can you just answer me? I know you've hurt him or..." She wavered at that, unable to bring herself to say the other possibility, that Magpie hadn't *hurt* Brandon but *killed* him.

"Fine," Magpie said, huffing a little, irritated now that Allison was in the world Magpie had made but unmoved by it, neither reverent nor awed nor, as if it were too much to ask, *scared*. "He's dead. I killed him. Are you happy now?"

Allison didn't cry. To be honest, the expression on her face hardly changed at all. She just nodded her head, as if to symbolize that she understood, and then she didn't say anything for a long time, and with every second that passed by that she didn't speak, Magpie grew angrier and angrier.

"You don't have *anything* to say?"

"What do you want me to say, Magpie? I can't beg you to bring him back. It doesn't work like that."

"Maybe it works like that here," Magpie countered.

Allison's eyes lit up with a tiny little light—a tiny glow of hope. "Does it?" she asked.

"Nope, sorry," Magpie replied, and she savored the way Allison's shoulders fell, the way Allison moved her hands to cover her face, the way, when she pulled them away, her cheeks had gone all red and blotchy.

"I hate you," she said, and the words were a scream even though they were no louder than a whisper. "I've always hated you. From the minute I met you. You know the problem with you, Magpie? How obsessed you were with me. At first it was fun, having you as a friend—you would do basically anything I asked; it was like having my own private cheering squad. But pretty soon it just became *pathetic*."

"Are you trying to hurt my feelings?"

"If I thought you had feelings to hurt," Allison retorted.

For a minute they just looked at each other.

And then—very suddenly—Magpie realized that Allison had started to cry.

"Fuck," she said, wiping at her cheeks with shaking hands. "You *killed* him?"

"He deserved what he got," Magpie said.

"Why, because he was mine, not yours? Because I would have picked him over you a thousand times over? Because he made you suck his dick at a party once?"

Magpie bit her bottom lip so hard that white dots swam in front of her vision.

"What did you say?" she asked.

"Do you think I was *happy* my boyfriend shoved his dick in your mouth, Magpie? Obviously not. But did he really have to die because of it?"

"You said—"

"Yeah, I know what I said. I said I didn't believe you, right? I said you were a shitty friend who was trying to steal my boyfriend from me, right? Don't make me laugh, Magpie. I *wish* you were interesting enough to do something like that."

Magpie could hear the sound of the ocean in her ears, and for a minute, she thought the waters had grown so close that the waves were even now echoing through her—but no. It was the sound of her own blood, thick and hot and bubbling inside her.

"You knew he did that to me and—"

"Give me a break, Magpie. If I had a dollar for every guy who slipped his dick in my mouth without asking, I'd be fucking rich and I wouldn't have needed Brandon Phipp's horse money. So yeah. I really fucking wish you hadn't murdered my boyfriend, but it's not so much because of how much I loved him as it is because of how you've sort of butchered my entire life plan."

Allison had stopped crying, and her face wasn't as red anymore, but her hands still shook. Only now Magpie realized that they shook not with sadness but with anger—the kind that had filled Allison's body from the very moment of her conception.

Wow.

And to think Magpie had ever *liked* this girl.

This poor, mean girl in front of her, in a too-short skirt and a bra that pushed her boobs almost completely out of her shirt. This angry, lost girl who had taught Magpie how to put on lip gloss and how not to lick it off and how to put a condom on a banana and how to braid her hair and how to act as if you didn't care about anything in the world. Magpie had thought that this last part had been a trick, just another ploy for Allison Lefferts to pick up guys, but it hadn't been like that at all. Allison really *didn't* care about anything in the world.

It was kind of refreshing, finally, to know that.

Not refreshing enough to change what Magpie had to do, but still. There was something nice about the fact that Allison was going to go out exactly as she had lived: like a raging, unforgiving bitch.

Magpie watched as a faraway figure opened the gates that kept the tiny town of Near safe from the encroaching sea. It had to wade through several feet of shin-deep water before the ground started slanting upward, then it was on the hill again, trudging dutifully toward Magpie and Allison.

"If you don't mind, I'd like to go home now," Allison said. But it was more like a demand. She crossed her arms over her chest, and out of the corner of her eye, Magpie saw the figure at the bottom of the hill pause, unsure of what it was supposed to do.

"Home?" Magpie repeated. "I'm sorry to inform you that's not an option."

"Are you trying to threaten me?" Allison snorted. "That's hysterical." She looked around impatiently. "A door brought us here, so I'm assuming that same door can get us out."

"I *said* it wasn't an option."

"Seriously, Magpie, are you going to *kill* me?"

A staring contest.

Magpie blinked first.

Allison looked around again, then paused, looking past

Magpie at something. Magpie followed her gaze and saw it, too: the thin outline of the door Magpie had drawn in Brandon's bedroom. She must have forgotten to pull it closed behind her because through it, in a shimmery sort of quality, as if she were looking at something through air gone wavy with heat, Magpie could see the outline of Brandon Phipp's bedroom—his unmade bed, the clothes that lay in a heap in front of his nightstand, the bureau where somebody had framed a picture of him and Allison laughing and sharing an ice cream cone. (Had it been a gift from Allison?)

Magpie took a step in front of it, blocking Allison temporarily, but she was too far away to reach back and pull the door closed. Plus, Allison had also seen the Near-shed, and the doorway that would lead her to Magpie's own backyard. The quiet, cricket-filled night of Farther. The glow of the moon on the still waters of an aboveground pool. A swan pool float made useless now by a thousand slashes from a razor blade.

The figure at the bottom of the hill was still standing motionless, and Magpie could feel something inside her that was stuck, too, like a gear that had stopped spinning, gunked up with years of misuse, of not being properly cleaned, of macaroni and cheese dinners standing over the kitchen sink while her mother vomited in the bathroom.

"You were my best friend," Magpie whispered.

Allison rolled her eyes. "Seriously? Name three things we

have in common, Magpie. You're like a leech. Or one of those things that will follow its friends off cliffs—"

"A lemming," Magpie whispered.

"First it was Eryn—I mean, Jesus, she's six years older than you, and it's like you expected her to be your best friend and hang out with you and take you everywhere she went. And then it was me, and now it's—who? Clare Brown? Ben?" Allison rolled her eyes again, and this time she laughed for good measure. "I've seen you sitting with them during lunch. Way to downgrade, Magpie. At least now you've got a fair shot of someone actually liking you back. Too bad they're losers."

"I don't believe you," Magpie said. "I don't believe you— we were friends for *years*, Allison, and you're saying—"

"I'm saying that you were annoying from the very beginning, that's exactly what I'm saying. But you were useful, too. You were always there whenever I was bored, whenever I wanted to do something. But then you got *un*useful really quickly, Magpie. Then you went and sucked my boyfriend's dick. See how that works out?"

"But I didn't—"

"Don't get blackout drunk and let a boy lead you into his bedroom. It's fucking obvious," Allison said.

"That's not how it works," Magpie said, and her voice was a little louder now, and the figure at the bottom of the hill took another shaky step upward. "It wasn't my fault."

"Whatever. Get on your little anti-slut-shaming soapbox. I'm not interested. And I'm going home."

Allison moved so quickly that Magpie was taken off guard, and before she really knew what was happening, Allison had pushed her hard, and Magpie went to her knees on the top of the hill in Near, the glaring sun beating down on her as she watched Allison march decisively into Brandon's nighttime bedroom, not looking back once as she slammed the door closed behind her, shutting out the hillside, shutting out the sunlight, shutting out Magpie, as she had done almost seven months ago when she'd taken Brandon Phipp's side and never spoken another word to Magpie again.

Magpie stayed on her knees. She let herself sink back onto her shins. She let the sun warm her face; she let the sound of the ocean drown out every other noise.

And then she took a deep breath, and she pulled herself to her feet.

What are you doing? I thought this was supposed to be the end of it.

But Magpie couldn't concentrate. She still heard her blood rushing around in her ears; her skin felt hot and sticky; she was filled with an anger that thrummed and pulsed through her, that showed no signs of slowing down, that needed to be let *out*.

And so she let it run free.

She let her anger take control.

And she took out her pen.

And she drew another door.

Magpie hadn't been sure that this would work because she had never actually been in this room before, but she knew as soon as she stepped through the door that she had succeeded. Here was the little minifridge in the corner. Here was the skinny twin bed. Here was the desk; here was the bureau. Everything generic and identical in its simplicity.

The yoga mat rolled up neatly in one corner.

A folded pair of exercise pants on the bed.

A poster on the wall showing a woman standing ankle-deep in the ocean. Flowery script above her read: *You only have yourself! See it! Do it! Be it!*

A khaki book bag leaning against a nightstand.

The cinder-block walls that every dorm room in America had in common.

Eryn wasn't home.

Magpie forced herself to be still. She located the anger flowing through her body and concentrated on calming it, focusing it, pinpointing it to a singular purpose.

She looked around the place that her sister had left home for.

There was not so much as a photograph of anyone in

the Lewis family. No, here was Eryn and a group of girls in yoga wear. Here was Eryn with a guy who might have been her boyfriend, their arms around each other, caught mid-laugh, his face angled toward hers like he might have just kissed her or perhaps was going to kiss her now. Here was Eryn in a complicated yoga pose, her legs folded in a way that looked almost painful, only one hand making contact with the ground. Her eyes were closed and her face looked utterly serene, as if the movement were effortless, natural, comfortable.

She picked up this last one, carefully undoing the back of the simple metal frame that held it, and she pulled out the photograph as if she were an archaeologist excavating something fragile and old.

There were two pictures of Eryn behind the first, both showing her in similar poses, with similar expressions of serenity on her face.

Magpie ripped them all carefully in half.

Then she turned her attention to the rest of the room.

And began, methodically, to destroy it.

In a little basket on top of the fridge, Magpie found a sharp kitchen knife, and she used this to slash Eryn's bedsheets and comforter and curtains, long deep slashes that sent feathers billowing up into the air when she reached the pillows. Next, she smashed the rest of the picture frames and tore all the photos inside to bits. She felt a particular sense of satisfaction when she ripped the poster off the wall—what the fuck did that even mean? *See it! Do it! Be it!* It was just like Eryn to put so much stock into inspirational messages that, when you actually thought about them, didn't make any sense at all.

With the knife, Magpie cut all of Eryn's clothes into ribbons, emptying the bureau and the small closet, making sure that nothing was left untouched. The sensible bras. The overpriced yoga pants. The shirts with words on them like *breathe* and *be* and *love*. Then she set her attention on Eryn's desk, shredding papers and upturning drawers, and finally, using a hammer she'd found in a small toolkit kept underneath her sister's bed, she ruined the laptop, beating it to smithereens, a million pieces of plastic and metal and wire. An unsalvageable mess.

She paused for a minute in the middle of it to look for Hither.

There it was, in one high corner of the room where wall met ceiling: a tiny little spider sitting on a tiny little web, watching her.

When she was done, she considered leaving a note.

But she decided to give her sister a little more credit than that.

She decided that if she really put her mind to it, Eryn could figure out exactly who had done this.

So she just made herself another door and left that mess behind her.

The next person she visited *was* home; Magpie could tell this instantly, in the way that you might feel your skin tingle if someone was watching you.

She was in the living room of a little house. A tiny blue love seat sat in the middle of the room facing a TV that was just a touch too big for the space. She could see the kitchen through an open doorway and a bathroom down a short hallway that ended with an open door.

That's where he was—Gabriel Lewis—fast asleep.

Magpie's father had always been one to go to sleep early. She'd often had to wake him up from the couch during the end credits to a movie he would inevitably remember nothing about. He was an early riser, always awake before anyone else in the house, always working on something for breakfast, sipping coffee out of a forest-green mug that said, in red letters, *#1 Dad!* A gift from Magpie and Eryn on some Father's Day past.

How inaccurate that mug had turned out to be; it was almost laughable. In fact, Magpie had to put a hand over her mouth now to drown out the rising giggle that was working its way up from her stomach.

She wondered if she could find a mug that said, *#1 Fuckup!* Or *#1 Asshole!* Or *#1 Ruiner of Families!*

Any of those sayings would have been more accurate than the one they had ended up choosing.

Well. You lived and you learned and you stopped buying cheap Hallmark mugs for people who didn't deserve them.

Magpie made her way down the hallway.

She saw Hither near the ceiling, a spider again. Still watching her.

She wondered for a brief moment whether she would find her aunt asleep next to her father, the two of them cuddled against each other in some affectionate, unconscious embrace.

She wondered if that would make things easier or harder for her.

If they had ended up together, did that change anything? Did that take away some of the insult of Magpie's walking in on them midcoitus; did that lessen some of the scarring she had inevitably suffered from seeing her father and aunt so exposed, so bare?

If it had been—as they say—*true love?*

Did that change anything at all?

Magpie didn't think so, but she was a little bit relieved when she pushed open the bedroom door and saw her father asleep alone, one leg sticking out from underneath the comforter. He snored quietly, the sound like a cat's purr.

She let herself watch him for one second, then she turned on the light.

He stirred instantly, putting his hand over his eyes, then rubbing them, then looking up, confused, blinking, adjusting to the sudden brightness.

"Magpie? Sweetheart? Is that you?"

267

Magpie made herself smile. "Dad. I have something so cool to show you. You're really going to love it."

She considered it.

Bringing Ann Marie into Near.

And she might have if Ann Marie had been home.

But the house was empty when Magpie finished with her father, and Magpie felt calmer now; the anger inside her body was subsiding moment by moment.

She couldn't find any left to direct toward her mother.

She even touched a hand to her own cheek to see if any sting remained from where Ann Marie had slapped her.

But that was gone, too.

She thought about leaving a note.

But what would it say?

You were kind of a shitty mom.

I'm in a better place now.

Everything she wrote felt too much like something a suicide note might say.

But this wasn't a suicide. This was almost the exact opposite. This was a whole new life.

So Magpie didn't leave a note.

Instead, she stood in the doorway of her mother's bedroom and tried to remember something nice. A happier time. A sober Ann Marie.

And she came up with this:

Eryn and Magpie. Magpie maybe four. Eryn ten. Laughing and giggling and still friends. Sneaking into their parents' bedroom on Christmas morning. The house smelling like pine needles and mulled spices. Crawling underneath the covers. Tangling up their limbs in the limbs of their parents. Softness and warmth. Someone kissing Magpie on the head. Someone calling her sweetheart. The blankets over her head making her feel as if she were underwater.

And then a summer night. Magpie five or six, Eryn eleven or twelve. Gabriel cannonballing into the pool. Ann Marie sunning on the swim platform. Magpie holding the pool's ladder to keep herself on the bottom. Eryn swimming underwater. Both their eyes open, meeting each other through the sting of chlorine, the burn of lungs needing oxygen.

It wasn't always terrible in that house.

If she tried, she could remember that.

But that happiness was faded, too. Just like the anger.

There was an emptiness that had taken its place.

She preferred the emptiness.

It felt homey, comfortable.

She changed into her bathing suit.

Magpie loved to swim in the moonlight.

Her skin looked silver when she held her hands underneath the water, and there was a gentle rippling quality to the light that made her look like something from the sea, a creature bred in the very depths of the ocean, just a visitor on land.

The pizza pool float knocked into the sides of the pool and floated back to her, then bounced gently off an arm or leg and continued its cycle.

Magpie floated on her back and looked up at the sky. If she cupped her hands on either side of her face, she saw nothing but the ring of treetops that surrounded their small property on Pine Street, the bright orb of the almost-full moon, the brilliant dots of light of thousands and thousands of stars. There were more stars in the night sky than you could even see. There were more stars in the universe than you could even comprehend. Magpie knew this, and it made her feel overwhelmed and happy and humbled and scared all at the same exact time.

She had been back in Farther for an hour or so.

Her father hadn't screamed when her Near-mother had stood in front of him and unhinged her jaw.

There had been a look in his eyes almost like...

Well. Almost like he knew he deserved it.

It had been such a long day.

Magpie's body ached with the effort of jumping from one world to another; her head pounded even as she soaked it in the cool water, even as she closed her eyes and pinched the spot on her hand between her thumb and index fingers that Eryn had once told her was a pressure point.

There hadn't been as much blood with her father.

Just one neat swallow, and it was over.

She had stayed to watch her Near-mother retreat slowly back down the hill.

"When will you come back to stay?" she had asked, and Magpie had smiled, and said, "Soon. I think I'm all done now."

But in this world, in Farther, her favorite thing had been to stay in the pool until her fingers were wrinkled, until her ears sloshed with water, until her eyes turned red from the chlorine, so that's what she chose to do, to let herself have just one more night in the empty, clear water.

The smell of chlorine.

It comforted her.

And so did the little patch of red on lime-green grass, and so did the sound Eryn's comforter had made as Magpie sliced through it with a kitchen knife, and so did the look on her father's face.

And so did being alone.

And so did the star-crowded sky above her, twinkling and glittering as if it were filled with diamonds instead of balls of luminous gas.

And so did the feeling of being weightless, of being supported by water, of being buoyant enough to float.

Are you finished now?

Magpie hadn't even noticed Hither, but there it was, resting atop the pizza float, a small catlike animal with claws that dipped so low that they skimmed the top of the water.

"It's nice to see you as something other than an insect."

It's good to be a quiet thing. You can sit and watch and not be bothered.

"Why don't you go ahead and keep sitting and watching? I'm not in the mood for any more lectures."

So far you haven't taken a single piece of advice I've given you. What makes you think I've come to try again?

"So why are you here, then?"

I am always here, whether or not you are aware of me.

"Well, fine. Just don't bother me. I was enjoying being alone."

We are never truly alone; we always have ourselves beside us.

Magpie snorted. "This is why I can't stand you. Nobody talks like that."

Ah, but you *talk like that*, it said, and then it was quiet, and when Magpie next looked, it had turned into something like a small child, face pointed upward, staring at the stars.

And because nothing good or peaceful lasts forever, Magpie became aware of voices.

A pair of them, their familiar cadences rising and falling and slipping around the house so Magpie knew who they were before she could see them, before they emerged into the moonlit backyard and paused, seeing her. One of them burst into laughter.

"See? I *told* you she was fine," Clare said, and before Ben could reply, she was stripping off her dress and climbing the pool ladder, then cannonballing into the pool with such a splash that even Ben, still three or four feet away, got wet.

"Clare, what the hell?" he said, wiping his hands on his shorts.

"Come in, grumpy! The water's fine!" Clare called back.

She was drunk. Magpie could smell it coming off her in waves even before Clare waded through the water to reach her, throwing her arms around Magpie's neck as if she hadn't seen her in weeks.

"Why did you *leeeee-ave*?" Clare whined. Magpie did her best to escape her death grip without seeming rude.

"That party was a drag," Magpie said. "Sorry."

"I agree," Ben added. He'd reached the side of the pool, and he leaned over the edge and let his hands float on the surface of the water.

Magpie took a step or two closer to him. She lowered her voice to a whisper. "I'm sorry about the movie. I just had to get out of there."

He shrugged. "Don't worry about it, Mags. I get it."

"Some other time," she said, and he seemed to brighten a little.

"Magpie, is your mom home?" Clare asked. "I have to pee. Should I just pee outside?"

"She's not home," Magpie said. "You can go inside. The door's unlocked."

"Oh, good. Whenever I try to go outside, I end up peeing all over myself."

"It's true," Ben said, when Clare had pulled herself out of the pool and was stumbling toward the house. "I've seen it happen."

"Shut up!" Clare shouted, then pulled the door shut behind her with a slam.

273

A moment of awkwardness as Magpie and Ben found themselves suddenly alone.

"So. How was the rest of the party?" Magpie asked.

"You didn't miss much. Allison Lefferts shut the whole thing down, like, fifteen minutes after we got there."

"Did she?" Magpie asked. She tried to make her face look surprised.

"Sorry. I know she's not your favorite person in the world."

"Not by a long shot, but don't worry, the sound of her name doesn't make me feel like spontaneously splashing anyone."

"Ha! Okay, well, I guess that's good for me. But yeah. It was really weird. She was acting like... totally bizarre. Like, just running around, turning on all the lights, cutting the sound system. When a few of Brandon's friends tried to talk to her, she just lost it. Went ballistic. I mean, she was throwing shit, screaming... She took one of their phones and called the cops. People started scrambling after that; I mean, you know it takes a week just to reach the street from Brandon's house. But I swear I heard her say on the phone that..."

"What?" Magpie prompted, when a few seconds had gone by and Ben hadn't finished his sentence.

"It's probably nothing. It was loud and sort of chaotic at that point, so I'm probably wrong... I just could have sworn I heard her tell them he was dead. Brandon was dead. That's what she said into the phone to the cops. That he was dead."

"Huh," Magpie said, and then, realizing that this was not

nearly enough of a reaction, she added, "Murdered. Wow. I mean. That's terrible."

"Not murdered—dead. She just said dead." He paused. "But honestly, she was kind of, like, tripping out. Seeing things, swiping at things that weren't even there. I don't think Brandon's actually dead. I think she probably just took some bad acid. There was some at the party, you know? I saw that junior girl, Nicole Lamb, having a full dialogue with a bathroom sink. I had to pee while she was in there because she wouldn't leave until they'd finished their conversation."

"Are you serious?"

"I got her some water, and she seemed okay otherwise."

"Well, I hope Brandon's all right," Magpie said, just a little flatly.

"Me too."

"But I'm not gonna lie. I would have liked to see Allison losing her mind like that."

"It was kind of entertaining, to be honest," Ben admitted, smiling.

"Are you telling her about Allison?" Clare asked, suddenly appearing next to the swim platform, pulling herself up with a bag of chips in one hand. "Can I have these?"

"Sure," Magpie said.

"It was *bonkers*." Clare lowered herself into the water, careful not to get the chips wet. "She was losing her *mind*. I'm so glad I don't do drugs. What's that famous commercial?

This is your brain on drugs? Well, I've seen Allison's brain on drugs, and it's a scary, scary place to be."

Magpie smiled. She really *would* have liked to have seen it, to watch Allison, confused and shaky and insisting Brandon was dead. If anyone could have emerged from their first visit to Near with any memory of the place, it was going to be Allison. Magpie almost had to give her a little credit.

"You've got the right idea, Mags," Clare said through a mouthful of chips. "This is the life, right here. I can't remember the last time I was in a pool."

Magpie laughed. "You were just in *my* pool the other week! Remember?"

"Oh, right," Clare said, but she looked a little confused, as if the memory was fuzzy, and instead of saying more, she put another handful of chips into her mouth, chewing slowly as Ben continued talking about the party, about meeting Luke's boyfriend before Allison had broken everything up.

But Magpie wasn't listening.

Magpie studied Clare.

It could just have been because she was drunk, but Clare's eyes were roaming around the backyard, as if she were trying to remember something.

Finally, her gaze landed on the garden shed.

She looked at it for a long time.

Ben kept talking. He thought Luke and his boyfriend made a cute couple.

Clare kept looking at the garden shed.

Magpie kept looking at Clare.

Neither of the girls blinked for at least a full minute, then Clare did, slowly, dreamily, as if she were emerging from a vision. She shook her head and turned back around, and they locked eyes, she and Magpie, and Clare had this expression on her face, as if there was something on the tip of her tongue that she could not quite name but was there all the same.

"We should go," she said loudly, probably louder than she had meant to, and Ben stopped midsentence to look at her.

"Go? We just got here."

"I have a curfew. My mom will lose her mind. And I don't want to walk home alone," Clare said.

Magpie didn't doubt that it was all true, that Clare almost certainly *did* have a curfew, that her mother *would* worry.

But there was something else, too, some slither of caution that had wormed its way behind her eyes.

Magpie knew Clare didn't remember.

But she knew, also, that Clare had realized there was *something* she didn't remember, and that being here, in this backyard, so close to the shed, to the doorway to Near, had reminded her of it.

Magpie didn't blame her at all.

It was natural to be afraid of the things we don't understand.

Even more natural to be afraid of the things we can't quite remember.

"It's all right," Magpie said, mostly to Ben. "We can catch

up this weekend. And then we'll have the whole summer. I won't even charge you guys admission to the pool."

Clare had already pulled herself onto the swim platform; she was dancing from foot to foot, trying to get dry enough to put her dress back on. Ben was still leaning against the edge of the pool, looking at Magpie as if the last thing he wanted to do was leave her.

Magpie smiled at him. "Can't let her walk home alone," she said, nodding her chin toward Clare, who was even now still so drunk that she was struggling to get her dress over her head.

Ben kept looking at Magpie, and she realized that in another lifetime, in another world, this would have been exactly what Margaret Lewis would have wanted for herself at sixteen years old: nights warm enough for swimming and moonlight so bright it was like midday and stars as far as the eye could see and a kind, lovely boy in front of her who looked as if, had Clare not taken that moment to dry-heave into the bushes next to the pool, he might have even kissed her.

He laughed. Magpie laughed. Clare moaned.

"I'll be out front," she said. "I think I drank a little too much. Mags, I'll call you tomorrow."

Magpie and Ben watched her go around the side of the house. Ben took a half step back, and Magpie could feel exactly what he felt: that the moment had passed. It was getting just a little too late. The magic hour had turned sour and stale.

"Ben," Magpie started, keeping her voice a whisper, a

secret from Clare and the entire universe. "What if I told you there was a place where you could have everything you wanted? Anything in the entire world, you could just wish it and it would appear in front of you."

Ben thought about it for a moment, and Magpie realized that this was just one of Ben's many refreshing qualities: When you asked him a question, he took the time to really consider it, to really hear you. He didn't just wait for his turn to talk.

"It sounds nice in theory," he said finally. "I mean... Of course there are things I want. There are things everybody wants."

"And you could have them. All of them," Magpie said, trying not to sound too eager, trying to keep her voice light.

"Hypothetically?" he asked.

"Hypothetically, yeah."

"Hypothetically, yes. Of course." He paused, looking upward, his eyes unfocused and faraway.

Magpie's head still ached. A steady thrum in the exact center of her skull.

He looked back down at her and smiled. "But I don't know. I'm pretty happy here. It sounds like that might get a little boring. Nothing to work for, you know? No challenges, nothing to accomplish. I don't know. It sounds like it would get old pretty quickly."

Magpie smiled.

And Ben cocked his head slightly, perhaps because he

couldn't figure out why his answer made Magpie's smile look so sad.

"Better get going," she said. "Clare's waiting."

"I'll talk to you soon, Mags, okay?"

"Yeah. Good night."

Ben gave her a little wave, then followed Clare around the side of the house.

I like him.

I like him, too, Magpie thought.

You could change your mind. You could stay. You could be with him.

"Let's say I did," Magpie said. She was talking to Hither, but at the same time, she was talking to herself. Or—those things were one and the same. "Let's say I stayed. And let's say we get together, Ben and I, and let's say—for the sake of argument—that the disappearances of my father, my English teacher, and my sexual abuser are never linked back to me. Let's pretend everything works out perfectly. It's a possibility, right? Ben and I start dating, Clare and I become best friends, Allison never fully remembers what happened in Near..." Magpie looked up at the stars. So many of them, each a million miles away. Each unreachable and impossible.

"Let's say all of that worked out. I don't fail sophomore year. My mother finally gets clean. My sister never reports me to the police for trashing her dorm room...

"But even if all of that happened, even if everything fell together, just so... Who's to say any of it would last? Ben and

I, we're sixteen. Would it last for a year, two years? Would we make it through college?"

Magpie took a breath. "So, no. I can't change my mind."

Not everything is about forever.

"But I can have whatever I want. Forever. And that's where Ben and I disagree; I don't think perfect gets boring."

And Magpie got out of the pool. She wrapped herself in her sister's towel: *ERL*. And—with Hither close behind her—she stepped through the garden shed into a world of her own making.

———

The little perfect town of Near was gone.

Underwater.

The crashing, expansive ocean had finally swallowed it up.

The hill was the only thing still green and untouched in this world, and Magpie stood on top of it in a long flowing white dress. (Had she wished this dress? Or had this place just given it to her?) Hither was beside her, a lion now, with teeth that glinted in the morning sun.

"I understand why there's water now," Magpie said.

What will you do?

"Just float," she replied.

She took the Near-pen from the pocket of her Near-dress and started to draw.

She had never been much for drawing back in Farther,

but here, in Near, the lines flowed from her pen as if she had studied art all her life. She concentrated with a singular purpose, and when she was finished, there was a perfect wooden sailboat in front of her, just big enough for her and Hither. There was a little cabin with a neatly made bed and a desk filled with maps and instruments that would allow her to navigate by the light of the stars. It looked almost exactly like the little sailboat in the painting hanging in Mrs. Henderson's office.

So I'm coming with you?

"You're always with me," Magpie said. "You've always *been* with me. The voice inside of my head trying to convince me that everything will be okay. And look—I'm stronger now. You've helped to make me stronger. My head isn't even hurting anymore. When I came back to Near—it just went away. I can stay here now. I can make whatever I want. Everything really *will* be okay. So maybe you'll finally take a little break."

She stepped into the boat, and Hither, a large seabird now, followed after her, alighting on the tall mast, cawing as Magpie unfurled the sail.

And together they turned toward the sea.

And the waters rose obligingly to meet them.

And they were on their way.

AFTER

It took another almost seven months.

Allison Lefferts, by the time the police arrived at the Phipp residence, could not remember for the life of her what she had meant on the phone with 911, what she had meant when she told the dispatcher that her boyfriend, Brandon Phipp, was dead.

The police assumed it was a prank.

The party was broken up.

Allison Lefferts neither slept that night, nor the night after, and she had only just managed to doze off on the third evening when the doorbell rang.

The police.

Brandon's parents had returned from vacation to find their youngest son missing.

Suddenly, people were interested again in what exactly Allison had meant when she'd told them he was dead.

There was an investigation.

For a little while, Allison was considered a person of interest.

But she stuck to her story that she didn't know anything, that she'd had too much to drink that night, that she couldn't explain why she'd called the police in the first place. And there couldn't be a murder without a body, without a single shred of evidence to suggest it, and eventually, the police stopped questioning her.

Summer came and went.

And then one ordinary Tuesday night, Mr. Franklin James—a missing person along with Brandon, Magpie, and Magpie's father—turned up at his own front door.

He patted his pocket for his keys but didn't find them.

He rang the doorbell.

He waited patiently.

Only a faint chill in the air suggested to him that something might be off.

Because he remembered that morning being warm. And now it felt almost like fall.

When his wife opened the door, she screamed and cried and seemed so very happy to see him. He couldn't understand it.

She called the police.

They showed him a newspaper; he told them he could

remember nothing of the entire summer. He remembered the inside of the classroom where he taught at Farther High, a very bright light, and then his own front porch.

He was wearing the same clothes he'd gone missing in. He was perfectly unharmed.

Brandon Phipp's parents never believed Allison had anything to do with their son's disappearance. They weren't naïve to their son's many shortcomings. They figured that probably Brandon had finally pissed off the wrong person.

They cleaned out his bedroom.

They invited Allison to the house one night for dinner.

There's a box of his things we thought you'd like to have. In his bedroom.

So she went to get it.

And for just a second—

But she was tired. Her eyes were playing tricks on her.

Another month passed. And another.

And one afternoon Ann Marie Lewis opened the door to find her former husband dirty and tattered and bruised on her front lawn.

Like Mr. James, Gabriel Lewis had no memory of the months that had passed between now and then.

Unlike Mr. James, he was slightly worse for the wear; he spent one week in the hospital, recovering (according to what Ben relayed to Clare in the cafeteria) from *a strange case of exposure.*

A few days after he turned up, Allison's cell phone rang.

It was Magpie's house number.

She stared at it for a long time. Wondering—was it her?

But the call went to voice mail, and when Allison listened to it, it was not Magpie's voice but Ann Marie's on the other end, her words sloppy and slurred as she begged Allison to call her back.

It was very late on a Wednesday night.

Allison *did* call back, because why not, and when Ann Marie answered the phone, she started crying.

Do you know where my daughter is?

Do you know where either of my daughters are?

I'm sorry. But I really have no idea.

Junior year had started.

Things at school were different.

Allison herself was quieter. She stuck to herself. She did her schoolwork. She avoided people in the hallway. She existed.

She sometimes ran into them in the cafeteria line or passing by their lockers—Clare and Ben. They seemed to always be together, the two of them, a little quieter, too, than they had previously been.

Ben talked to Allison only once. Outside calculus. A quick touch to her wrist to get her attention. And he'd leaned in and said:

Do you know anything?

She had, for a moment, been tempted to pull away. Call him a name. Tell him to fuck off.

But those things felt like too much effort now.

So she just shook her head.

And said no.

And he didn't bother her again.

And once, in English class—

But no. That was silly.

And then winter came to Farther, and with winter came hot apple cider and wreaths made of dark evergreens and holly berries and Christmas. And with Christmas came Christmas trees.

Allison went to the Christmas tree farm with her parents, trailing behind them in a white knitted hat that covered her ears and made the world sound muffled, distant. She liked that.

It had been a hard almost-seven months for Allison. A weird almost-seven months.

For a little while, after Mr. James and Gabriel Lewis had returned, she had started to hope that Brandon might show up soon, too, confused and hurt but ultimately *alive*. But then she'd decided that wherever Brandon had gone he was almost certainly never coming back.

She pinched an evergreen needle between her fingers and smelled it.

Her father called from somewhere. She spun around but didn't see her parents; she must have wandered away from them.

Coming!

And she started to follow the sound of his voice, but—

Well, that was odd.

It almost looked like...

If she turned just the right way...

She saw something impossible.

It had taken almost seven months, but finally Allison saw what she had seen two times before and hadn't let herself believe.

You cannot open up a doorway to another world and expect the cracks to go away when you close it again.

Allison reached out into the darkness.

And her hand found purchase.

She gripped the doorknob of an impossible door, and she stepped through into an impossible world.

A world made almost entirely of water, just the tip of a green hill left rising above the waves.

A world that was bright and shining and new.

Well, almost new.

And she remembered now.

She had been here before.

Do you like it? Magpie had said. *I made it myself. It's called Near.*

And Brandon really *was* dead.

Magpie had killed him.

Allison closed her eyes.

The sun was hot above her, glinting off the water and the waves of this place. Of this world.

She held her hands in front of her stomach, squeezing her fingers one by one.

She smelled chlorine.

The smell of chlorine had always reminded Allison Lefferts of summer.

And summer in turn reminded her of Magpie's pool.

Was this ocean made of pool water?

She had loved Magpie's pool. They had played Marco Polo, the two of them. They had pretended to be mermaids. They had seen who could hold their breath the longest. They had been friends once. They had met in a pool and they'd grown up in a pool and they'd grown older in a pool and at some point—Allison couldn't quite pinpoint when—they'd grown apart in a pool.

She had said so many terrible things to Magpie.

I hate you. I've always hated you. From the minute I met you.

But that hadn't really been true at all.

Because she hadn't always hated Magpie.

And she didn't even really hate her now.

Maybe a tiny bit.

But mostly she just felt sad.

With her eyes still closed, with her nose filled with the smell of chlorine, she felt, for the first time in a long time, the gentle breeze of happiness. Caressing her skin. Slipping into her blood. Warming her body.

How many hours had she spent lying on an oversize swan

pool float, Magpie next to her on a float shaped like a piece of pizza, gently bumping into each other, letting their skin burn in the hot summer sun?

It was all she wanted now. To be back on that swan. To be back on the water.

To just float.

She opened her eyes.

And it took them a moment to adjust to the bright, bright sun of Near.

But then she saw it. On the grass next to her.

An oversize swan pool float.

As if she had dreamed it into existence.

She turned back around to the doorway she had stepped through.

She pulled it closed.

Oh, Magpie. Don't you know to always lock the door behind you?

And she stepped gently onto the float.

And pushed herself out to sea.

ACKNOWLEDGMENTS

If I could dream up the perfect place like Near, it would include all the wonderful people who helped bring this book to life (and I promise none of them would get eaten by impossible monsters). To everyone at Little, Brown Books for Young Readers, and especially to Megan Tingley, Jackie Engel, Alvina Ling, Erika Breglia, Lindsay Walter-Greaney, David Hough, and Hannah Milton—I couldn't be more grateful for your commitment to this book. And a huge and special thank you to Parrish Turner for lending your keen eye to a sensitivity read.

The paperback version of *You Must Not Miss* is especially dear to my heart because the artwork was made by the incredible Tran Nguyen and the cover design was executed perfectly by Karina Granda. Ladies, you saw Magpie so fully, and, Tran, you brought her to life in a way I will be forever grateful for. The birds, the rage—perfect! And speaking of Magpie, I am so grateful for all the behind-the-scenes support she received— from Elena Yip, Stefanie Hoffman, Natali Cavanagh, Valerie Wong, Siena Koncsol, and Victoria Stapleton.

And, of course, to a person who deserves her own magical door-creating fountain pen, my editor Pam Gruber, who made this book so much better: I'm so happy Magpie brought you into my life.

Always, always, always, thank you to my agent, Wendy Schmalz, a tireless, lovely force of a woman.

I first had the idea for this book in May of 2016, while lying on a pizza pool float in Palm Springs, California. I had my straw hat over my face and suddenly I knew her, Magpie, as clearly as if we'd grown up together. The very first person I introduced her to was my great friend and great writer Aaron Karo, and I'm so excited that almost exactly three years later, I get to introduce Magpie to all of you. (Careful, she bites.)

I have so many supportive, wonderful people in my circle—my family, my friends, my dear readers who have been with me from the beginning. (You know who you are!) Thank you especially to Shane, a continuous, never-ending beacon of support who is proud of me even when I am not proud of myself. And vice versa, of course.

Writing these acknowledgments is a distinct pleasure because it means I have been allowed to publish one more book. And although writing can sometimes feel like a hugely private, reclusive affair, these acknowledgments prove that it isn't. I am surrounded by great people. I wish I could buy you all a box of macaroni and cheese, a pizza pool float, and an ocean of chlorinated water to go with it.

© Jaimee Dormer

KATRINA LENO was born on the East Coast and currently lives in Los Angeles. She is the author of *Horrid, You Must Not Miss, Summer of Salt, Everything All at Once, The Lost & Found,* and *The Half Life of Molly Pierce.* She has a habit of peeking into garden sheds to check for impossible worlds. You can visit her online at katrinaleno.com.

You Must Not Miss
KATRINA LENO'S
Books

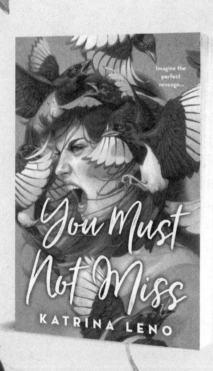